THE

Elephant Keeper's Daughter

ALSO BY JULIA DROSTEN

The Lioness of Morocco

THE
Elephant
Keeper's
Daughter

JULIA DROSTEN
Translated by Deborah Langton

Published by AmazonCrossing, Seattle

www.apub.com

Amazon, the Amazon logo, and AmazonCrossing are trademarks of Amazon.com, Inc., or its affiliates.

ISBN-13: 978-1542048552
ISBN-10: 1542048559

Cover design by Shasti O'Leary Soudant

Printed in the United States of America

Anyone who torments others also striving for well-being will find no happiness in the next life.

Anyone who protects others also striving for well-being will find happiness in the next life.

—Dhammapada, third century BC

Table of Contents

Part One

The Jungle Kingdom of
Five Mountains
1803 to 1818

Chapter One
Senkadagala (city of Kandy), Lanka (Ceylon), 1803

"Samitha, what are you doing here? Why aren't you in bed?" The maid set the stack of hand towels on a chest and hurried to the half-open door.

With a defiant look, the child slipped into the room, but Kalani grabbed her arm.

"No, Samitha," she said.

Samitha tried to wrestle her arm away. "Let me go! I want Mama!"

She peered anxiously toward where her mother lay on a large bed. The dancing flames of oil lamps cast shadows across the woman's pale face. Seeing her daughter, she tried to sit up but flinched and let out moans of pain as she sank back into the cushions.

The maid released Samitha and ran to the bed. "Wait, I'll help you, ma'am." She supported her mistress with care while arranging cushions at her back.

"Mama!" The little girl ran over and nestled up to her mother. "Are you sick?"

Anshu forced a smile. "No, my darling. Your brother is ready to come into the world."

"Oh!" Samitha's mouth fell open in amazement. Timidly, she looked at the curve of her mother's huge belly.

Anshu stroked her daughter's hair. "You must get to bed now and sleep. If you're good, you can come and see your brother early tomorrow morning. Kalani, take Samitha to her room."

"Of course, ma'am." The maid picked up the little girl, dodging her flailing arms. But just as they reached the door, Anshu let out a cry of anguish.

"I'm coming, ma'am!" Kalani hastily put Samitha down again, pushed her from the room, and bolted the door.

Samitha stood stock-still in the empty hallway. She'd been so excited about her brother's arrival, but seeing her mother like this frightened her. She knew she should go to bed but wanted to stay by her mother. She peered uncertainly down the dark hallway. All the doors were shut. Through the ornate window grilles, a gentle breeze carried the song of night birds and the loud chirping of cicadas. An elephant roared in the stables, making Samitha jump. She remembered her father saying at dinner that he was going to take another look at the pregnant elephant, Yakkhini. Jeeva Maha Nuvara was the *Gajanayake Nilame*, the most senior keeper of the sacred elephants belonging to King Vikrama Rajasinha. He took his responsibility very seriously indeed.

Samitha looked again at the closed bedroom door. She could hear her mother wailing, Kalani murmuring something in return, and all of a sudden, she knew what to do. She would run to her father and tell him her brother was on his way. Her father would embrace her and be happy with her, and this would chase away all her fear.

Like all the king's high-ranking officials, Jeeva lived with his family on Astawanka-veediya, the elegant boulevard connecting the palace to the elephant stables. It was bordered by imposing houses, their walls whitewashed and their roofs tiled red. An avenue of luxuriant areca and coconut palms offered some protection from the tropical sun by day, but the heat lingered into the night. Sweet jasmine wafted from the gardens, and the silvery moon lit the little girl's way as she raced down the empty street.

She could hear distant music, voices, laughter, and the repeated trumpeting of elephants. Samitha knew tonight was a special night, the culmination of a lavish, ten-day festival in which the people of Kanda Uda Pas Rata celebrated the most sacred relic of their faith: the left eyetooth of Siddhartha Gautama, the enlightened Buddha. This holy relic was kept safe in a temple in Senkadagala.

Still only five years old, Samitha was too young to join the celebrations. She had heard her parents recount tales of the magnificent nightly processions in honor of the Enlightened One, with dancers, singers, musicians, and richly bejeweled elephants. The night of the full moon marked the high point of the festival, when the biggest and most noble of the king's bull elephants would bear the Sacred Tooth Casket through the city. The king himself took part in the procession, his golden coach pulled by eight white horses.

Samitha had reached the stables. These consisted of three long buildings not far from Mahaweli Ganga, the longest river in the kingdom. Colorful carvings inlaid with gold leaf decorated the gables, and the royal standards at the entrance gates rippled in the breeze.

Each stable had ten gated stalls topped with ten open skylights. Behind them ran a narrow alleyway used by the *mahouts* when they fed or mucked out their animals. The three buildings framed a large square where the elephants were trained for their military or processional tasks. King Vikrama Rajasinha owned thirty elephants: twenty bulls and ten cows. All belonged to the Chaddhantha caste, the highest of the ten elephant castes. They were huge, powerful creatures with skin so pale it was almost white, long trunks, and expressive amber eyes. The bull elephants nearly always boasted magnificent tusks. The biggest and most valuable bull was known as the *mangalahasti*, or state elephant.

Samitha stood looking at the stables. The sweet smell of the animals pervaded the air, but she didn't hear their usual snorting or noisy rooting in their feed. The gates to the empty stalls stood open, nearly all the elephants off taking part in the full-moon procession.

Only one gate was closed. There was a sudden, shrill trumpeting sound, then agitated male voices. Samitha realized it was her father and Eranga, Jeeva's top mahout. She hurried over and found them in the alley. Yakkhini's mighty pale-gray head loomed above them. Her ears flapped noisily back and forth, her trunk whipped up and down, her frightened eyes bulged in their sockets. She trumpeted again and kicked against the walls of her stall. The mahout was holding an *ankus*, a wooden stave with a leaf-shaped metal point and an iron hook. He used it to tap the elephant gently on her hindquarters, talking to her in a low, soothing voice, "Ho, ho."

The men were giving all their attention to the troubled animal and did not notice Samitha, who was so alarmed that she'd hidden behind a huge pile of palm leaves intended for the elephants' breakfast. Cautiously, she peeked out between the green fronds. The elephant held her tail high and stiff, her legs splayed. A sudden flood of bloody water spurted from an opening under her tail and hit the floor with an alarming splash. The elephant moaned and grunted and arched her back, her rear legs almost buckling with the strain. A small, white bubble appeared, growing larger and larger until it burst. At last, a baby elephant, wet and dark, tumbled to the ground. Blood and water gushed from the elephant's womb, washing over the motionless little creature.

The elephant tried to turn, but a strong tether held her in place. She trumpeted in rage, stamping her back feet dangerously near the baby.

"Eranga, what's wrong with the calf?" shouted Jeeva. "Why isn't it moving?"

Eranga threw aside his ankus, squatted down behind the cow, and in one movement heaved the calf into the alley. Jeeva snatched two rough towels from a hook and threw one to the mahout. Then he knelt down on the mud floor and started to rub down the calf. His white shirt and the white sarong tucked around his hips quickly soaked through with blood and mucus.

The mahout was horrified. "This is no work for you, master!"

"Now is not the time to worry about caste! The king expects a healthy calf from his favorite cow."

The two massaged strength into the little animal while Samitha, holding her breath, watched from her hiding place.

"Master!" Eranga exclaimed, his face glowing with happiness. "Look!"

A small trunk stretched upward like a signaling flag in the wind, and the calf tried to lift its head.

Jeeva folded his hands across his chest in gratitude. Then he and the mahout got the little elephant to its feet.

"Eranga, I thank you. Not only are you a courageous fighter, but you are also thoroughly deserving of your office as first mahout."

Fifteen months ago, Eranga had distinguished himself fighting against the British. In gratitude for helping to keep Kanda Uda Pas Rata the last remaining free kingdom on the island, the king had decreed that Eranga be promoted to first mahout.

Jeeva and Eranga studied the elephant baby. Next to its enormous mother, it looked tiny. Its skin hung in folds. The trunk did not yet reach the ground, and between its ears some bristly black hair stood up straight. It moved its head from right to left and looked around with cautious, bright eyes.

"It looks healthy," said Jeeva, relief in his voice. "But that dark skin and bristly hair make me doubt its father belonged to the Chaddhantha caste."

"Only Yakkhini knows who the father is," said Eranga with a smile. He himself had captured wild Yakkhini in the jungle not long before, without realizing she was pregnant. Now he bent and looked underneath the baby. "This is no bull. It's a little cow."

Jeeva's face fell. "Not a Chaddhantha and not a bull. The king will use her as a working elephant or give her to the Moorish traders, who'll sell her on to the British. They will pay anything for them."

Yakkhini puffed loudly and turned to look at her child. Her expression was full of concern and her honey-brown eyes full of tenderness. Gently, she extended her trunk, and the calf attempted its first stumbling steps. If the mahout had not supported the clumsy creature, she would have toppled over.

Samitha giggled in delight.

Jeeva whipped around. "Samitha! How long have you been there?"

"I saw the little elephant fall out of Yakkhini's bottom." The child scrambled through the palm leaves.

Jeeva frowned. That his daughter could sneak to the stables in the middle of the night without anyone noticing displeased him greatly. "You should be in your bed."

"But I was frightened, Papa." Samitha snuggled against his legs.

Softening a little, he stroked her hair. "Why didn't you go to Kalani if you were having a bad dream?"

"It wasn't a bad dream. And Kalani is with Mama because my brother's arriving tonight. Mama told me so. If I'm good, I can see him in the morning. Please don't tell Mama I'm here, or she'll be angry and then Mihiri will get to see him first." She snuggled even closer to him.

Jeeva looked down at his daughter's mop of dark hair in disbelief. "Your brother's arriving tonight? Did Mama really say that?"

He was torn between joy and alarm. After two daughters, five-year-old Samitha and three-year-old Mihiri, he was desperate for a boy. The court astrologer had predicted only a minimal chance of an heir, and yet Anshu felt sure she was expecting a boy. She referred to her "son" so often that Jeeva had come to believe it. But this was too soon—the baby wasn't supposed to arrive quite yet.

"Who is with her now?" he asked Samitha.

"Kalani," she replied.

Jeeva pursed his lips. Kalani was a skilled healer, but Jeeva had wanted a doctor present at the birth, too. No risks were to be taken with his son.

"Help the calf latch on to her mother, make sure she's feeding, and give Yakkhini plenty of palm leaves. She needs to stay strong," he instructed Eranga.

Without waiting for the mahout to reply, he scooped up Samitha and hurried from the stables.

"Ma'am, will you not look at your daughter?" Kalani cried. She held out the little bundle, all wrapped in white, but Anshu turned her head.

"Take her away, Kalani."

The old servant was not to be put off so easily. She had been at her mistress's side through childhood and marriage alike, and had attended the births of her other babies. She loved Anshu as she would her own flesh and blood. But she loved Anshu's children, too, and the newest addition, so longed for and now, apparently, so unwanted, moved her deeply.

Very gently, she held the freshly bathed, sweet-smelling baby against Anshu's chest. "Just look how pretty she is," Kalani cooed, her finger caressing the baby's chin. "Feel how silky her hair is. Her skin smells like honey, her fingers are so tiny." With the greatest of care, she placed the little girl on Anshu's belly. "Ma'am, hold your daughter."

Whether Anshu wanted to or not, she had to hold the little bundle tight to stop it slipping from her belly. "What use is it to me that you're pretty?" she whispered sadly.

The baby seemed to give a little frown, looking back at her mother with big, dark eyes.

"Since I conceived you, little one, I've prayed and offered up sacrifices every day, but still I have not been favored with a son." Anshu let out a deep sigh. "There's only one solution. I'll have to conceive again as soon as I can."

Kalani shook her head. "It took nearly three years for you to conceive after Mihiri, and the pregnancy has been so hard. Don't forget how you've had to lie down for months, ma'am, to be sure the baby stayed in place, and then, after all that, she has still come early. Perhaps it is your fate to have no more children."

"Then I shall disappoint my husband deeply." Anshu groaned.

As if she had understood, the baby's little face crumpled, and she started to cry, loud and clear.

Instinctively, Anshu bent toward her daughter and cradled the baby in her arms. "You can't help it, my little one," she murmured. "I'm the one who has failed. Your father will take a new wife, one who bears sons. Oh, why in this world are daughters not valued so greatly as sons?" She leaned over the baby and gently stroked her dark, shining curls, her golden-brown cheeks, and her sweet little nose.

Kalani bent to pick up a bloody sheet that had fallen from the bed and threw it in the palm laundry basket. She knew well how much Jeeva yearned for a son. He had been overjoyed with Samitha because she was the firstborn. But with Mihiri, his enthusiasm was noticeably dampened. The maid wondered how he would react to the news that the third child was another girl.

The front door slammed. Anshu and Kalani looked at one another in horror.

"Ma'am, your husband is back from the stables," whispered the maid.

Footsteps hurried down the hall, then stopped right outside the bedroom. Someone tried the handle, but the door was still bolted from the inside.

"Anshu?" came Jeeva's voice. "Is everything all right? Kalani, open up! I want to see my son." The door handle rattled.

Anshu's eyes widened. "Who could have told him?" she whispered.

As if in reply, Samitha's voice piped up. "Mama, let us in! We want to see my brother."

"Tell him I'm asleep," Anshu begged her maid. "I can't see him yet."

"Be brave and accept fate, ma'am—whatever it may be," replied Kalani.

But Anshu shook her head. "I can't. Help me, please!"

There was more rattling at the door. "Kalani, open up immediately!" thundered Jeeva.

"Quick! Give me the child," said the maid firmly.

"What are you going to do?"

"Leave everything to me."

Kalani marched to the door, drew back the bolt, and Jeeva almost fell into the room.

"Master," said Kalani, holding the child out to him. "Please greet your newborn son."

The next morning Jeeva walked through the palace garden with a basket of ripe fruit and colorful flowers. Today was not a day for his usual plain garments. He had chosen the traditional dress of the court aristocrat, an embroidered jacket over his white shirt, loose white pants, and a broad, golden belt. His shoulder-length hair was oiled and adorned with an embroidered cap, his moustache carefully trimmed.

He was glowing with joy, delighting in the sight of the sun as it rose from behind the woods surrounding Senkadagala, and smiling at the screeching of the gray monkeys that played above him amongst the boughs of cinnamon and fig trees.

He had just paid a visit to Yakkhini and her calf and was pleased to find both in good health. Now, by invitation, he was on his way to an audience with the king. First, however, he wanted to go to the Sri Dalada Maligawa, the temple where the Buddha's tooth was worshipped. This huge complex of white buildings was in the palace district and, like the king's residence, was surrounded by high walls and a deep moat full of crocodiles.

Jeeva walked over the bridge and through the gate to reverential greetings from the guards. At the main entrance to the temple, he removed his sandals and, barefoot, crossed the *sandakada pahana*, a circular slab of stone set into the floor. He paused briefly, looked at the sumptuous ornamentation symbolizing the eternal cycle of life and death, then took the stairs up to the temple, where the casket containing the Sacred Tooth was kept. Jeeva wanted to make an offering to thank the Enlightened One for giving him the gift of a son.

He had been so happy last night when Kalani had shown him the baby. It had looked so small and fragile, but Kalani assured him the child was healthy. He had held his son for a long time, cradled him and kissed him. Kalani had snatched the baby back when Jeeva tried to do a more thorough examination. "Master, it is too soon," she had said, swiftly pinning the cotton toweling back together. "The wound left by the umbilical cord mustn't be exposed."

Jeeva opened the silver-studded door to the inner sanctum and entered a windowless, candlelit room. Warm air, mingled with the sweet perfume of sacrificial offerings—lotus and frangipani flowers, ripe mango and jackfruit—enveloped him. The inner chamber was lined with gold brocade. The casket was in its center. It was inlaid with gold leaf and encrusted with precious stones. Before it stood a number of small crystal figures of Buddha.

Jeeva set down his basket of fruit and flowers close to the other offerings at the shrine, laid his palms across his chest, and remained like that for several moments, deep in thought.

"I thank you, Enlightened One," he whispered, his voice unsteady. "I thank you for hearing my prayers."

Not long after, Jeeva was bent reverentially forward on the floor of the king's audience chamber, his forehead touching the cool stone, listening to the creaking of the handles cranked by palace servants as they raised the red velvet curtain concealing the ruler on his throne.

"We have been informed that this night you have received the gift of a son," came the pleasantly rich voice of the monarch.

Jeeva lifted his head and straightened up on his knees. "Yesterday my wife gave birth to a healthy boy, Your Majesty. I am a happy man."

Sri Vikrama Rajasinha, ruler of Kanda Uda Pas Rata, the jungle kingdom of five mountains, sat beneath a canopy of gold embroidered brocade and looked down at his chief elephant keeper. Lofty pillars of carved palm wood supported the high ceiling. From the walls hung silken rugs depicting scenes of court life. These rugs also covered the floor around the gallery. Behind the king's throne, two mighty elephant tusks framed the flag of the Nayaka dynasty: the golden lion, heraldic beast of the Sinhalese people, on a red background.

The young ruler was dressed in the most exquisite garments, decorated with gold thread and jewels. A golden sword adorned his girdle, golden sandals his feet. A servant stood behind him, holding over the monarch's head the royal parasol of white silk. Another servant, who was crouching next to the throne, held out a banana leaf heaped with sweet, sticky rice balls. The monarch took one and devoured it with relish.

Other important court figures kneeled around the gallery. Their supporters squatted behind them with standards bearing the symbols of their masters' power and honor.

Vikrama Rajasinha looked kindly at Jeeva. "Your son was born the same night as our elephant calf."

"That is so, Your Majesty. Permit me to say how happy I am that Yakkhini and her calf are in good health."

"I'm told that your son's spirit came into the world early," the king noted as he took another rice ball. "The spirit decided to become flesh at the same time as our elephant."

"You are right, Your Majesty."

"We have consulted our astrologer, and his interpretation has shown us the way." The king placed the delicacy in his mouth and chewed reflectively.

Jeeva nodded solemnly. The fate of all earthly life was inseparable from the course of the heavenly bodies. This was why it was imperative to speak to an expert on the stars before making any major decision. Taking heed of his interpretation would ensure good karma for future incarnations.

Vikrama gestured with his right hand, heavy with rings. A young man with a shaven head, dressed in the orange robes of the Buddhist monks, stepped forward and handed him a talipot-palm leaf that had been dried and shaped into a square.

The king thanked him and looked at the leaf, which was covered in small, round, interlinked characters. "As our astrologer, Mahinda Dharmapala, assured me," he said, nodding toward the young monk, "the simultaneous birth of a sacred elephant and your son on the night of the Esala full moon is an extremely unusual event and one of great significance. The two new spirits are linked, and we are duty bound to respect this." He paused and considered his senior elephant keeper with a gentle smile. "Jeeva Maha Nuvara, we have decided to reward you for your loyalty and exemplary care of our sacred animals and make you a gift of the little cow elephant. Please accept this in the name of your son."

"Most esteemed Majesty, I owe you my eternal gratitude." Jeeva bowed low until his forehead brushed the floor. His heart was pounding with joy. First the son he had longed for had been born, and now the king was rewarding him in front of the whole court. With this gift, the ruler was certainly also making it clear to all that the important office of Gajanayake Nilame would remain in Jeeva's family for the next generation.

"Tell us when you have set the date for your son's rice festival. Then we'll instruct our astrologer to draw up the child's horoscope." With a wave of his hand, Sri Vikrama Rajasinha brought the audience to a close, and Jeeva left the chamber, bent in reverence, never once turning his back to the monarch.

"My husband was beside himself with joy to hear he had a son. I've never seen him like that before."

Anshu looked out through the open window at the garden. But she seemed to notice neither the glorious blooms nor the birds singing on their boughs, for her face was solemn and pensive. With a sigh, she turned to the mixture of rice flour, palm sugar, and coconut milk Kalani had served her in bed. But she pushed the tray away, the bowl still half-full. "I should have stopped you from telling this lie, Kalani. It will bring us a lot of bad karma."

The baby, who had been sleeping alongside Anshu, awoke, gave a big yawn, and flailed her little arms in the air. Anshu smiled and tickled one of her tiny fists.

"Ma'am, you should put her to the breast. She's bound to be hungry. And you yourself need to eat more so you can nourish your baby." With a disapproving shake of the head, Kalani carried Anshu's tray to a table by the door. Then she went to a chest of drawers and took out some fresh toweling and a little bottle of oil. A contented smile lit up her old face when she turned and saw the baby nursing eagerly.

"When you've fed the little one, I'll change her and rub her tummy with sesame oil. It's good for the digestion."

With her free hand, Anshu stroked the back of the baby's head. "You're not even one day old, and your mother has already burdened you with the most difficult of destinies," she said softly.

Kalani's eyes filled with tears. "Oh, ma'am, you're not responsible for this. I am."

"I know you meant well," replied Anshu. "I know your loyalty to me. But our secret cannot remain a secret forever."

"Have no fear of your husband, ma'am. He is a good man with a kind heart. And he loves his child."

"Because he believes it's a boy."

The nanny gave a decisive shake of the head. "Trust me, ma'am. I've seen in his eyes the power of his love."

Six months later they reached the day the king's astrologer had chosen for the baby's rice festival. It was the fifth day of Duruthu, the month in which the Buddha had first set foot on Lanka Island, and today the child would be blessed beneath the sacred Bodhi tree and given her name and horoscope.

Soon after sunrise, Kalani brought Anshu her breakfast, then went to the *almirah* and took out her mistress's jewelry box and her most beautiful sari. Then she set the little silver tub on top of a chest, filled it with warm water, and fetched fresh towels and the white embroidered gown the child was to wear for the celebration.

"Ma'am, are you wondering what name the venerable Mahinda Dharmapala has chosen for the little one?" asked Kalani while she arranged the sumptuous silk of Anshu's sari over her mistress's shoulder.

"I hope for a name that augurs strength and happiness for my child." Anshu wound her hair into a knot at the nape of her neck and added a couple of orchids for decoration. Then she sat down at the dressing table and opened her jewelry box.

"This little girl will need all the strength she can find. The burden we have placed upon her will grow heavier, not lighter, with the passing years." She took from the box a pair of long gold earrings set with sapphires.

"Don't despair, ma'am; we don't yet know what fate holds for your youngest daughter." Kalani picked up the baby and set her in the bath. At six months, the little girl was a healthy, happy child, her first teeth coming through. When Kalani dipped the sponge and let the water trickle over the baby's head and shoulders, the child laughed and reached out, trying to catch the drops.

"Mama, Mama!" Samitha and Mihiri burst into the room, ran straight to their mother, and snuggled against her. They, too, were in their best clothes, their long hair combed out to perfection.

"Papa said that Yakkhini and her baby will be here soon," Samitha gushed.

Jeeva came in after his daughters. Decked out in his court gown, he beamed at the sight of the happily splashing baby. "Today is a great day for you, my son. You and your elephant will be named today."

He stepped toward the baby, but before he could get there, Anshu blocked his way.

"My husband, have you nothing more important to attend to than women and children? Why are you not seeing to our guests?"

"I want first to wish my son all good things on his special day." Placing his hands on Anshu's hips and smiling, he moved her aside.

Anshu looked to Kalani in horror. The maid had positioned herself in front of the tub in such a way that she could support the baby and still shield her from her father's view. "Master, your son is bathing. Would you not rather come back when he is dressed?"

"No, Kalani, I want to see him now." Jeeva pushed the maid to one side and lifted the baby out of the water. "Good morning, my—"

His voice faltered and he stared at the naked child. Then he turned to his wife with the baby held out like something dangerous or dirty. "Explain this to me, please."

Anshu opened her mouth, but nothing came out.

Mihiri piped up. "What are you doing, Papa?"

"Go outside, girls. Leave the grown-ups alone," Jeeva ordered.

Mihiri's lip trembled, but Samitha grabbed her by the hand and they scurried from the room.

"Anshu, I am waiting." Jeeva's calm voice carried menace.

"Master!" wailed Kalani. "It's all my fault. I am the one deserving of your anger."

Jeeva's icy gaze shifted from Anshu to the maid. "What is going on in my house? What are you women plotting?"

"Nothing, I swear on my life!" Anshu cried.

"Do you wish to see me disgraced at court? The penalty for deceiving the king is death. And what a monstrous deception this is." He gently swung the baby, but it responded only with happy gurgling.

Anshu dropped her head. "I never intended anything like this."

Just at that moment an elephant trumpeted loudly from the street, and there came a knock at the door.

"Master," a servant called, "Yakkhini and the calf are here. All the guests have arrived. The procession is ready to depart."

Jeeva looked at the baby still suspended in his grip. "I ought to call everything off," he murmured.

Kalani took a step toward Jeeva. "Master. Your wife can bear no more babies, so this must be your son. Nobody knows the truth apart from us, not even the girls."

Grim-faced, Jeeva looked back at her. He knew only too well how long it had taken for Anshu's womb to be blessed again after the birth of Mihiri and how difficult this pregnancy had been. Even the doctor who had examined her could offer no hope of another.

Further, he saw no way of resolving the problem without causing a scandal that would be the talk of the court for years to come, so he gave a brief nod. "Anshu and I will greet our guests. Get the child dressed. But after the celebration I want to know what drove you two to do this."

Jeeva's neighbors ran along Astawanka-veediya as the procession passed by. Laughing and waving, they scattered flowers on the street and wished the family happiness and plenty.

At the head of the procession was one of Jeeva's supporters, bearing the Maha Nuvara family standard, a white elephant on a gold background. Then came drummers and people playing flutes and tambourines. Behind them walked Yakkhini and her calf. Both were decked out in magnificently colored blankets which covered their heads, ears, and trunks. Around Yakkhini's legs were lightweight chains with bells that jangled loudly with every step. Eranga rode between her ears, guiding her gently with his feet and his voice. Just behind him was a *howdah*, firmly strapped to the elephant's back. Here, beneath a canopy, sat Jeeva, Anshu, and the baby. Anshu held the child while Jeeva waved to all sides in a stately fashion. His face gave no indication that only moments before he had discovered that his son was really a daughter.

The rear of the procession was made up of Kalani with Samitha, Mihiri, and relatives who had come to celebrate the new arrival. They held sunshades with one hand and, with the other, carried baskets of offerings for the Buddha. Jeeva's grandfather, the oldest member of the family, proudly wrapped his gnarled hands around a small bowl of boiled rice, the most important of all offerings.

Mahinda Dharmapala awaited the procession beneath a superb Bodhi tree in the temple area of the palace. The guests set their offerings on the ground around the tree and then lit small candles.

At a signal from her mahout, Yakkhini knelt so that Jeeva and Anshu could climb down in comfort. Jeeva took the child and, with Anshu, stood before the monk. Mahinda opened the ceremony with a traditional chant, telling of the ancient sutras that augured happiness. Then he burned incense in a small bronze container. When the smoke began to rise, spreading its scent of cloves, cinnamon, and sandalwood, he went to Yakkhini and her calf and swung the burner in front of the baby elephant, saying, "You shall be called Siddhi, after the third wife of Ganesha, the elephant god. May you be happy all your life and blessed with many offspring."

Then he turned to the baby, who was watching him with her big, dark eyes, and said, "You shall be called Phera. May you be wise and astute, passionate, courageous, and persevering, just as your name augurs."

"A girl's name?" Jeeva's outburst disturbed the solemnity of the moment, and all the guests looked at him in alarm.

Anshu quickly took his arm and put on her most conciliatory voice. "Phera is a good name, and it can be for boys as well as girls." But she, too, had jumped in fear when the monk spoke.

Mahinda's gaze rested on the baby, then on Anshu, before moving to Jeeva. "The name came from the depths of my consciousness while I was meditating on your child," he replied calmly. "You do not have to accept it."

Jeeva cleared his throat. "Forgive me, venerable *hamudru*, I have been disrespectful. The child will be called Phera."

Now Jeeva's grandfather stepped forward with the bowl of rice. He pinched a few grains between his fingertips, carefully placed them in the baby's mouth, and announced, "Phera is your name."

The monk bent to pick up a brass singing bowl and gently circled its rim with the accompanying rod. A high, even tone of pure beauty resounded over the assembled company before eventually fading to an echo. Anshu took a deep breath. She knew the interpretation of Phera's birth sign would come next.

Mahinda had already straightened up and taken a piece of palm leaf from inside his habit. This was where he had drawn out Phera's horoscope: a big square subdivided into smaller squares symbolizing the twelve astrological houses. Within these were the twelve star signs and the nine *grahas*, consisting of the seven principal planets and the two moon nodes. How to interpret the celestial constellations had been revealed to wise men in times of light and truth, now long past. That knowledge helped through the joys and sorrows of life every soul incarnate on Earth.

Mahinda held the leaf high so that all present could see and declaimed, "The soul of the child Phera has become incarnate in the sign of Kataka, Cancer, the sensitive one, which reflects the eternal alternation between birth and death, leaving and returning. But Kataka's ascendant, Vrishika, the poisonous Scorpio, can prevent the soul from following its destiny. Vrishika's influence means that Phera's mind is as sharp as a newly whetted blade. But if it is not used wisely, it can turn dangerous and deadly, like an untamed elephant. The ruling planets in Phera's horoscope are Chandra, the sentimental Moon, and Mangal, the aggressive Mars. They strengthen the opposites, Kataka and Vrishika."

The monk lowered the palm leaf and looked at Jeeva and Anshu. "Your child will feel as if there are two souls living in, and tearing at, its body," he said. "If the child wants to realize the characteristics of Kataka and Chandra, then Vrishika and Mangal will immediately pull in the other direction. This child's *dharma*, its goal in life, has to be to tame and unify the souls fighting within."

The assembled company gasped to hear that Phera's soul would have such a thorny path through life in this incarnation. While Mahinda went on to explain the significance of the twelve astrological houses, the interrelationship of the planets, and the influence of earlier incarnations, Anshu's thoughts drifted back to the day of Phera's birth. She regretted with all her heart that she had burdened her daughter so, and wished she had revealed Kalani's lie. But it was now too late for remorse; her innocent child would have to bear the burden of what they had done.

"Nothing happens by chance!" Mahinda's voice tore Anshu from her thoughts. "Everything is embedded within the great cosmic order and is borne along with it just as waves are borne by the ocean." He stepped before Phera. "There will be times when you will feel so lonely, as if you are alone in the world. But don't despair. People will come, people who will recognize your true being and will know that you were born to break new ground." He positioned his hands like a protective canopy above Phera's little head. "May evil stay far from you and goodness draw near. May you always walk on the path of the eight virtues so that no pain can follow you, only love and kindness."

Late that evening, when all the guests had gone home, Jeeva went to his wife's bedroom. Anshu was sitting up in bed, Phera at her breast. When Jeeva came in, the little girl broke off, turned her head, and gave her father a beautiful smile. He sat down on the bed with a deep sigh.

"Are you angry with me?" asked Anshu in a soft voice, as she put the baby to her breast again.

"Do you think I've forgiven your deception just because we've all enjoyed such a wonderful naming day?" He sat on the edge of the bed and watched the baby peacefully suckling. "What on earth were you thinking of?"

She touched his hand, but he pulled it away. "I know I've done you a grave injustice," she said slowly. "But I also know how much you longed for a son. I prayed for one out of love for you, and out of that same love, I remained silent about the truth. I've often been close to telling you, but in the end, I couldn't find it in my heart to destroy your joy in our child."

"But now that joy has been destroyed," he shot back. "You and Kalani have put me in an impossible position."

"Kalani's not at fault in this," Anshu retorted. "She knew how sad I was about not giving you a son." She lifted Phera from her breast and dabbed the baby's little mouth with the corner of a towel. "Just look at our child." She placed the baby on Jeeva's lap. "And then tell me whether your feelings for her have really changed."

Jeeva squinted at the baby, who, sleepy with milk, returned his gaze. "Everything has changed."

"She is your daughter," Anshu said. "But who says she can't manage with the tasks a son would? 'Don't be sad that you have a daughter, because she is going to be every bit as good as a son.' That's what the Buddha said to the king of Kosala as he walked with him in his garden."

"I can't possibly go to the king and tell him my wife and her maid have made a fool of me!"

"Were you not listening to the monk's horoscope?" Anshu leaned close to Jeeva and looked into his eyes. "She has been born to break new ground. It is Phera's destiny to take a path never before taken by any woman. Until a few hours ago, this child was a son for you. You treated her as a son and had no doubt in her strengths and capabilities. That need not change just because you now know she's a girl."

Jeeva looked perplexed. "What are you trying to say? That Phera should—you mean, a man's life?" He shook his head in disbelief. "That's quite impossible."

Anshu reached for his hand again, and this time he did not pull away. "The heavens determined Phera's destiny on the day of her creation. This means she is your heir and will take the place of the son you will never have."

"Phera? Take on my position as senior keeper? Out of the question!" Jeeva shook his head again. "Elephants are too big and strong to obey a woman."

"They're too big and strong to obey a man, yet they do," replied Anshu. "We will raise Phera as your son, and we will hand her to the mahouts for training—"

"—so she'll learn all the things a son would have learned," Jeeva slowly finished the sentence for her. He thought hard for a few minutes and looked at his daughter, now sleeping peacefully in his arms. "After the lie we've told, this is the only way left open to us." He leaned toward his wife, across the sleeping baby's head. "We are guarding a dangerous secret, Anshu, a secret which Kalani, you, and I must keep forever. And we must instill this secrecy in Phera as soon as she is old enough to understand. Should the tiniest hint come to light, I would be executed, and you and the children would be banished from any caste."

Chapter Two
Senkadagala, Lanka, 1815

"Daha!" shouted Phera. "Walk on!"

Siddhi hardly needed the command. She waded eagerly into the shallows of the Mahaweli Ganga, Phera on her back. The cow elephant was now almost twelve, and nearly as big as Yakkhini.

"Well done, young man," said Eranga approvingly. "Next time, give the spoken instruction at the same time that you squeeze your toes behind her ears. That way she'll learn the language of your body, too. Now it's time for you to praise her."

Phera opened his shoulder bag and took out a banana. Siddhi had already reached around with her trunk in anticipation of the tasty tidbit.

"She knows she's earned a reward." Phera laughed. "Shall I wash her now, Eranga?"

"Yes. Be sure to get all the grime out of her skinfolds. And remember to check her over for any injuries. Pay special attention to washing off any urine traces between her back legs."

Phera nodded seriously. Eranga had been his instructor since his fifth birthday.

"You know that Eranga is my first mahout," Jeeva had said. "Nobody in the kingdom knows these sacred animals like he does. Always listen to him very carefully and follow his instructions."

If Phera was to take over his father's position as royal elephant keeper, he would not actually do the work of a mahout. But it was important for him to know everything the work entailed.

"Can you remember the command for Siddhi to lie on her belly?" asked Eranga.

Phera's reply was drowned out by a babble of voices: "First in the water's the winner!" Bare feet slapped against the ground as a group of six boys emerged from the bushes and ran into the water.

"There's Phera!" called one of them. "Phera, d'you want to swim with us?"

He groaned inwardly and pretended he hadn't heard. The invitation was not a real one, because the boys knew Phera never joined any rough-and-tumble.

One of them was already goading him. "Scared of the water, Phera? Are you still a baby?"

"Or are you too grand to come swimming with us?" called out another. In mocking imitation of a peacock, the boy strutted back and forth in front of his friends, earning howls of approval.

Eranga shooed them away as he would a horde of monkeys. "Go away! Leave the young gentleman in peace!"

Phera's expression hardened. The boys had been mocking him for years. Like him, they were the children of palace officials and had all grown up in the same neighborhood. Once upon a time, they had climbed trees together, built camps of palm leaves, and played hide-and-seek amongst the palace's many buildings. But that had stopped long ago.

"Phera's a coward, Phera's a coward!"

The chanting pained him deeply. But he fought bravely against the tears welling up. Crying in front of his tormentors was out of the question.

"Leave him alone, all of you."

Phera was taken aback to hear Tharindu's voice. Tharindu was fourteen, older than the others, and he never joined in the teasing.

Still, the singsong continued. "Phera's scared of water! Phera's a coward!"

High atop Siddhi's back, Phera clenched his fists. Small and slight, he knew only too well he would get the worst of any fight.

All this time Siddhi had been standing quietly in the cool water. But now she turned to get the boys in her line of sight. She whipped her ears back and forth in warning, then began to charge.

"Hold back your elephant, Phera!" shrieked the ringleader.

"Who's the coward now?" Phera yelled. He urged on Siddhi, plowing determinedly through the water.

The boys splashed their way toward the bank. Phera saw the panic in their faces as they looked back and realized the elephant was gaining on them. Out of the corner of his eye, he spotted Eranga running back and forth at the water's edge, brandishing his ankus.

That'll do, thought Phera. *They've learned their lesson.*

"Ho!" he called out. "Ho, Siddhi. Stop!"

But the elephant took no notice and charged on, her trunk outstretched, ready to attack. Phera started to panic. Much as he despised his tormentors, he did not want to see them trampled. He knew it was not uncommon for an elephant, even a tame one, to attack a human. His father always had such creatures put down immediately. The thought was unbearable.

"Stop, Siddhi!" he called out again. "Please!"

But the creature took no notice. Phera had never felt so small and helpless.

"Eranga!" he shouted fearfully. "Help me!"

The mahout was already trying to block Siddhi's path, but he was too far away. Within seconds Siddhi had reached the fugitives, rounded them up, and blocked their way to the bank. Phera clung to her back, paralyzed with fear.

All of a sudden, Siddhi lifted her trunk high and sprayed a powerful jet of water at the boys, making them shriek with surprise. Then she turned around and marched contentedly back into the deeper water. Phera smiled at the sight of the boys' dripping faces. He leaned forward to stroke Siddhi's rough gray head.

"Thank you, my friend."

He glanced over and saw the boys playing a safe distance away, acting as if he and the elephant were not even there.

Phera ordered Siddhi to lie down on her belly. Then he took from his shoulder bag a piece of neatly cut coconut shell, dipped it in the water, and began to carefully scrub at the elephant's hide, so thick and yet so sensitive. He kept an eye on the boys, now playing bare chested in the waist-high water. Glistening drops cascaded down their brown skin. As Tharindu plunged headfirst into the current, Phera's eyes traced the well-defined muscles of his broad shoulders. He saw Tharindu's firm buttocks and the sinews on the back of his thighs. Phera's chest tightened. Then he experienced the strangest feeling, a tingling sensation between his legs, so overwhelming he had to press himself against Siddhi's neck. But this only increased the tingling. It overtook him completely, wonderful but frightening.

"Phera!" called Tharindu as he broke the surface again, energetically tossing back the wet hair from his face. "Come into the water with us. I'll make sure the others don't mess with you."

Phera blushed deeply. He said nothing in reply, just bent over Siddhi's head in confusion and scrubbed at it with the coconut brush.

After a few minutes, curiosity overcame him and he stole a look over his shoulder. Tharindu was horsing around with the other boys. He jumped high, then tried to knock his opponent off balance and push his head under the water. When the lower part of Tharindu's body emerged from the water, Phera had to stifle a gasp. The older boy's sarong, knotted at the hip, had slipped aside, and Phera found himself staring in amazement at Tharindu's thighs and the fleshy pipe dangling between them.

He remembered an incident six years earlier, when Tharindu and the other boys were still his playmates. One of them had suggested a competition to see who could pee the farthest. Tharindu had lifted his sarong, and Phera had seen between his legs the same fleshy thing, only smaller than now. It had shocked him then, too. He didn't have anything like this on his body. His shock had turned to horror when the other boys had lifted their sarongs and he'd seen it between their legs, also.

What's that? six-year-old Phera had asked himself. *And why don't I have one?*

He'd bolted from the competition, running off to Kalani with his worrying discovery. "Don't concern yourself, young master," Kalani had said. "Yes, boys are born with this piece of flesh, but it dries up and drops off. In your case, that's already happened."

Now Phera stole another glance at the boys romping in the shallows. Several of their sarongs had slipped, and it was clear that their fleshy pipes had not dropped off any more than Tharindu's had.

So Kalani had lied to him. But why? He remembered how his father and mother had talked to him very seriously after that early incident and explained it was not acceptable for the son of a high-level palace official ever to be seen naked or carelessly dressed. After that they would no longer let Phera leave the house without an adult. From then on Phera's only playmates were his sisters, Samitha and Mihiri, boring girls who just wanted to play with dolls and who would cry if Phera pulled their hair.

Phera plucked uncertainly at his sarong, lying smooth and empty where his thighs spread left and right on Siddhi's neck. There could be only one explanation for Kalani's untruth and his parents' behavior: it was not the other boys who were deformed; it was him.

He slid off the elephant in a flash. "Eranga, take care of Siddhi, please!" he cried and ran toward home, paying no attention to the dumbfounded mahout.

◆　◆　◆

"Kalani! Kalani!"

The elderly maid, seated on a bench in the shade of the veranda, looked up in surprise from the basket she was weaving. Phera came racing around the corner of the house.

"Young man! What's happened?" She set her work down next to her on the bench.

Phera stopped in front of her, panting. "Am I sick, Kalani?"

"Sick?" repeated the maid. "Do you have a fever?" She lifted her hand and rested her worn fingers on Phera's cheek, flushed from running.

Phera shook the hand away in impatience. "I don't mean sick with a fever. I mean sick from the accident I had when I was little."

"Accident?" Kalani shook her head. "There was no accident."

"Don't lie to me again!" shouted Phera, close to tears. "I'm deformed. Here." He tugged at his sarong, knotted below the hips. The lines on Kalani's careworn face seemed to deepen. She reached out, but her little charge shrank from her.

"You lied when you said it would drop off the other boys!" Phera screamed. "Why? Why didn't you admit something happened to me? Or was I born like this?"

"You're not sick, my child." Now tears were pouring down Kalani's cheeks.

"So what happened?"

Kalani shook her head. "Let's go to your mother. She will tell you everything." With difficulty, she got to her feet.

They found Anshu in the drawing room. She was sitting in a beautifully carved high-backed chair, and before her knelt the cook, as was seemly for someone of the lower castes. When Kalani and then Phera entered the room, the two women were in the middle of discussing the food for Samitha's wedding party in four weeks' time.

"Ma'am," said Kalani. "Phera would like to speak to you."

Anshu looked up. "Can't it wait?" she asked, a little annoyed. But when she saw the distraught look on Phera's face, she waved away her cook. "You can leave us now."

"Mama," Phera began as soon as the cook had gone. "Kalani says I'm not sick. But I saw the other boys bathing and I know I'm different. My body's not right."

The color drained from Anshu's face. "Kalani, send one of the men to fetch my husband from the stables. Tell him it's urgent."

The elderly maid hobbled away as fast as she could.

"Sit, my child." Anshu gestured at the sofa near her chair. Phera anxiously obeyed. He tried to catch his mother's eye, but Anshu avoided his gaze. Her restless fingers toyed with a small silver bowl in her lap. She removed its lid, took out a piece of betel nut, placed it in her mouth, and chewed nervously. Then she offered Phera some. But the boy shook his head.

"You are not sick, my child," said Anshu gently. "You're just as you should be. That's all I can say until your father arrives."

This reply only upset Phera further. After all, he had actually seen that he was deformed. They couldn't lie to him anymore. An agonizing silence hung in the air. Time itself seemed suspended. At last the front door opened, steps hastened along the hallway, and Jeeva threw open the drawing-room door.

"What happened?" he panted.

Anshu took a deep breath. "It is time," she said, a slight tremble in her voice. "We must tell Phera the truth."

Jeeva's face froze. He turned to his child and stared.

Phera cleared his throat. "I saw the other boys when they were in the river. And now I know I'm deformed." He swallowed hard. "Do I have a disease, Papa? Am I going to die?"

Anshu stifled a sob.

Jeeva went to Phera and crouched down in front of him. "You are not deformed and you're not going to die, my child. But on the day of your birth, you were dealt a special destiny." He placed his hands on the child's knees in a protective gesture. "You were not born as our son, Phera. You were born as our third daughter. Yet you are not permitted to be our daughter."

Then he told the young boy—the girl—what had happened the night of the birth and in the months that followed. Phera listened without interrupting, her eyes growing bigger and bigger. When Jeeva finished speaking, there was another long silence.

Eventually, Phera said quietly, "So I'm not a boy." She looked down at her own lap and thought of what she had seen today. "All these years I've had to be a boy, when I'm not a boy at all."

"That is your destiny," responded Jeeva. "Without you, I have no son, no heir to my office as senior elephant keeper. This office has been in our family for generations. The respect we are shown and our high rank at court all rest on this. There are jealous people who are after the position, but they won't get it. I am the ninth Gajanayake Nilame from the house of Maha Nuvara. You shall be the tenth."

She remained silent, her heart full of questions she longed to ask.

Jeeva went on. "Heaven sent us a sign that you were chosen to take the place of a son when the king bestowed on you the elephant born the same night. With your birth horoscope, that sign was confirmed.

Your mother and I know you bear a difficult destiny. But it would not have been decided for you if you couldn't live up to it."

Phera tried to understand what her father was saying, but everything he talked of was either too long ago for her to remember or somewhere in the distant future. She understood one thing and one thing only. She was not a boy, as she had believed herself to be for the last twelve years, but a girl. She had loved being a boy, but certain things began to make sudden sense.

Her thoughts went to Tharindu and the sensation she had experienced watching him, and mixed with all her confusion was the tiniest bit of happiness. She tilted her head to one side and asked shyly, "So I took the place of a son, but may I be a girl, too?"

"Never!"

Phera trembled. "I don't understand, Father."

He shut his eyes and took a deep breath. "When the king made you the gift of Siddhi, he signaled that the post of senior elephant keeper is to stay in our family—with you. And such a high office may be held only by a man."

"But one day I'll be a woman," Phera persisted. "And I know plenty about elephants. Eranga says I'm the best pupil he's ever had."

"You must not ever think that one day you'll become a woman, Phera," answered Jeeva. "For the king, for your mother and me, for the whole world, you will remain forever my son, just as you have always been."

Again she thought of Tharindu and her throat tightened. "But what if I don't want to be a boy forever?"

"Silence! Don't let me ever hear those words again!" He seized her by the shoulders. "I demand obedience, Phera. You are a boy. You will accept your destiny."

Tears streamed down her cheeks.

Jeeva let go of her shoulders and held her head with both hands so that she had to look straight into his eyes. "You mustn't cry, child. Be strong, as befits my son and heir. And never forget: the well-being of our entire family depends on you. You must keep your secret until death."

Several weeks passed, during which Phera turned her father's words over in her mind endlessly.

Her father behaved as if the day's events had never happened and continued to treat her as his son, just as before. Her mother often looked at her with concern and seemed to hesitate before addressing the child as her son. Anshu tried to make Phera's life as a boy seem attractive for her. "Just think of the education you're getting," she would say. "Your sisters have learned only how to read, write, and run a household. While you have learned to do arithmetic and will, one day, be invested with a position open to very few men, and never to a woman."

But when Phera asked why she could not learn and hold an important position as a girl, her mother had no answer.

Kalani took special care of her, making sure that the cook prepared her favorite foods and that there was always a bath and a fresh set of clothes ready after her work with Siddhi.

"Don't quarrel with your destiny, young man," Kalani said. "You cannot change it, so you must resign yourself to it."

In these confusing weeks, Phera buried herself in the activity she had always loved best: spending time with Siddhi. Whenever she busied herself with the young elephant, keeping her clean, feeding her, and tending to her needs, she could forget her own inner turmoil. Deeply affected to learn that she carried the fate of the family on her twelve-year-old shoulders, she understood that she must never reveal her secret. For other people, she was a boy. But her last thought at night before falling asleep, and her first in the morning when she awoke, was *I am a girl.*

"Today Mother bought some fabric from the Moorish merchants from Colombo," she confided in Siddhi one day. "We're all getting new clothes for Samitha's wedding. Samitha's sari will be gold silk, and Mihiri's will be pink. If I were allowed to wear a sari, I'd love to have one the same yellow as the *ruk attana* flowers in our garden. And I'd put some blooms in my hair, too."

She sighed ruefully. For the wedding party she would wear a new sarong, a shirt, and a short, embroidered men's jacket. Her uncles would wink as always, asking if she had any peach fuzz on her cheeks yet.

She rested her arm for a moment and lowered the coconut shell she had been grooming Siddhi with, so she could lay her forehead against the animal's shoulder. "I wish I didn't have to go to the wedding at all."

The young elephant wrapped her trunk protectively around Phera's waist and made a gentle rumbling sound.

The monk, Mahinda, had compared the horoscopes of bride and groom and set the wedding date for the new moon in the last month before spring. The bride's relatives began to arrive several days beforehand, while the groom's family sent gifts for Samitha every day. There were bangles, necklaces, rings, and earrings of gold and precious gems. Oxcarts piled high with household goods went daily from Jeeva's house to the bride's future home, only a stone's throw from Astawanka-veediya.

Her bridegroom, Upali Amarasekere, was considered a young man of great promise. At the court of Vikrama Rajasinha, he had the important job of overseeing the kingdom's revenue and expenditures. His father, Psindu, was amongst the king's most powerful supporters. Psindu was the *dissava*, the administrator of the province of Uva, and represented the ruler's power there. Both families belonged to the high Radala caste and had agreed that a marriage between their children would be advantageous.

The wedding took place in the garden of the bride's house. There, beneath a huge mango tree, workmen had set up the wedding *poruwa*, a wooden platform with a baldachin decorated with flowers, beneath which the bridal pair would seal their vows.

The garden was full of excited guests, all dressed up for the occasion. The groom's relatives had already gathered on the right side of the poruwa, the bride's on the left.

Directly in front of the platform stood the master of ceremonies, at his side the groom, nervously jigging from one foot to the other.

Mihiri turned to Phera. "Look how nervous Upali is. Do you think he loves our sister?"

"I don't think so. He's only met her once, with Mama and his mother chaperoning."

"But if it's true love, one look is enough," said Mihiri. "You're still too little to understand that. And anyway, you're a boy."

Phera winced. The sound of trumpets and flutes on the street drew nearer.

"It's starting!" As Mihiri craned to get a good view, the servants opened the gates to the garden. Phera watched in surprise as her mother and aunts all took handkerchiefs from their handbags and dabbed at their eyes.

Then came the musicians, dancing through the gates. With her arm linked through her father's, Samitha stepped from the house and joined the procession. A sigh rippled through the crowd. Samitha was radiant. Her eyes, full of joy and expectation, were directed toward the groom; and when he gave her a shy smile, her face glowed. She cut a graceful, womanly figure, and her sari hugged her hips and her full breasts.

I want to look like that, too, Phera thought.

Her own breasts had been developing for a while, and although they were still no more than bumps, her mother made her bind them flat with strips of linen. Kalani always pulled the cloth so tight that Phera felt she could barely breathe.

"Doesn't Samitha look beautiful?" said Mihiri with a sigh. "I'll be next, in just a couple more years. Maybe I'll marry your friend over there, the one waving. He's handsome and looks strong. Then again, I don't want a husband who's younger than me."

Phera followed Mihiri's gaze to Tharindu, and her stomach filled with dread. Ever since her discovery, she had avoided him and the other boys more than ever.

"He definitely wouldn't want to marry anyone as old as you."

"You're just in one of your moods again," Mihiri snapped back at her.

Phera fixed her eyes on the procession and pretended she hadn't heard.

Samitha and her future husband stood face-to-face and greeted one another, their palms flat on their chests. Upali led his bride up the two steps of the poruwa. When both stood side by side under the canopy, the master of ceremonies handed them a tray bearing betel-pepper leaves, the symbol of a happy marriage. Then Upali hung a golden chain around Samitha's neck. Next Jeeva placed his daughter's right hand on Upali's. The couple linked their little fingers, and over this an uncle of the groom poured water from a silver pot. At the end of the ceremony, Anshu handed her daughter a bowl of boiled rice, and the couple fed one another. Finally, Mihiri and the other girls sang the "Jayamangala Gatha," a song extolling the Buddha's virtues and believed to bring luck to the newlyweds.

At the end of the performance, Phera lowered her head so no one would see her tears. It was hard to share her sister's joy when she herself could never marry—not as a woman and surely not as a man. She wiped her eyes on her sleeves.

"You feel lonely, don't you?"

Phera whipped around to find herself looking at Mahinda Dharmapala. As the monk's gaze rested on her, she felt he was looking into the depths of her soul.

"Don't despair, Phera," he said, "for you are strong."

"I don't feel strong," she answered faintly. "I feel weak and helpless."

"Let those feelings pass through you like a breath of wind. Be fearless and brave, and know that your spirit is eternal and indestructible."

She understood that he wanted to do more than comfort her. He wanted to convey something of great importance, a message to strengthen her in hard times. But the loneliness remained in her heart. She looked at Tharindu. He was standing close to Mihiri now and must have been telling an amusing tale, because she was laughing and inclining her head so close to his mouth that her ear brushed his lips.

"Will I ever marry, venerable hamudru?" Phera asked.

He smiled gently. "One day someone will come, someone who will recognize your true being." For a moment he placed his hand on Phera's shoulder. Then he turned and left.

She watched until the orange glow of his robe vanished into the crowd.

"I shall bear my destiny," she told herself. "But I'll never stop hoping. And apart from the one big secret that I did not seek out for myself, I shall have my own secrets that belong to me and me alone."

A lavish feast of rice, spiced meats, ripe fruits, coconut milk, and palm wine lasted until long after sunset. The servants lit torches in the garden, and the company was entertained by singers, musicians, and dancers. Anshu sat under one canopy with the women, Jeeva under another with the men. The bride and groom, together with the younger guests, organized lively games. They had great fun hurling cotton bolls at one another. Anyone missing a catch got a generous spraying of water.

Phera did not join the games. After the meal she took a couple of pieces of fruit and stole out of the garden to see Siddhi. Since earliest childhood, she had always spent much of the day with her elephant friend. But today the wedding party had kept her away.

It was already close to midnight when Phera reached the stables. After the evening feeding, the mahouts had put out all the lights, and the stable was lit only by pale starlight, a gentle gleam coming through the skylights and the open door. Phera paused a moment in the alley, breathing in the warm scent of the animals and listening to the slow, regular chewing as they ground down leaves and rice straw in their powerful jaws. Then she went to Siddhi's stall, located roughly in the middle of the long row. Siddhi turned as much as her rope allowed and greeted Phera with that familiar rumbling.

"*Ayubowan*, my friend." Phera squeezed into Siddhi's stall and stroked the animal's crinkled cheeks. "I know I'm a bit late today, but I've brought you a couple of special treats: breadfruit and mangoes and, yes, your favorite, too."

Siddhi's trunk explored Phera's fingers until it found the banana.

Once she had fed the elephant all the delicacies, Phera sat down on the rice-straw-covered floor, caressing Siddhi's trunk and gazing at the powerful head high above her. Behind it the animal's back rose like a dome. Siddhi's small eyes sparkled in the dim light, and her ears moved slowly back and forth. The tip of her trunk gently played over Phera's hair, then puffed at her neck.

"That tickles!" Phera giggled.

"Let's talk in here." A male voice came from the stable door. "So nobody can see us or hear us."

Phera gave a little jump. She knew all the mahouts' voices, but this one was unfamiliar. It was hoarse and croaky, as if its owner were about to cough.

Someone was creeping into the stable. Phera ducked behind Siddhi's front legs, which towered in front of her like pillars, and held her breath as the footsteps came closer and closer. The feeble light of an oil lamp lit up the floor. The man passed the other cow elephants, snuffling in quiet concern about a stranger in their midst, and stopped almost directly in front of Siddhi's stall.

"Is it safe?" asked the croaky voice from the entrance.

"Yes, sir. There's nobody here," replied a second voice. The first man then felt his way into the stable and joined the other.

Phera peered cautiously from between the elephant's legs. Two pairs of human legs stood on the patch of mud floor lit up by the oil lamp. One was draped in a sarong reaching almost to the ankles, the feet in expensive gilded sandals, much like those her father wore. The other pair of feet was unshod and the sarong hitched up to the knees. Siddhi's huge body blocked any view of the men's top halves.

"Turn down the lamp," ordered the croaky one. The flame faded to give the smallest light. "You have news for me?"

"A letter from the British general, sir," replied the second man.

There was some rustling. Phera heard a dry crack as a seal was broken, then again the rustling of paper. There was silence for several minutes. At last the one with the croaky voice said, "This is good news. You have earned your reward." There was a soft clinking of coins.

"I thank you, sir. What answer shall I convey to the British general?"

Another silence followed; then the first man responded: "Tell General Brownrigg that I, and my loyal supporters, stand ready. Vikrama Rajasinha is finished."

Phera gasped, then quickly clapped her hand to her mouth. Too late. The men's feet swiveled in her direction.

"What was that?" asked the first one under his breath.

"It came from the elephant stall. Might be a monkey, having a go at the feed." The second man clapped a few times.

Phera held her breath. The elephant barely moved a muscle either. Only her trunk gently stroked Phera's shoulders.

"A monkey would have cleared off by now! There's someone here," the first man hissed in annoyance. "Someone's listening."

Phera watched, petrified, as the legs moved toward the stall. Then Siddhi stepped in. She stamped her feet in anger and swung her powerful hindquarters from side to side.

"We can't go in, sir; the elephant will crush us." The second man sounded scared.

"Turn the lamp up," the first man ordered. "Someone's been listening."

Phera jumped up and pulled at the bolt that secured the outside gate. But it was jammed. She was trapped. Her heart pounded. She looked around in search of an escape route, and her eyes landed on the skylight directly above her head. But it was far too high. She clenched her fists in frustration. Siddhi seemed to sense her fear and gently stroked her tensed fingers with the tip of her trunk.

Oh, my dear friend, even you can't help me, thought Phera and clasped Siddhi's trunk. Then something struck her. *Yes, you can.*

She stood up straight and whispered: *"Rangu!"*

Phera had started practicing this just recently with Siddhi and was not at all sure whether the elephant had gotten the hang of lifting her truck on command.

The lamp grew brighter as one of the men tried to shine it into the stall. Luckily, Siddhi's enormous body was still obscuring the view.

"Rangu!" repeated Phera and tapped Siddhi's trunk. After a moment's hesitation, the elephant lifted her trunk into the shape of a swing. Phera sat on it, and Siddhi tensed her muscles to hoist her little load. In a flash, Phera drew level with the skylight. She could have wept with relief.

"Thank you," she whispered to Siddhi.

She grabbed the lintel with both hands and pulled herself up, getting first her upper body and then legs through. She looked down from the high roof.

"There's a boy out there!" she heard the second man yell.

"We have to catch him," shouted the first one. "Go!"

Phera closed her eyes, summoned all her courage, and jumped. She hit the ground hard, and pain shot through her ankles and knees. But she recovered quickly and ran for it.

She knew these stables so well, she could have found her way blindfolded. The cinnamon trees surrounding the cows' stables were surrounded by thick, prickly bushes. With the courage born of desperation, she plunged in. Thorns scratched every bit of exposed skin.

Bravely, she swallowed her yelps of pain and banished from her mind all thoughts of the spiders, poisonous snakes, and terrifying black scorpions she might have stirred into activity. She rolled herself into a ball under the bushes and listened. The men were already very close, and she could hear their footsteps and low voices.

"Where on earth did he go?" asked the second man. He beat at the bushes with his hands, right above where Phera lay.

"Stop that!" said the croaky voice. "Do you want to get attacked by a cobra?"

Their footsteps receded, and Phera heard them darting amongst the cinnamon trees.

"He got away, sir," the second voice said. "If the child warns the king, we're dead."

"Nobody will warn the king. My own people are guarding him tonight," he retorted. "They will let only General Brownrigg through so he can take Vikrama Rajasinha captive, and that'll be before daybreak. Now take my message to the general. I must get back to the wedding before anyone misses me."

Phera lay beneath the bushes, rigid with fear, listening to the sounds of the night. Elephants shuffled in their stalls, owls hooted in the trees, and small rodents rustled through the undergrowth. Her scratches stung, but she just gritted her teeth.

Once she was sure the men would not return, Phera climbed warily out of the bushes and raced through the moonless night to her parents' home. It was clear to her that enemy soldiers were at the gate of the city and the king was in danger.

The wedding party was still in full swing when she rushed back into the garden. Fire-eaters, jugglers, and acrobats were showing off their tricks to enthusiastic applause.

She found her father with several of her uncles. Seated on comfortable chairs and sofas, goblets of palm wine in their hands, they were all deep in discussion.

"Papa! Papa!"

"What is it, Phera? I'm busy at the moment," he said. But as he turned to shoo her off, his eyes widened. "Child! You look as if you've had a fight with a leopard." He reached out toward the red marks on her face and hands. Her shirt and sarong were spattered with blood and dirt.

"I have to tell you something, Papa!" Leaning close to his ear, she whispered everything that had happened at the stables. The more she recounted, the more dismayed Jeeva's expression became.

In the seventeen years he'd been on the throne, this was not the first attempt to depose Vikrama Rajasinha. His former patron, the first *adikarm* or most senior minister, Pilima Talawe, had offered to kill the king for the British twelve years ago if they would help him take the Crown. This plot failed, but Vikrama Rajasinha later had the man executed for high treason. Jeeva had thought it a mistake when the king then appointed, of all people, Pilima's own nephew, Ehelopola, as first adikarm, and had not been surprised when the king discovered that Ehelopola was also plotting against him. Unlike his uncle, however, Ehelopola managed to flee to the territory under British rule. Hearing Phera's tale tonight, Jeeva immediately suspected the man's involvement.

Jeeva's eyes ranged over the guests. The most important of the king's palace officials, generals, district administrators, temple superintendents, and monks were all in his home for this great occasion. Feeling uneasy, he wondered if he should bring the party to a close, send the guests home, and take his family to safety. With a slight shake of the head, he decided against it. This would only arouse suspicion and do nothing to help the king.

He took some deep breaths and placed his hands on Phera's shoulders. "My child, you have done the right thing, and I am proud of you. I'll take care of everything else myself. Go to your mother and stay close."

Jeeva stood up. He had to warn the king. Phera had reported that the king's bodyguards counted amongst the traitors, so he would find a way of forcing his way through to his monarch. He would have to hurry if the king was to reach the safety of his highland fortress in Hanguranketha. Once the British had crossed the Kadugannawa Pass, the capital city and the king would lie exposed before them.

Jeeva cleared a path through the crowd, smiling to left and right as he went and trying to arouse as little attention as possible. A guest seized his arm. "You don't want to leave your own party before the end, now do you, Jeeva Maha Nuvara?" His voice was croaky, as if he were about to cough.

Jeeva was wondering if he should take the man into his confidence. This guest was, after all, the second adikarm and a close confidant of the monarch. But he dismissed the idea. He could trust nobody. "I'm looking for the servants who are to prepare the fireworks, Deepal Sirisena."

The second adikarm nodded jovially. "Afterward I would very much like to talk to you about our children. My son and your daughter seem to like one another." With a smile, he looked over at Tharindu and Mihiri. They were sitting on a sofa, their heads close together.

"Indeed, Deepal." Jeeva hurried onward, but just before he reached the gate, a servant rushed up to him, shouting.

"Master! Foreign soldiers are in the city! They're coming down Astawanka-veediya now."

A wave of panic spread through the gathering as these words were passed from ear to ear. Voices rang out in disbelief, and everyone spilled out onto the street. Jeeva scoured the crowd for his family. Upali had put his arm around Samitha and pulled her behind the stage with the acrobats, where they were protected from the jostling throng. Mihiri and Tharindu were stuck in the middle of the most densely packed group, but Anshu and Phera weren't far away. Jeeva tried to reach them, but the mass of humanity swept him up and out to the street.

The residents of Astawanka-veediya lined the street, watching in bewilderment as foreign soldiers took up positions on every corner, barking orders in a strange language. Apart from a few Indian sepoys, all the soldiers were English. Very few citizens of Senkadagala had ever seen a European. White faces and light hair glimmered eerily in the dark and left them shocked, as did the cannons rumbling down the street behind prancing black horses.

"Papa!"

Jeeva spun around and found Phera and Anshu pushing through the crowd to reach him. Phera seized his hand and he pulled her close. He put his other arm around Anshu. The three of them clung to one another, staring at the royal palace.

"Mother, Father!" Mihiri appeared, flinging her arms around her parents. She hugged Phera, too.

"Tharindu stayed by me. He made sure nothing happened." She gestured toward the boy standing next to her, tension etched on his face. Jeeva thanked him absently. His eyes were still on the palace. Lights blazed from the windows, and torches burned at the gates. The foreign soldiers hurried back and forth before the walls.

"So they've finally managed it," said Jeeva, his voice choked with emotion.

"What do you mean?" asked Phera.

He sighed deeply. "The year you were born, the British tried to conquer Kanda Uda Pas Rata, but our own soldiers drove them back across the Mahaweli. The jungle took care of the rest. Their men and horses died of heat and fever, and a regiment of Indian sepoys came over to our side. The only reason the British have beaten us tonight is because they had the help of traitors. They must have shown them our secret routes through the jungle."

"If only I'd stopped those men," Phera wailed.

"It wasn't just those two." Jeeva looked at the palace again. The thought of Sri Vikrama Rajasinha being abducted by British soldiers grieved him deeply. Strangers from the end of the world had conquered the jungle kingdom of five mountains; the last free ruler on Lanka had fallen.

"There you are, my son. I've been searching for you everywhere!"

Slowly, Phera turned to look. She would have recognized that croaky voice amongst thousands. It belonged to an imposing-looking man in noble dress. Phera knew who he was, even though she had never met him. She would never have dreamed that Tharindu was this traitor's son. Instinctively, she tugged the sleeves of her shirt down over her scratched fingers and hid behind her father's shoulder.

The second adikarm looked at the palace, too. "From now on, there'll be better times for all of us," he boasted. "We shall unite behind the British and regain access, at long last, to the sea, so that we can trade with the whole world."

Jeeva's jaw dropped, and he hissed at the man in disgust. "The king trusted you, Deepal Sirisena! You are one of his closest advisers, and you have betrayed him!"

"Don't you dare speak to my father like that," Tharindu shouted as he moved toward Jeeva, but Deepal restrained him.

"I want no fight here, son." He looked first at Jeeva, then Phera, and lifted his eyebrows quizzically. "You have some interesting scratches on your face, child. Might they have anything to do with the thorny bushes around the stables?"

Phera edged even closer to her father and gave no reply.

Jeeva snorted. "If you threaten my child, Deepal, it will cost you dearly."

"Jeeva, please! Why so hostile?" Deepal replied. "I wish you no ill, nor your family. You call me a traitor, but you are wrong. My intentions are pure, and my actions serve the interests of the kingdom. The

British already rule half the world, and they are on the way to becoming masters of it all. Do you imagine our little Kanda Uda Pas Rata can stand in their way? We must join them while we can still dictate terms."

"What terms?" Jeeva growled.

"That the British guarantee respect for our laws, and that high offices in the law and the military will be occupied by our ministers and officials. That they will support Buddhism over other faiths, and protect our temples. These things would not otherwise be so, Jeeva."

Jeeva stared again at the palace. The foreign soldiers were lowering the Sinhalese lion flag. The Union Jack was soon fluttering from the mast. "What about the king?"

"His reign is over. He will go into exile," replied Deepal. "Don't put yourself on the losing side, Jeeva. I've known you a long time; you're a capable man. Join us. I'm counting on you, and I'm counting on a bond between our children, too."

Chapter Three
Kandy, Ceylon, 1815

Two weeks later, at the spring's new moon, Jeeva was standing in the audience chamber with a hundred of the most important dignitaries in the kingdom. They were listening to an interpreter reading out in Sinhalese a contract between the British and the deposed king.

While the interpreter declaimed all twelve paragraphs of the Kandyan Convention, Jeeva looked at the podium. Where the king had previously held court beneath his white sunshade, there now stood a few chairs and a modest table. On one of these chairs, surrounded by his officers, was the British supreme commander, Lieutenant General Sir Robert Brownrigg, a strapping man with white hair, inexpressive eyes, and a strangely florid complexion. His uniform of high boots, indecently tight trousers, and an equally closely fitting red jacket was disturbingly alien. On the wall behind Brownrigg, where the lion flag of the Nayaka dynasty had always hung, was an image of George III, King of England.

Jeeva looked at Ehelopola, who was seated next to Brownrigg, and narrowed his eyes. With a show of apparent modesty, the one-time first adikarm had refused the governor's offer of high office and satisfied himself with the title "Friend of the British Government." But his conceited smile did not escape Jeeva.

"This is a big day for us," said a croaky voice behind Jeeva.

He turned and came face-to-face with Deepal Sirisena.

"I see you continue to hesitate. But trust me, friend, good times are dawning for our country," said Deepal. He bowed his head slightly and climbed the two steps to the platform.

After all the dignitaries, including Jeeva, had signed the document, Brownrigg stood to attention in front of the portrait of George III. "God save the king!"

A gun salute sounded on the square outside, followed by loud cheers. But Jeeva slunk toward the exit. A day of celebration for some, but the day the mighty kingdom of Kanda Uda Pas Rata became the British territory of Kandy was a black day indeed for him.

He felt someone tug at his jacket. It was Mahinda Dharmapala.

"I didn't expect to see you here, venerable hamudru," said Jeeva. "Are you amongst those who believe that good times are dawning for our country?"

"Has any conqueror ever brought better times?" replied the monk. "I am here because our king wants to see you."

Soon Jeeva was crossing the square in front of the audience chamber. The new rulers' Light Dragoons Regiment had been massing here since morning. With bayonets fixed, they were there to warn against unrest during and after the signing.

He entered the king's palace to find the place teeming with more soldiers. They stood guard over the servants packing the king's possessions into crates, dragging out his furniture, and bearing away huge stoneware jugs filled with gold and silver coins. Jeeva saw the king's wives in one of the halls. Surrounded by their ladies-in-waiting, they huddled in a corner, nervously watching the comings and goings. Guarding the doors to the deposed monarch's private quarters was more of the British military, but they let Jeeva through when they heard his name.

Jeeva entered a little reception salon, then stopped dead in his tracks. All the precious furnishings, rugs, vases, and statues had vanished. But the sight of King Vikrama Rajasinha shocked him even more. No jewels, no jacket adorned with precious stones, no golden slippers. He was barefoot, like an ascetic, dressed only in a simple white shirt and sarong. He sat cross-legged on a straw mat.

"Your Majesty!" Jeeva sank to his knees, bowing so deeply his forehead touched the floor.

"Ayubowan, my dear friend. Please do get up. I am no longer the master to whom you have to bow your head."

Vikrama Rajasinha's deep, mellifluous voice was tinged with sadness, and he refrained from the royal "we." He gestured toward two men Jeeva had not noticed before. They nodded in acknowledgement.

"May I introduce my companions? Major Greene and Mr. Doyle. Mr. Doyle will translate our conversation for the major." After a short pause, he went on. "I have heard the gun salutes. So the conquerors are celebrating the end of my reign. My throne, my sunshade, and all insignia of my previous power are already on their way to Great Britain. They now belong to the new king and are to be exhibited in his castle. They tell me it is called Windsor."

"I am truly sorry," murmured Jeeva.

Vikrama Rajasinha raised his hand. "I forbid you from mourning. I have accepted my destiny. In the next few days, my wives and I will be taken to South India and Vellore Fort. This is where I shall live under the supervision of the British."

Jeeva could not speak. It was no secret that the king had to go into exile, but to hear it from the lips of the man himself, the man he had served for so long, touched him deeply. The Nayaka dynasty had ruled the country for almost eighty years and had always been linked to the fate of the Maha Nuvara family. The end of the Nayaka rule left Jeeva feeling he had lost his own roots.

Vikrama Rajasinha looked at him long and hard with his dark eyes. "Before we say farewell forever, please allow me to thank you for your loyal service." He grasped Jeeva's right hand and put something in his palm. Jeeva caught sight of a tiny figurine, an ivory elephant. The king clasped Jeeva's fingers and closed them to make a small fist around the little figure. "You know what I am entrusting you with, Gajanayake Nilame?"

Jeeva felt a shudder run down his spine. "Yes, Your Majesty."

"You will take good care of it?"

Involuntarily, Jeeva glanced over at the two Englishmen by the window. The interpreter was translating everything in a quiet voice, but the officer seemed to show no interest. His only reaction consisted of a suppressed yawn.

Jeeva let out a deep breath. "I will give my life for it, Your Majesty."

"Another bloodsucking beast! Heat and mosquitoes, that's all this appalling country has to offer!" The young Englishman in a Royal Engineers uniform slapped at his own neck. "How could I ever have thought Ceylon would be an adventure?"

His associate laughed. "Don't be silly, Charles. In India it was even hotter, and there were midges there, too." He wore no uniform, just a brown suit, a white shirt with a high collar, and a cravat. Both men were in their early twenties. They were tall and slim, with dark hair, dark eyes, prominent noses, and sensual lips.

The mosquito-plagued captain was openly ogling a group of women on the other side of Astawanka-veediya, and now he whistled at them. The women drew the veils of their saris over their heads and hurried away, their faces averted.

"Indian women aren't prudish like that," he complained. "And they're prettier, too."

"Watch out Major Thompson doesn't hear you," chided the civilian. "You know his orders, Charles."

"I know, I know. Respect the locals and leave the women alone. But you're not going to tell on me, are you, Henry?"

"No, but don't overdo it."

"There you go being softhearted again, little brother. You know I'm bored to death in this hole. Since we marched in two weeks ago, we've had nothing to do. No women, no drink, and not even a jungle trip for a spot of elephant and leopard hunting. Gosh, Henry, just look at that fellow there!" He pointed toward a Sinhalese man coming down the other side of the street. His upper body was naked, a sarong wrapped round his hips, and his long hair was tied up in a bun. "Another of these effeminate chaps! It's disgusting! Why do you men in this damned country dress yourselves up like women?" Charles advanced on the man, who froze, staring at him in amazement.

"Answer me, you brown monkey!" Charles's hand went to the hilt of his saber. The Sinhalese's eyes were wide in fear and disbelief. He moved to run, but Charles seized him by the arm so hard, the man cried out in pain.

"Release him immediately!" Henry pushed his brother aside.

The Sinhalese man stumbled backward and rushed away. The two brothers glared at each other for several seconds, ready for a fight. Eventually, Charles's hand dropped from his saber, and he walked away.

"You never were any fun," he snarled at his brother.

Henry followed him. "Since we've been here, I don't recognize you. Why are you being so detestable?"

"For heaven's sake, you needn't take everything so seriously. This loafing about is unbearable. And anyway, what do these monkeys mean to you?"

"You mean 'people,' Charles."

"Let's stop talking about it. Have I told you Brownrigg has finally given me permission to commandeer a few elephants?"

"No." Henry shook his head. "What on earth do you need elephants for?"

"Brownrigg wants me to do an inventory of the local transport system, if you can call a couple of rough tracks a system. And I'll be doing some surveying. The elephants are supposed to carry our equipment. Maybe we'll ride them—though I'd much rather hunt them. Then, the elephants I don't need, I'm to sell. Did you know people will pay a fortune for one of those gray beasts?" He broke off. "Look, those are the elephant stables over there. Very fancy."

Henry was looking at the gleaming white buildings. "I did hear most of the old king's elephants were to be sold. The first ten are setting off for Colombo soon." Henry gave a sigh. "In fact, I'm meant to examine the elephants, see that they're fit to travel."

"You're to do what?" Charles stared at Henry. Then he burst out laughing. "My little brother, demoted from assistant to the regimental surgeon to an elephant doctor. If you'd gone to the Royal Military Academy like I did and become an engineer, you'd have spared yourself such nonsense."

"I wanted to be a doctor and help in that way," retorted Henry. "And it doesn't bother me in the slightest if I sometimes examine animals, too. As a matter of fact, I find elephants fascinating."

"You keep accepting stupid tasks, and you don't even have a military rank. But that's what idealists like you get. You're eternally on the losing team." Still grinning, Charles put his arm around his brother's shoulders. "Heavens above, what is going on over there?"

The brothers watched as a Sinhalese boy hopped around in anger at the entrance to one of the stable buildings and shouted at the military guard refusing him access. They walked toward the doors.

"Why's he making such a fuss?" asked Charles.

The soldier saluted. "I don't know, sir. He has been raging around here for about half an hour. I can't understand what he's saying, and I have orders not to allow inside anyone I cannot identify."

The boy had listened to the soldier's explanation. Now he gave vent to another torrent of words.

"What does the rascal want?" Charles asked his brother.

"He wants to get to his elephant," Henry explained. "He says he has to bathe it." He leaned down to the boy. "Are you a mahout?" he asked in Sinhalese.

The boy stopped midsentence and stared at him.

"Are you a mahout?" repeated Henry, adding, "I'm a doctor. I am to examine the elephants. And this"—he pointed at Charles—"is my brother."

The child gave each of them a long, hard look, then turned to Henry. "Tell your guard I want to go to my elephant. I come here every day because I need to care for Siddhi, and every day I explain to him yet again who I am and what I do. How slow and stupid are you English people?"

Henry suppressed a smile. He translated, skipping the last bit, and said, "I think it's all right to let him in."

The soldier moved aside. Before Phera slipped into the stable, she turned to Henry again. "And no, I'm not a mahout. My name is Phera, and I am the son of the Gajanayake Nilame, the highest royal elephant keeper." Her head held high, she disappeared inside.

"What did he say?" Charles wanted to know.

"That he's the son of the head elephant keeper," answered Henry.

"Just the man I need!" Charles exclaimed. "Tell him to fetch his father. On the double."

A little later, Jeeva, Henry, and Charles were standing together on the square where the elephants used to practice. Henry explained to Jeeva that Charles needed some elephants as working animals.

"You want to use the king's prize elephants as beasts of burden, heaving boulders and tree trunks?" Jeeva stared at them in horror. "These animals belong to the Chaddhantha caste. They are not intended for the menial work you want to burden them with. And you have absolutely no right to sell them!" He folded his arms across his chest.

"What's he saying?" Charles, impatient now, poked his brother in the ribs.

"It would appear that the elephants belong to a caste that forbids them from bearing loads. I had no idea there was a caste system for elephants."

"What utter rubbish!" snorted Charles. "Does this madman really think that a couple of dozen elephants can be allowed to eat and excrete ad libitum at the cost of the British exchequer? Tell him any disobedience will be deemed refusal to obey orders and the governor will put him up against the wall."

Five days after this encounter, Jeeva was sitting in his drawing room with Eranga. "Early tomorrow, ten elephants are to set off for Colombo. They'll be loaded onto ships and taken to foreign lands. Yakkhini was selected—the mangalahasti, too. The British captain ordered me to ensure that the mahouts are ready at daybreak. He has also downgraded a number of elephants to working status, including Siddhi. The rest will be sold off later."

"The king's state elephant? Taken out of the country?" Eranga was aghast. "And Yakkhini, too?" He shook his head in sorrow. "How has your son taken the news about Siddhi?"

"He doesn't know yet." It pained Jeeva to think how this would affect Phera. "We must put our plan into action tonight."

"The mahouts are ready, sir," Eranga replied solemnly. "I'll convey your orders straightaway. When it's all over, they'll flee to their home villages. They'll be safe there—the British can't get through the jungle." He stood up and left the room.

Jeeva got to his feet, too. He found Anshu in the garden, beneath the old mango tree. She was seated on a cushion, feeding chopped nuts to two small, gray long-tailed monkeys. Jeeva sat down next to her.

In hushed tones she said, "I saw Eranga on his way out. Is this really it?"

He nodded. He had taken Anshu into his confidence from the start. "Upali will take you to his father's country house this afternoon. I've let people think you're paying Psindu a visit on matters of health. I'll follow you as soon as everything's done here."

Anshu put her dish to one side, and the monkeys scrabbled greedily for it. "Our things are packed. Samitha, Mihiri, Phera, and Kalani know they have to be prepared. But Phera is so worried about Siddhi."

"There's no need for that. I'll take Siddhi to our hiding place."

Anshu looked around the garden, at the luscious blooms on the trees and bushes, and she breathed in the sweet, familiar scents. "Will we ever come back here, Jeeva?"

He reached for her hand. "I don't know. It hurts me, too, to have to leave our home. But I will not serve our new ruler."

"Everything has changed overnight. Once we thought we knew what the future held for us. And now it's all so uncertain." She slipped her hand in his. "Perhaps there is one good thing in all this change. Jeeva, Phera no longer needs to carry on being a boy. Do you remember how she asked us if she could live as a girl? We shouldn't deny her anymore."

Jeeva looked doubtful. "I deceived the king. Where will I be if people find out?"

"That was a long time ago," replied Anshu. "Things have changed. Phera need no longer be bound to this fate."

The soldier on night duty at the elephant stable sniffed the air. No, he was not mistaken; his nose had picked up the smell of smoke on the breeze. Then he saw the blaze, flames leaping from palace windows in the dark night. Just as he opened his mouth to raise the alarm, a hand came from nowhere, stifling his shout. He felt a searing pain in his back and collapsed to the floor, lifeless.

"Well done." Jeeva stepped out from behind a cinnamon tree and took a look at the dead Englishman.

Eranga knelt next to the corpse, wiping a bloody blade on the man's uniform. "I may not be so young anymore, sir, but I haven't forgotten how to kill an Englishman." He sheathed his dagger and stood up.

"Load him onto Yakkhini. In the jungle, we'll throw him to the leopards."

The first mahout nodded. Then he heaved the dead man over his shoulder and carried him into the cow elephants' stable.

Jeeva kicked at the sand with his sandals to try to conceal the blood. Then he raised his hands to his mouth and imitated the call of an owl. The mahouts slipped silently from behind the trees and into the stables. All were dressed in black, like Jeeva and Eranga, so they blended into the shadows. Jeeva was still standing alone on the square, looking at the palace. Fire flickered behind the widely spaced windows. The soldiers' shouts of alarm carried on the wind, and ghostly figures ran frantically back and forth before the palace walls.

The fire had been Eranga's idea. It had been started by servants who, although working for the British now, were still loyal to Vikrama Rajasinha. Jeeva was saddened by the thought of the palace being damaged, but the plan had met its objective: distract the British.

He turned and hurried to the stable where the mangalahasti would be. As he reached the stall of the huge lead bull, he tightened his grip on his ankus. The mangalahasti was the king's personal elephant, and Jeeva was not sure if he would tolerate anyone other than his master on his back. But to his surprise, the animal greeted him with a deep rumbling and moved his powerful body to the side.

"Your master has gone and won't be back," he explained softly to the bull, while unbolting the door and pushing it open. "This is why we're giving you and your companions your freedom." He knelt down and cut through the rope that bound the elephant to a post. The mangalahasti gently blew warm breath against Jeeva's neck. As Jeeva turned to him, he saw the animal had raised his front leg, as if inviting him to climb aboard.

The mahouts had opened the other gates, untied their animals, and mounted. Now they looked at Jeeva expectantly. A little squeeze behind the elephant's ears from Jeeva's toes, and the mangalahasti led the way through the open gate. Already waiting in the training square were the elephants from the two other stables, together with their mahouts. None of the animals seemed nervous.

Jeeva looked at them all. He knew these men trusted him completely, and that's what made the responsibility weigh so heavy on his shoulders. If anything went wrong, it was not only the lives of his own wife and children that would be affected but those of his brave men, too. He calmed himself and again used his toes to urge on his elephant. Soon afterward the training square stood empty, deserted.

The elephants headed east, moving almost silently on their cushioned feet through the night. They could keep up an astonishing pace for their heavy build. Not a soul was about, with every available soldier busy containing the fire at the palace.

After a few minutes, they had reached the edge of the jungle, which stood like an impenetrable black wall between them and the Mahaweli Ganga. Jeeva felt his burden ease and a sense of liberation take its place.

He turned to Eranga, riding behind him with Siddhi on a lead rope, and raised a fist in triumph.

The group took the narrow path through the jungle that led to the elephants' bathing place. Luckily, the moon was almost full, and its silvery glow cast enough light. It was not long before they saw the river glistening ahead. The mangalahasti scented the water. He raised his trunk hopefully and was happy to be directed onward. The other elephants followed without hesitation. Eranga pushed the dead soldier off Yakkhini's back before riding right into the water. There was a dull splash.

The group had left a clear trail behind them to the riverbank. But now the water could wash away any further traces. From here on they were almost invisible to the British. The hardest part was behind them.

Psindu Amarasekere's country house lay a day's fast march southeast of Kandy, hidden in dense jungle on the Badulu Oya in Uva Province. A village of fifty families nestled at the edge of the clearing, surrounded by virgin forest. While the country house was made of wood and had a tiled roof, the farmers' huts had clay walls and roofs of palm straw. To protect the country house from the Badulu Oya, which sometimes rose in the monsoon season, it stood on posts. The front door was reached by steps leading to a veranda that wrapped around the whole house. Living areas and bedrooms were in the front of the house, while the larders and kitchen were to be found at the side.

The farmers' huts were small. Here people lived and slept in the same room. They cooked outside, sheltered by the overhanging roof. A few hens scratched freely here and there, and sometimes there was a cow, too. Each family had its own vegetable garden. Rice was grown in communal fields around the village.

But Anshu, Samitha, Mihiri, Phera, Kalani, and Upali didn't reach their hiding place until the fourth day of travel, shortly before sunset. The journey had been tougher than expected, and everyone was exhausted from being on the move from dawn until dusk. Only Kalani, on grounds of age, had been allowed to ride on the oxcart. They had spent the nights in the open, clustered around a small campfire intended to scare off leopards and bears. When they at last reached Upali's father's large home, Psindu was already standing there, waiting to welcome them. They were relieved to have palm-straw mats again, after sleeping on the bare earth. Before falling asleep, Phera thought of Siddhi. She hoped that her father, all the elephants, and their mahouts were safe, and that they'd arrive soon.

When the sun rose, she got up and walked to the riverbank. After making sure there were no crocodiles close by, she squatted on the bank, beneath the canopy of a fig tree, in a flat spot between its huge roots, and stared for hours at the ford she had waded across the previous day. Overhead, monkeys shrieked and green parrots squawked. The sun had climbed high before she heard the sound she had been longing for—an elephant trumpeting. There was a cracking in the undergrowth, immediately followed by the sight of Siddhi's distinctive shape on the other bank. She had scented Phera a while ago and was trotting happily into the water, her trunk held high and her ears forward. On her back was Jeeva. His weary face lit up at the sight of Phera. At last he knew that his family had reached safety.

Phera jumped to her feet and ran into the shallows to welcome her father and her friend. Siddhi had already reached her and wound her trunk around Phera. With joy, she lifted the little girl into the air. Jeeva slid down, and father and daughter threw their arms around one another.

"The elephants and their mahouts have successfully fled," he said. "We set the elephants free near the fort at Hanguranketha. They disappeared into the jungle straightaway. Only Siddhi refused to go, as if she knew I'd bring her to you."

Tears filled Phera's eyes. "And the mahouts, did they all go? Even Eranga?"

"Eranga didn't flee to his home village but has gone back to Senkadagala. He wants to scout things out, see how the British behave after losing the elephants. He'll come here in a few days to give me a report." He took Phera's hand and smiled awkwardly. "There's something else I want to say to you, my child. Before we fled, your mother made a request, and I have come to see that she is right." He paused for a moment. "I know we've placed a burden on your shoulders, Phera, and you have borne it courageously. But now things have changed. You will no longer become the next Gajanayake Nilame of Kanda Uda Pas Rata because this office no longer exists. So, my daughter, if you wish, you may put your earlier life behind you and be the girl you were born to be."

Chapter Four
Uva Province, Territory of Kandy, 1815 to 1818

Immediately after his arrival, Jeeva called together his family; his son-in-law, Upali; Upali's father, Psindu; and the faithful Kalani. His youngest child stood next to him, straight backed and proud, as he revealed to the little gathering that Phera was not a boy but a girl.

While Jeeva explained, concisely and without emotion, why Phera had been raised as a boy for the first twelve years of her life, Anshu and Kalani broke down in tears, grateful to be relieved of their secret. Samitha and Upali stared at Phera, both speechless. Mihiri sniggered but lowered her head in shame when Jeeva threw her a warning glance.

Psindu rose from his armchair. "I'd have done exactly the same, Jeeva Maha Nuvara. You needed an heir and had none. What else could you have done?"

"You're right, my dear father-in-law!" Samitha got to her feet, too, went over to Phera, and embraced her.

And Upali put his arms round her, also. "Now I've got another lovely sister-in-law."

Last of all came Mihiri. She stood in front of Phera and looked her up and down, her head to one side. "If you want, I'll teach you how to look like a girl." Smiling broadly, she took her younger sister into her arms.

At first Phera saw her girl's life as a wonderful game. It was fun to have her sisters show her the right way to put on a sari or weave flowers into her hair. Best of all she loved not being made to cinch down her chest. However, when Kalani and Anshu explained that as a girl she should not race around, shout, or climb trees, but must always be sweet, charming, and compliant, she felt as constricted as she had in her enforced life as a boy. *Being a girl is too complicated,* she thought. Just putting on a sari took so much longer than pulling a shirt over her head and tying a sarong. A girl's life began to seem so monotonous and subject to so many rules.

Thank goodness she still had Siddhi. She was utterly devoted to her elephant and spent as much time as possible caring for her, feeding her, and bathing her in the river. When her mother implied it was not seemly for a girl to work with an elephant, Phera would lose her temper. Siddhi was her best friend, the living creature she trusted most. She would never allow anyone to dictate her relationship with her elephant.

Phera resolved not to accept all the ridiculous regulations that limited women's lives. She would decide for herself what would happen, or be allowed to happen, to her.

And that included wearing a sari only when she felt like it. She went in search of the village tailor and asked him to cut down one of her saris into wide pants tapered at the ankle, just like Sinhalese noblemen wore. They gave her wonderful freedom of movement, but Anshu was shocked.

"She looks indecent dressed in those things! You must forbid her from wearing them."

But Jeeva let his daughter prevail. "We have already burdened her with so much in her young life. Let's allow her to move through this huge change as she must. You'll see, she'll be copying her sisters in no time."

When Eranga arrived a few weeks later, Phera herself told him the truth and asked if he would continue to instruct her.

"I know that girls cannot become mahouts," she said. "But Siddhi's my friend. She wouldn't understand if I stopped working with her all of a sudden."

"You're right," replied Eranga after some reflection. "I shall continue to instruct you and your elephant."

Phera beamed at him. "Thank you, oh, thank you!"

He gave a little bow of the head. Then he disappeared into the house to deliver his report to Jeeva.

"The British are sure it's you that planned the disappearance of the elephants, master, because you are the Gajanayake Nilame. And that Upali assisted because he is your son-in-law. They also hold you responsible for the disappearance of the soldier who was on watch the night we fled." Eranga gave Jeeva a long, hard look. "They have already tried you in their court for his murder. They have sentenced you to death and have confiscated your property, your villages, your rice fields, and your house in Senkadagala." Eranga swallowed hard. "Sir, I bear the guilt for your misfortune. This is why I shall now return and give myself up. You shall not pay the price for my deed."

Jeeva raised his hand in protest. "You will not, under any circumstances, give yourself up. You must bring me reports from town."

Eranga bowed. "So be it, sir."

"Do the British suspect I'm here?"

"They do not have the slightest idea. Nor do they know where the other mahouts and the elephants have vanished to," replied Eranga with a smile.

Jeeva gave a hearty laugh. "They know neither the tracks through the jungle nor the fords and bridges to get across our rivers. These Britons are half-wits."

And yet as the months passed, Jeeva changed. It pained him to have lost office, status, and property overnight and become dependent on the goodwill of Psindu. He became taciturn, his face drawn and partially covered with a thick black beard that lent him a stern appearance. Only when Eranga brought him news from town did he seem enlivened.

The mahout told how discontent had become widespread amongst the local population. It infuriated the nobility that even the lowest British soldiers failed to show due respect to their caste. The people did not wish to serve some distant English king. They wanted a Sinhalese king right there with them, a Buddhist, a sacred figure to revere. In their temples, they began openly to pray for a new king and the expulsion of the British.

Jeeva had been living with his family in Psindu's house for two years when the people's prayers were answered. In Badulla, the largest village in Uva, a monk named Wilbawe, claiming to be a descendant of the deposed ruling dynasty, declared himself the new king of Kanda Uda Pas Rata.

When the news reached Jeeva, Upali, and Psindu, they seized their sabers and journeyed to Badulla to pay homage to the new ruler. On their return they reported that Mahinda, former astrologer to Vikrama Rajasinha, had seized the Sacred Tooth of the Buddha from the temple in Senkadagala and brought it to Badulla, whereupon King Wilbawe called on the whole country to rebel against the hated British. The fire of rebellion burned in everyone, from the highest noble to those with no caste, for they all knew that only he who has the Sacred Tooth in his safekeeping could be the rightful king of Kanda Uda Pas Rata.

From then on, Jeeva, Upali, and Psindu disappeared for days at a time, meeting up with other rebels. Eranga always stayed behind to protect the women, while his master, together with Upali, Psindu, and the young men from the village, went to war against the British.

Faced with a heavily armed enemy, they relied on ambush, not open battle. Skillfully, they blocked pathways with fallen trees or set traps in pits disguised with thorny undergrowth and filled with sharpened wooden posts. The unfortunate British would fall in only to be subjected to a volley of flaming arrows or rifle bullets fired off from mounted *jingals*. Before the British could see what was happening, they were dead and their attackers long gone into the jungle.

After almost a year of bitter fighting for freedom throughout Kandy, domination was slipping away from the British, and the Sinhalese sensed the final victory ahead.

"Ow!" complained Phera. The knife slipped from her grasp and fell to the ground. She struggled for air, trying unsuccessfully to free herself from Eranga's grip.

"If this had been a real fight, you'd be dead, young mistress." Eranga released her, bent to pick up her weapon, and handed it to her. "Again."

Concentrating hard, she planted herself in front of him once more and acted as if she had not seen the looks the boys were giving her, both admiring and appalled. She was now fifteen and the only girl in the group that was learning how to fight and shoot a bow and arrow. Psindu had asked that Eranga train the local farmers' sons as resistance fighters. When Phera heard about this, she had pestered her father until he agreed she could join them.

Anshu had covered her face in horror, but Jeeva took a very positive view. "It's good for her to learn this," he had said. "Maybe one day it'll be useful to her."

The farmers' boys had never before seen a woman fighting, let alone trained alongside one. And because Phera belonged to a higher caste, they did not dare speak to her. Eranga was the only one to treat her normally. He neither coddled her nor gave her any advantage, simply insisted she do her best. For him, it was irrelevant whether she was a boy or a girl. If his master wanted him to teach Phera how to handle weapons, then that is what he would do.

Eranga struck the pose of an attacker and jumped at Phera, his knife drawn. Quick as a flash, she turned, grabbed his knife arm, and used all her strength to twist it behind him. Eranga fell to his knees and dropped the knife.

"Well done, young mistress," he grunted, rubbing his elbow.

Phera whooped and danced about in triumph and looked over to the veranda where Anshu, Samitha, and Mihiri sat idly in high-backed chairs and chewed betel nut. Kalani was on a low stool, crouched over her embroidery. Hearing Phera's victory cries, she looked up and smiled with pride.

But her sisters made sour faces.

"I've tried so hard with her, but she'll never be a proper woman," Mihiri said with a shake of her head. "I doubt whether any man will ever want her."

"I fear you're right," sighed Samitha. "Only yesterday I asked her when on earth she's going to start behaving like she should."

"And what did she say?" Mihiri asked.

"Absolutely nothing. She just walked off."

Kalani put her work down in her lap and looked at the two sisters. "My young mistress Phera hasn't found herself yet. She's searching but hasn't found herself."

A little later Eranga brought the combat practice to a close, and the young men returned to their homes.

"Please, will you help me harness Siddhi?" Phera asked the mahout. "A tree's come down in the rice field by the river. Siddhi can drag it away much quicker than the oxen."

Eranga and Phera had made a harness for the cow elephant using leather straps and rope and had taught her to pull heavy loads. But Siddhi did not simply haul fallen trees; she pulled the plow, too. She carried out jobs she would never have done in her earlier life in the royal stables. She was keen to learn and seemed to enjoy every new task.

Phera found the elephant behind the house. Since coming here, Siddhi no longer had a stable, nor did Phera want to tether her. At first Eranga had been scared she would run off and join a group of wild elephants. But Siddhi seemed determined to stay close to Phera and never went far from her new home.

Eranga and Phera were in the process of harnessing the elephant when suddenly Upali, Psindu, and Jeeva stepped into the small clearing.

Phera shouted with joy. Her father had been away for nearly two weeks. But instead of running to meet him, she stood still, as if rooted to the spot.

A fourth man had stepped into the clearing. He was tall, imposing, and wore the traditional clothing of a Sinhalese noble. Under Vikrama Rajasinha, Rajapaksa Keppetipola had been a powerful dissava and overseer of the Temple of the Sacred Tooth. In spite of his high rank, he had gone over to the British in 1815. Jeeva had often said that Keppetipola was a disgrace. Now Phera could not imagine why her father would have shown him where the family was hiding. There was disquiet on the veranda, too. Anshu, Samitha, and Mihiri rose from their seats, their hostility toward Keppetipola clear.

Eranga positioned himself next to Phera. "What's this traitor doing here?" His fingers closed around the handle of his knife.

Jeeva's steady gaze moved from one family member to another, coming to rest on Eranga. "Keppetipola Dissava is with us now."

"He's not to be trusted, sir! He'll betray us to the British!"

But Jeeva held up a pacifying hand. "Keppetipola has come over to our side and brought five hundred men with him. He's fighting for the rebellion now."

"It could be a trap," snarled Eranga, his hand still on his knife.

"Your mistrust shows that you are a clever man." Keppetipola gave Eranga a long look full of respect. "Our kingdom has been in darkness for a long time. But now, with Wilbawe, a new king has appeared, someone to give us the light of hope. I'll be a loyal servant to this king until I die."

Eranga frowned and looked at his master.

"Come into the house with us. We want to discuss the next steps against the British."

Eranga bowed and turned to Phera. "Can you finish harnessing Siddhi on your own?"

She nodded. "We'll get that tree out of the rice field."

She was about to check the strap across Siddhi's chest when she saw two more men entering the clearing. Deepal Sirisena and his son, Tharindu. The three stared at one another. Phera held her head high and gave them a challenging look. Deepal looked baffled, while Tharindu seemed thunderstruck.

Jeeva cleared his throat. "Deepal and Tharindu are with us, too. They bring from Senkadagala important news about the British." He turned to them. "Deepal, Tharindu, you already know Phera, my daughter."

Without further explanation, he turned and went into the house. Upali, Psindu, Keppetipola, and Deepal followed him. Deepal gave Phera a cursory nod before he vanished from view.

Only Tharindu stayed. His eyes roved over Phera's face and figure, lingering on her braided hair and the breasts clearly outlined beneath her blouse.

Phera tossed her head to flick the braid back over her shoulder and stuck out her chest. "Tharindu Sirisena, what an honor. You probably don't recognize me now." Her voice was cold and mocking to hide her uncertainty.

Tharindu was now seventeen, a young man. He was even more handsome than she remembered, and her heart raced at the sight of him.

"No, well, yes—" he stammered. "Of course I recognize you." He blushed and looked away in embarrassment.

Secretly, she had hoped it would please him to see her as a girl. It was disappointing to learn he did not find her appearance in any way appealing, so she took refuge in malice instead. "Let's hope you have more of a clue when it comes to fighting the British!"

Before he could reply, she instructed Siddhi to raise her front leg so she could climb up. Moments later she and her elephant had vanished into the jungle.

Tharindu stared after them, still not believing his eyes.

"Not even Samitha and I knew until we got here. Isn't it weird?" He hadn't noticed Mihiri was now standing beside him.

He shook his head, still looking troubled. "Now I understand why he, er, I mean, she never wanted to play with us boys," he said, more to himself than to Mihiri.

"You understand her? Then you're ahead of the rest of us."

When Phera awoke the following morning, heavy rain was drumming on the roof of the house. The monsoons had set in after the summer full moon two months ago. Bowls stood on the floor to catch the water that forced its way through the roof. Even the Badulu Oya, usually a narrow river, had swollen to a roaring, elemental force, dragging with it sludge, dead animals, and entire trees. Fortunately, the village and the country house were a sensible height above the bank, out of the water's reach.

Phera gave a big yawn and looked across to where Mihiri always slept, curled up under her rug and blissfully unaware of the noise. Phera fished around on the floor next to her palm-straw mat for her pants and shirt. Like every other morning, she was eager to check on Siddhi. She slipped into her clothes and rapidly braided her hair while looking out onto the clearing. Siddhi loved the powerful monsoon rains and often stood out in the open to enjoy the downpour. Today, however, the elephant wasn't out there.

Phera ran barefoot onto the veranda. On the way she grabbed a couple of bananas for Siddhi from one of the dining-room baskets. She paused briefly outside the closed door of the room where Tharindu was sleeping. Yesterday's meeting with him had been so strange. He had reacted to her with wariness and unease, as if to some mythical creature. It still pained her to think of it.

But I can't change it, she thought, with a touch of stubborn pride. *I can't make him like me.*

Outside, the sound of raindrops pelting on clay earth was deafening. But the sheets of rain didn't bother Phera. The warm water felt as if it could cleanse her body from top to toe. It pooled all around the veranda. The green of the jungle gave off an even more luscious glow than usual. Raindrops bounced off the leaves, fell like shining pearls to the ground, then rose again to the heavens in a gentle mist, the breath of Mother Earth.

Phera hurried across the clearing to the jungle's edge. She was looking for Siddhi but found her mother instead. Anshu was seated on a round rock beneath a huge Persian ironwood tree. Her sari was drenched. Her dark hair hung long and loose, glistening with rain. The rays of the rising sun shone through the tree's branches and down onto Anshu as she sat there, motionless. Her eyes were closed, her face calm and concentrated. Before her was a small gold figure of Buddha that she had brought from Senkadagala and a dish of fresh orchid flowers.

Sensing her daughter's presence, Anshu opened her eyes. "I'm praying for our men," she said, trying to make herself heard above the rain. "They've all left now."

"All of them?" asked Phera in surprise.

Anshu nodded. "They set off overnight. The men from our own family, together with Eranga, Keppetipola, Deepal, Tharindu, and the men from the village. Only old folk are left. Eranga took Siddhi."

"Just took her, without asking me?"

"That's how your father wanted it. She'll help our men with the next strike on the British. Deepal has reported that a British company from Senkadagala is marching on Badulla to capture our new king, Wilbawe. Our men set off to stop that happening."

Phera didn't know what to think. She was proud that Siddhi was fighting against the hated British, but at the same time she was deeply concerned that something could befall her friend. "I hope Eranga is taking good care of her."

"The British have to pass through the Uva Ravine. Our men plan to block their way out with logs and boulders. Siddhi will help them drag everything into position. When the British enter the ravine, our men will attack them from above."

Phera knew the narrow ravine with its steep and rocky sides. "They'll destroy the enemy. I know they will!" She sat down excitedly under the tree next to her mother. "I'm going to pray that Siddhi and all our men come back safely."

◆ ◆ ◆

One week later Phera was sitting in a comfortable chair on the veranda, idly watching a few stray hens from the village as they hunted for worms in the puddles. Rain had fallen all morning, but now the sun had broken through and a heavy, humid heat had descended over the jungle.

After their midday meal, the other women had all gone to rest. Phera was pleasantly sleepy and full. Her fingers toyed languidly with the silk of her sari. With Eranga and Siddhi gone, she had nothing to occupy her. Fight training was no fun without an opponent. Out of sheer boredom, she had taken to putting on a sari every morning and using kohl on her eyes. She even let Kalani rub sweet-smelling oils into her hair and adorn her wrists and ankles with bangles. Anshu was delighted that at last her daughter wanted to be a real girl. She didn't realize that Phera had no intention of giving up her comfortable pants, her combat practice, or her work with Siddhi.

At a sudden trumpeting from the jungle, Phera leapt to her feet. Siddhi! She hitched up her sari and ran down the steps. The chickens scattered noisily as she raced past them in her bare feet, and a huge, gray shape materialized in the dense foliage. Eranga was close behind.

"Siddhi!" Phera ran, stumbling, through the thick undergrowth. "Siddhi!"

The elephant responded with loud trumpeting.

Phera's eyes filled with tears as she snuggled close to the animal's broad chest. Siddhi's trunk wrapped around her, gently caressed her cheeks and ears, and then delved into the folds of her sari to hunt for treats.

"I'm so sorry, there's nothing there! I didn't know you'd be back today." Phera giggled as Siddhi's trunk tickled her. Then she turned to Eranga. "I am so pleased you're back safely."

He laughed, and the lines on his sunburnt face deepened. "We are both well, young mistress. We have won and not lost a single man. A few were injured, but they will recover."

"The British walked into our trap like blind men, and we slaughtered almost all of them," added a voice from above her head.

Phera realized that her brother-in-law was riding on Siddhi's back. His head and left shoulder wore a dressing of banana leaves. "Upali! Oh, you've been wounded!"

"I was grazed by a bullet, that's all," replied Upali, gently tapping at his left shoulder. "That's how I fell and hit my head on a rock. My head's thumping as if I've had too much palm wine." When he saw the worry on Phera's face, he put on a brave smile. "Don't you worry. It'll be all right. Siddhi helped us enormously. She dragged logs across the exit, then rolled boulders down onto the English once they were trapped. She has the courageous spirit of a true war elephant." He patted the elephant's broad neck.

"I've always known that," said Phera with pride.

"If you will allow me to, young mistress, I'd like to tend to Siddhi," said Eranga. "Then you can go and welcome your father."

She nodded, and he moved off across the clearing with Siddhi and Upali. Anshu, Samitha, Mihiri, and the servants came running out of the house. Kalani was the last to reach the veranda, leaning heavily on the cane Eranga had fashioned from a sturdy branch. Samitha shrieked when she saw her husband was wounded. But as soon as he slid down from Siddhi's back and folded her in his arms, she regained her composure.

One by one, the other men emerged from the jungle. Tharindu was in the lead, the image of the victorious warrior, a spear in his right hand. Impaled on its tip was the blanched and bloody head of a Briton.

As soon as he spotted Phera, he began to swagger, swinging the spear from side to side. "Just look at this! It's the head of Sylvester Wilson, the man sent by the British government to capture our King Wilbawe. Killed by my arrow. We could've killed all the British, but we spared a couple of lives and sent them to Senkadagala with Wilson's body and the news of our victory. Now the British will flee Kanda Uda Pas Rata like the rats they are." Tharindu tilted the spear so that the dead Englishman's grotesque face was eye level with Phera.

She flinched. Much as she delighted in the victory, those lifeless eyes seemed to fix her with a hostile look. "Didn't the British put up a fight?"

Tharindu laughed. "We didn't give them the chance. Our arrows and rocks pelted down on them like a thousand rainstorms." His gaze took in her made-up face and body. "You look nice."

She concealed her pleasure with a snappy reply. "Only just noticed?"

He laughed. "When we hold our victory celebrations, my beauty, I want you at my side." Without a backward glance, he moved off across the clearing, still brandishing his trophy.

Her cheeks burning now, Phera turned away and searched for her father amongst the warriors continuing to stream out of the jungle. Some had wounds protected by nothing more than banana leaves, but their faces glowed with pride. Many were now clad in enemy headgear or jackets, the cloth stained with blood. They brandished in triumph all the weapons they had plundered from the British.

"Phera!" Jeeva was there, ready to embrace her.

She hugged him in relief. "Oh, Father, I'm so happy you're back."

"There was no need for you to be worried, my dear daughter. Keppetipola is a fine warrior and led us to an important victory. We have wiped out the regiment sent to Badulla by Brownrigg. Our King Wilbawe is saved!"

Phera looked around. "So where is Keppetipola now? Was he wounded?"

Jeeva shook his head. "He's gone back to Badulla with his men in order to receive further orders from our king." He held Phera close again, then hurried toward Anshu.

Phera watched him go, one moment feeling triumphant, the next desperate. They had been living here in hiding for over three years. Would this mean it was all over? Would they all go back to Senkadagala and resume their old life? And what did that mean for her? The royal elephants were gone, and even if they had still been there, she would no longer have been able to be her father's successor.

"Our victory may seem major, but these British were easy game. They were hopelessly exposed. Their gunpowder was damp, and they couldn't make any use of their cannon and rifles," came a croaky voice, cutting through her thoughts of home. Next to her stood Deepal Sirisena, his hand on the bridle of an enemy horse. "Our men are drunk with victory. They'll be celebrating until dawn. But the British don't give up easily. Masters of the world won't take a defeat like that without retaliation." He looked darkly at the fighters as they continued to fill the clearing. Women and children from the village had come running to cheer for them. Servants had brought palm wine, and goblets were passed round. Voices struck up triumphal harmonies, and people clapped in time with the songs telling of heroic deeds.

"Silence, you prophet of doom!" Psindu was suddenly there, next to Deepal. "Let's cook all the rice we have and enjoy the palm wine. Today we're celebrating our victory over the British invaders. We've well and truly routed them. The children of the lion are stronger than these white-skinned bastards!"

"You're telling me they beheaded Wilson, took his head as a trophy, and then sent you here to me with his body?" Governor Brownrigg brought down his hand so hard on the huge writing desk and bellowed so forcefully that the sounds echoed through his office in the king's old palace. "I demand an explanation, Captain!"

On the other side of the desk stood Charles Odell, saluting. His uniform was torn and dirty, his face drawn and exhausted, and yet his voice shook with rage. "The brown monkeys lured us into a trap. We couldn't defend ourselves because the damned rain had made our gunpowder wet. Those hounds slaughtered us. I led the advance and had almost traversed the ravine with my men when we discovered the way out was blocked. We thought it was some earthquake or avalanche, not unusual in the monsoon season. I was about to shout a warning when a shower of arrows rained down on us, followed by huge lumps of stone. Hardly anyone escaped injury. Wilson was one of the first to perish. They shot my horse to the ground, a bit of luck, really, as it meant I could take cover behind his body. By God, I was sure I'd breathed my last."

"It was a terrible slaughter," added Henry Odell, the third man in the room. "The only reason they left a couple of us alive was for us to bring you Wilson's body and the news of the rebels' victory."

The young doctor looked as bewildered as his brother. His right knee was heavily bandaged. He had been dragging a wounded colleague to safety beneath a rocky outcrop when he himself caught a hail of enemy rocks.

Brownrigg raked his fingers through his silver-gray hair. "How many men have survived, Dr. Odell?"

"Eighteen."

"Eighteen! Eighteen out of two hundred and fifty?"

"With regret, sir, I have to report that half of those eighteen are going to die," Henry clarified, his voice subdued. "There is no hope for those hit by arrows and spears. Sadly, my medical skills are limited to fixing broken bones and crush injuries. And many of the soldiers have been weakened by the climate. They are suffering from malaria, and their bodies lack the strength to heal."

"What about your superior, Dr. Bell? Is he still alive?"

"He fell, Your Excellency, while we were tending to casualties during the onslaught," replied Henry.

Brownrigg's expression hardened. "That means the Fifteenth Infantry Regiment needs a new senior surgeon. Odell, you will take on this post with immediate effect." He gave a brief nod in Henry's direction and turned back to Charles. "Is this ravine the only route to Badulla?"

Charles shrugged. "There might be one or two trails through the jungle. If there are, it's unlikely they're suitable for a unit the size of ours. Keppetipola led the Sinhalese. It's because of him and his five hundred men that they had the strength to conquer us."

The governor looked at him, long and hard. "Was Keppetipola the only one leading the ambush?"

"No. With him there were six altogether. Deepal Sirisena and his son were there. They've changed sides, just like Keppetipola. The other three are well known to us. We've been after them for years: Psindu Amarasekere; his son, Upali; and Jeeva Maha Nuvara. They all vanished over three years ago, together with the royal elephants."

Brownrigg looked deep in thought. "This needs considered action."

"With respect, Your Excellency," Charles said, "if we can get those men, the entire rebellion will collapse."

"But how are we to find them? The rebel leaders have the full support of the population. The people will never give away their hideout."

"I don't see it that way, Your Excellency. Up to now we've let the brown monkeys walk all over us. Now it's time to use the only language they understand." Charles gave the governor a meaningful look. "I'm referring, of course, to starvation, fire, and the sword. Anyone—and here I include the women and children—who refuses to toe the line will be killed."

"I agree the rebel leaders must be punished, but only through a civilized judicial process," Henry broke in. "An eye for an eye is not acceptable, most particularly where women and children are involved."

"There should be no exceptions!" retorted Charles. "It's the women who give birth to the next generation of rebels."

But Henry persisted. "When we arrived in Kandy, many Sinhalese welcomed us. We should be asking ourselves why that's changed."

Brownrigg was listening attentively. "And what do you think, Doctor? Why have the Sinhalese changed their minds about us?"

"We have not adhered to promises made in the Kandyan Convention, Your Excellency. We do not respect their Buddhist faith. The people hold that against us."

The governor looked puzzled. "What do you mean? We don't stop them going to the temple."

Henry shook his head. "The missionaries we brought from England forced local people to send their children to Christian schools. This antagonized the monks, the people held in the highest of esteem by the population. When the monks spoke out against us, the people listened to them. That's what really fueled the rebellion."

"What are you suggesting, then, Doctor?"

"The utmost tact in our dealings with the native population and greater respect for their traditions."

"Don't listen to my brother, Your Excellency," Charles said, his voice betraying impatience. "Where would we be if we let every savage in the colonies do whatever he felt like? Every one of us is here to serve the monarch. How do you suppose London will react if other colonies hear about our defeat and more uprisings break out as a result? Do you really want it to come to that?"

"You're right, Captain." Placing both hands on his desk, Brownrigg rose to his full and commanding height. "Nobody treats British soldiers like this. We will destroy this rabble."

Chapter Five
Uva Province, Territory of Kandy, October 1818

As day dawned, Phera opened her eyes and was immediately struck by the silence. For the first time in more than two months, the daily pounding of rain on the roof had not woken her. The month of Asvina, known as October on the British calendar, had come and with it the end of the monsoons. Through the window came the sounds of the jungle: soft rustling and crackling, birdsong, and then the shrill cries of a monkey.

She sat up and listened carefully. The house was still quiet, too. Since their fighters had come back from Uva Ravine, life seemed to have come to a standstill. Everybody was waiting for news from Eranga. After the victory celebrations, the mahout had gone to Senkadagala to observe how the British took the overwhelming defeat. He was to break into the British munitions store and steal bullets and gunpowder for the fighters to use with the plundered weapons. And, more importantly, he would buy sacks of rice—the tiny village's rice fields could not feed all the extra mouths. He had set off two weeks ago and taken Siddhi with him to carry the goods.

Keeping quiet as a mouse so as not to wake Mihiri, Phera slipped on her pants and shirt and rolled up her sleeping mat. Her thoughts drifted to Tharindu. On the night of the victory party, when revelers had eaten all the food, the fire was out, and most fighters were so full of palm wine they had fallen asleep where they sat, he had kissed her. Quite taken aback, Phera had pushed him away. Tharindu, surprised by his own boldness, had turned on his heel and hurried into the house.

But in secret, Phera often thought about the kiss. She was not sure whether it had felt nice, exactly, but it had certainly been intriguing. While she braided her hair, she thought how she would like to try kissing Tharindu again. The trouble was he spent all his time with his father and the other rebel leaders and seemed to be avoiding her.

She went to the window and peered out. The jungle still lay like a dark wall before her. And yet the deep, velvety blue of the night sky was growing lighter, and the shapes of the huts near the jungle began to come into view. A morning mist rose at the jungle's edge, drifted up to the treetops, and melted away, clearing the way for a gentle, golden sun.

Phera's eyes went to the spear bearing the head of the British government's representative. Tharindu had rammed it into the soil in the center of the clearing. Her scalp prickled at the sight of rotting skin hanging from the bony skull, two gaping holes where birds had pecked the eyes from their sockets. Every day she resolved to ignore the skull, only to find herself somehow bewitched by it, repeatedly drawn back to this gruesome sight.

Just then she glimpsed a shadow moving rapidly down the spear to the earth below. A cobra. Rearing up, it opened its hood. It was motionless for some time, then shot forward, spat, and hissed. Phera followed the snake's line of sight but could not work out what had provoked the creature. When she looked back, the cobra had disappeared.

Phera squinted into the jungle. There! Something was rustling in the foliage. A leopard, ready to attack a cow in the farmers' stalls, or maybe the horse captured at Uva Ravine? She whipped around at the sound of a branch snapping. Instinct made her step back from the window.

Suddenly, a torch flared up between the huts, closely followed by another, then another and another. They formed a ring of fire around the village. Phera's heart was racing so fast, she could hardly breathe.

I must warn everyone, she thought. But she was paralyzed with fear.

Terrifying sounds broke the silence. It was like the bugles blown by the monks in the sacred temple of Maligawa in Senkadagala, but far more threatening.

Mihiri woke with a start. "What was that?"

Men in red uniforms emerged from the jungle in droves. They all had blazing torches or rifles with fixed bayonets. As they ran past the farmers' huts, they hurled torches through the windows. The palm-straw roofing and outside walls were too damp to burn, but the fire took hold inside. Several torches landed on Psindu's veranda but went out before the wood caught fire.

Mihiri screamed as a torch landed in their room. Phera grabbed her straw mat and beat it out.

Smoke and flames poured from farmers' huts. Terrified families came stumbling outside. Mothers clutched babies in one arm, pulling bigger children behind them with the other. The men carried the old and frail on their backs. Panic-stricken, many ran blindly into the firing line. Anyone not felled by the hail of bullets was slit open by a bayonet. Screams and sobs mingled with gunfire. Fatally wounded mothers tried to shield their children with their own bodies, as did men their wives. The village boys grabbed stones and hurled them as they ran for their lives. But they stood no chance against the well-armed British.

The animal stalls, too, were on fire. Some of the cattle had already gotten out and were running through the village in terror. Their attackers drove them through vegetable gardens and rice fields, where the animals trampled on crops and tender, young rice plants. The enemy set fire to the store sheds and destroyed any reserves the farmers still had.

Under orders from their commander, soldiers stormed Psindu's house. Heavy boots pounded across the veranda. The wooden door was hacked open. Phera searched desperately for a hiding place. Apart from a trunk and some rugs, there was no refuge. The British were inside the house. Rifle butts forced open more doors. Mihiri scuttled to the corner of the room, whimpering. Jeeva's and Anshu's voices rang out, as did the harsh yells of the soldiers, then a shot. Phera ran to the window and dove onto the veranda. She vaulted over the railing into the mud, then wriggled under the deck. On all fours, she crept behind the posts that the house stood on and cowered there like a terrified kitten. She could hear her mother and sister weeping above, the thud of boots, and the tap of bare feet as the residents were driven from the house. The footsteps stopped almost directly over her.

The air was thick with the smell of fire, and she clapped her hand across her mouth to keep from coughing out loud. Her eyes streamed from the smoke. She dug into the mud with her free hand and smeared it on her face as camouflage.

Above her head, the imperious voice of an attacker shouted a question. A different voice interpreted: "Your names, you rebels."

One by one, Jeeva, Deepal, Tharindu, and Upali gave their names and titles. Phera did not hear Psindu at all.

The first man's voice came again, and the second followed. "Who is the master of this house?"

"The man your leader shot when he forced his way in here," replied Jeeva. "Psindu Amarasekere."

Phera kept a tight grip on herself so as not to cry out. The first Englishman burst out laughing and said something more. "Governor Brownrigg will be delighted by this news. We are here on his orders to"—the interpreter broke off; there was a short, sharp exchange between him and the commander before he completed the sentence—"punish you for your rebellious conduct toward us, your rightful rulers."

After a brief pause, the commander roared in apparent rage, then the other man relayed, "Is that the impaled head of Mr. Wilson?"

Phera's stomach turned, bitter-tasting bile filling her mouth.

"Yes, that's him." Jeeva's voice shook with anger. "He and all the others have only themselves to blame for their fate."

The commander gave an order. Boots tramped over Phera's head again and then into the clearing. She saw the spear with Wilson's head on it being torn from the ground and borne away.

The commander spoke again. "Jeeva Maha Nuvara, you speak as if you are the rebels' leader."

"I am one of many who are fighting to drive you intruders from Kanda Uda Pas Rata," Jeeva told him through the interpreter.

"You have a new ruler, our King George, whom you have deprived of the elephants of Vikrama Rajasinha. You have joined traitors and rebels and have murdered British citizens. Surely you must know that you have been sentenced to death in absentia? You will now receive your punishment. But first," continued the commander, "I'm going to teach you and this rabble to show complete obedience to your British masters." This time he did not wait for the interpreter but went to the railing and roared something to his soldiers. A burst of applause and cheers followed, with gunfire added to the howls of delight.

Piercing screams from the women followed. Children wailed, and Phera heard the men begging the soldiers. A few shots and they were silenced.

"Come on, lads! There's plenty of skirt on the loose here. Show them what you're made of, redcoats!"

The men stepped up to the mark with no hesitation. Not a single village woman still alive escaped their clutches.

"Have you truly lost your mind?" Henry shouted at his brother.

His face white and drawn, he looked at the remains of the meager village. Smoke still billowed from the huts, the little vegetable gardens and surrounding rice fields were irretrievably damaged, and the dead and the dying sprawled everywhere. Men bayoneted mothers' bellies, spilling guts and blood where the women still lay shielding their children. Infants, children, the elderly had all fallen victim to the massacre. Cattle had been slaughtered indiscriminately, too, but a handful of goats had escaped, now wandering around amongst ruined homes and corpses.

"This must stop now!" Henry seized his brother by the arm. As a doctor, he was unarmed, a status he now regretted for the first time in his career. Had he had a gun, he would have turned it on his own without a moment's hesitation. But as it was, he was powerless, forced to watch this atrocious behavior.

A malicious smile played around Charles's lips. "Don't be so damned priggish. I know you haven't had a woman for ages. You must need a rut just as much as the men do. Get on with it. Take one." He looked over the women on the veranda. "Which one would you like, my dear brother? That one?" He pointed at Mihiri, trying to hide behind Kalani. "Or this? No, you're not having that beauty." He sneered lasciviously at Samitha, who clung desperately to her husband. Charles's eye found the women's mother. Her hair loose, dressed only in a thin nightdress, Anshu clutched a sheet against her body as if to protect herself. "What about this one, brother? No young filly but well broken in." Charles stepped forward and tore the sheet from her. Anshu cried out and folded her arms across her breasts.

"Damn it, Charles! Where is your honor?"

Henry was about to pull his brother back, but Jeeva got there first. He shoved aside the soldier guarding him and gave Charles such a powerful blow to the chin that the Englishman stumbled backward and almost fell. Two soldiers, bayonets at the ready, seized Jeeva, but Charles called out, "Just tie him up, don't kill him." He addressed Jeeva directly. "So that's your wife, elephant keeper? Now you'll see what happens to the wives of troublemakers."

Jeeva struggled ferociously against the soldiers. But one struck him across the head with a rifle butt and brought him to his knees. The wound opened, blood flowed, and the soldier tied Jeeva's hands behind his back.

Tharindu rushed at Charles with a howl of rage. He reached under his shirt for his secret dagger and lashed out. But the soldier standing next to Charles was faster. He buried his gleaming steel bayonet deep in Tharindu's chest. The young man collapsed, gasping, and was dragged to the railing and hurled over the side.

"My son, oh, my son!" Deepal stood staring in shock at the bloody bayonet. He made no attempt to resist the soldier who, at a nod from Charles, seized and bound him.

Tharindu's body had landed with a dull thud not far from Phera. His face was horrifying. From her hiding place, she had seen nothing but heard everything. It was clear that most of the village had been murdered. The same fate now threatened her own family. Psindu had fallen already, and now Tharindu.

She heard him groaning pitifully and saw him attempting to lift his head. In vain.

"Tharindu," whispered Phera, still full of hope. "Look at me."

There was a slight movement in his shoulders. Slowly, he turned his head toward her. She could see how hard it was for him. Her eyes tried to hold his gaze.

"Stay," she begged him softly. "Please stay with me."

He grimaced in pain. His eyes widened, then froze. Phera pressed her hand over her mouth, trying desperately to silence her anguish.

Henry cleared the railing in one bound, landed next to Tharindu, and carefully placed two fingers on the boy's neck. When he felt no pulse, he took him by the shoulders and laid him carefully on his back.

Although he had expected as much, he was dismayed by those life-less eyes. The boy had barely reached manhood and yet had not shown a moment's hesitation in defending the rebel leader's wife. His courage had cost him his life. Henry reached out and gently closed the dead boy's eyes. As he looked up, he noticed something beneath the veranda.

A mud-covered creature stared back at him, wide-eyed, its crouched body tensed like an animal poised to flee. Henry knew he should report the creature, but everything in him fought against that. This mud-smeared native seemed even younger than the boy at his feet. He would not hand another child to his bloodthirsty brother.

Slowly and deliberately, he lowered his head to signal he would not give the child away. But the creature showed no reaction, and he had no idea whether his message had been understood.

"Time for some fun!" Henry was roused from his thoughts by Charles's voice. He looked up and saw his brother walk over to the rebel leader's wife, grab her roughly by the hair, and push her toward the soldier who had killed the boy. Jeeva roared, struggling in vain to free himself. Samitha, Mihiri, and Kalani wept helplessly.

"Soldier, your reward. You've earned her." Charles gave the man an encouraging nod. Then he saw Henry's expression. "Something wrong, brother dear? Shall I choose one for you, then?" He grabbed Mihiri. She fought back, trying to scratch his eyes out. Holding her at arm's length, Charles took a long look. "Well now, a little wild cat. Do you want her, Henry? She's probably never had a man before."

Henry sprang to his feet and raced up the steps. "Leave the girl alone!" He pushed his brother against the railing. Taken aback, Charles released Mihiri. She scurried to Kalani.

Then Henry dashed toward the soldier who held Anshu. "Stop! That is an order!"

Uncertain for a moment, the man faltered and looked over at Charles. He guffawed. "You're a civilian, Henry! You can't give orders to anyone, not even an ordinary soldier."

At that moment Kalani groaned in agony and clutched at her heart. Mihiri tried to support her, but she fell to her knees. She was gasping for breath as she dragged herself toward the house and leaned against it.

"Kalani, Kalani!" Mihiri crouched down near their maid, but two soldiers dragged her away. Kalani saw her but seemed defeated. The blood had drained from her face. Slowly, her eyes closed; she swayed and slid to the floor. Henry ran forward but was too late.

"She's dead." His eyes full of reproach, he looked at his brother. "Heart failure."

"Oh, I might just cry!" Charles's face showed his disgust. "Do you realize you are overstepping your powers as regimental doctor and showing a dangerous level of sympathy for the rebels?" He raised his pistol, stepped toward Henry, and pressed the weapon to his brother's chest. "You know the punishment for military disobedience."

Henry did not flinch. "Who are you? What on earth has happened to you?"

"Go to hell," hissed Charles. He turned to a nearby soldier. "Dr. Odell is disputing my military authority. Tie him up and take him away!"

"You can't mean that!" Henry was so amazed, he offered no resistance as his hands were bound behind his back.

"Killjoys have no place here!" declared Charles after his brother had been forced into the house by two soldiers. Then he clapped, shouting, "Take the women, comrades. Do whatever you want with them, as often as you want. The party hasn't even begun!"

The soldier who had killed Tharindu ripped off Anshu's nightdress, hurled her naked body to the veranda floor, exposed his erection to all, and then rammed it between her legs.

Two soldiers seized Mihiri and bent her over the railing. A third pulled up her sari, grasped her by the hips, and forced his way inside her. Mihiri howled in pain. Behind her stood a line of soldiers, waiting to take their turn. They had found the palm wine and were drinking and jeering while they each took Mihiri, one after another. With every new torturer, her cries weakened until she was reduced to whimpers. She eventually fell silent, seeming almost to lose consciousness.

Jeeva raged against the ropes that tied him. Tears streamed down his face.

Samitha was trembling, struggling not to scream out all her fear and horror. Upali kept his arms tight around her. Her eyes wild, she looked from her mother to Mihiri as the soldiers subjected them to the most abhorrent acts, things she could never have imagined even in her darkest dreams. The lecherous voice and lustful glances of the British commander had not escaped her. As he came and stood in front of her, a suggestive smile on his face and a pistol in his hand, she knew she was next.

And so did Upali. He lunged for the commandant's throat. Charles had raised his pistol, and fired. The bullet went into Upali's forehead. Like lumber he fell to the floor.

"Clean this up," ordered Charles, without so much as a sideways glance at the body. He looked into Samitha's eyes. Then he put his free hand around her throat. His thumb stroked her pulse, almost gently. But then he squeezed hard. Samitha choked and tried fruitlessly to turn away from him.

"Frightened, little one?" Charles whispered in her ear. "I like that." His hand slid from her throat, first to her right shoulder, then to her left, and ripped away her nightdress. He took a long look and licked his lips. Then he grabbed one of her breasts, digging his fingers into the delicate flesh. She winced with pain but made no sound.

"You want to stand up to me, do you? I like that even better." Charles pushed his knee between her legs and forced them apart. He pushed the barrel of his pistol between her thighs.

Phera still crouched, motionless, beneath the veranda. When the Englishman who had discovered her hideout had argued with his commander, she had felt the smallest flicker of hope. This man had not betrayed her. Perhaps he was trying to help her family and the few survivors. But when she'd heard him rebuked and taken away, Phera's tiny flame had died without a trace. She had wept silently with Mihiri's cries. Her mother's groans of agony and her father's sobs had nearly driven her out of her mind, and she hardly dared wonder what was in store for Samitha and Upali. As if to answer the question, a shot rang out directly above her, and a weight hit the wooden floor. Drops of blood trickled through the planks and fell onto Phera. She rubbed wildly at her face, as if possessed. To stop herself going insane with fear, she bent forward, pressed her forehead against her knees, wrapped both arms around her head, and rocked back and forth.

By the afternoon, a petrified silence hung over the village. The cries of children, the moans of the women and the pleading voices of their husbands, the shooting and drunken roars of the soldiers had all fallen away. Intoxicated on palm wine, most of the soldiers now lay in the shade of the trees, sleeping it off. Only the soldiers under orders to guard a few survivors had not joined the carousing.

The pungent odor of fire hung over the clearing, mingling with the sickly smell of the dead. Dark swarms of flies hovered and hummed in the heat over the rapidly decomposing corpses.

The British had hung from the strongest branches of the Bodhi tree the twenty village men not killed in the massacre. This desecrated the sacred tree of the Enlightened One, but none of the survivors were capable of protest.

Anshu was sitting on the veranda floor, wrapped in her torn nightdress. She fought to ignore the persistent pain in her belly and looked at Jeeva. The soldiers had tied up her husband and Deepal back-to-back and left them in the middle of the clearing, where they had been mercilessly exposed to the burning sun for hours. Some of the women had attempted to bring them water, and Anshu wanted to tend to Jeeva's wounds, but the guards had repeatedly driven them back.

Deepal stared into nothingness, impassive. Jeeva, his jaw set, had found a fixed point on the ground between his feet, and refused to return Anshu's gaze. He had been forced to stand by while his wife and Mihiri had been raped. The commander had abused Samitha with his pistol right there on the veranda, then pulled her into the house. Jeeva's grief and shame was bottomless.

Anshu wanted to tell her husband he should feel no guilt for these barbaric acts. But she could not reach him.

Her thoughts turned to their children. All her hope rested on Phera, who had somehow managed to escape the house. Now Anshu prayed with all her remaining strength that at least one of her children was unscathed.

It was agony not to know what was happening to Samitha. After dragging her into the house, the commander had not reappeared for hours. Then, sated and smug, he had swaggered out onto the veranda, legs wide apart, and made a show of buttoning up his pants. But of Samitha there was no sign. If Anshu had been able to hear her weeping and calling out, she would have felt less frantic. Instead there was a strange stillness that gave her little hope that her eldest daughter was still alive.

Anshu stroked Mihiri's head. Her attempts to untangle the girl's hair came to naught, her mind filling repeatedly with appalling images of the day's events.

After the soldiers finished with her, Mihiri had slid from the railing to the veranda floor and not moved since. Had Anshu not been able to see the almost imperceptible rise and fall of her back, she would have taken her for dead. The British had not stopped Anshu from moving her daughter into the shade, at least. Mihiri was unconscious, blood pouring from between her thighs. And while Anshu tried frantically to staunch the flow, her daughter quietly breathed her last.

Anshu closed her eyes and took another deep breath so as not to lose all composure. In silence, she offered up *paritta* prayers to protect the soul of her dead child on its way to the other world. She tried to find the strength to recall the good, the wonderful and happy events in her daughter's life. In the end, Mihiri would find joy in looking back at her mother from the other world. But Anshu could only weep. She knew Buddha was displeased by selfish mourning, but she could not control the pain in her heart. She kept asking herself which of Mihiri's deeds in an earlier incarnation could have warranted such a cruel price in this life.

Charles bounced into the room where his brother was locked up. He had just completed his tour of inspection around the burnt-out village and noted with great satisfaction what a resounding success his retaliatory action had been. Every last one of the settlement's huts, fields, and reserves had been destroyed.

He thought about the young Sinhalese woman he had just been enjoying to the full. She had done all she could to fight him off, had struggled, scratched, spat, and kicked. She had behaved just to his liking, and he had taken pleasure in disciplining her. Once he had finished with her, he strode out without a backward glance at the young woman curled up on the floor. Now he felt a new man, ready to lead the last strike against the rebels.

He observed Henry, who stood in front of the window, his back toward him. His brother's legs were secured at the ankle, his arms bound behind him. Two soldiers were on guard.

When will this idiot see that the army is not a playground for sloppy sentimentality? Clearing his throat, Charles asked, "Have you calmed down now?"

"Why did you hang those men? Brownrigg gave no order to obliterate the whole village."

Charles shrugged. "He gave the order to make an example of them. But I'm not here to argue with you, brother. I'd like to invite you for tea."

Henry looked at him suspiciously as Charles took him by the shoulders and made him turn back to the window.

They watched two soldiers setting up a small table and two camp-stools on the veranda. An assistant to the regimental cook appeared, carrying a basket from which he took a white tablecloth. He placed it on the table, followed by napkins, a set of bone-china cups and saucers, and teaspoons. Last of all came a silver teapot, a bowl of sugar, a small jug of milk, and a platter of sandwiches.

"This can only be a bad joke," Henry murmured.

"Sadly, we have to go without cake. But I have arranged entertainment that will make up for the pitiful lack of provisions," replied Charles.

"You mean not all the women have been raped and the men murdered?"

"We've dealt with all the women, but not the men. Two rebel leaders are still alive."

"And what does this little drama have to do with that?" Henry nodded at the tea table.

Charles gave him a look of mock reproach. "Didn't you hear me? Didn't I promise you a show? While we enjoy our tea, the two rebel leaders will be beheaded."

"Again you go too far! It is your duty to pass sentence only through an official court."

Charles waved aside his brother's objections. "I'm the court around here. Besides, the two traitors were given death sentences in absentia a long time ago."

"I'll report you to Brownrigg," threatened Henry.

Charles's eyes narrowed. "Then I wish you every success. You know perfectly well that Brownrigg's commission is to subdue the rebellion in Uva. I have fulfilled this commission to such perfection that I am justified in hoping for military honors." He smoothed the front of his uniform. "It might actually be you in front of the war tribunal. Plenty of my soldiers have been witness to your repeated opposition to my orders." He pushed his fist hard against Henry's chest, making him stumble and fall to the ground.

Charles spun on his heel and went to the door. "Untie him," he ordered the guards. "Take him outside and sit him at the table. But stay with him. I don't want him to move an inch."

After they had freed Henry's hands and feet, they led him to the veranda and pushed him down onto the remaining seat, next to his brother. Charles picked up the silver teapot and poured. "Nothing beats a good afternoon tea, eh? I do so hate missing it."

Henry's jaw tightened but he stayed silent. He looked at the empty clearing and racked his brains for how to stop his brother carrying out these executions. Nothing came to mind. His mind felt hollow.

Since becoming an army doctor, he had learned only too well the bloodiness of war. And yet the barbarity he had experienced here today shook every fiber of his being. His own brother seemed to have lost all humanity. He was taking a frenzied revenge not only on the rebels but also on the elderly and sick, on women and children. What was even worse for Henry was seeing how much satisfaction Charles got from causing suffering.

A troop of soldiers approached, bringing with them the two surviving rebel leaders. Deepal seemed detached, as if he had already finished with life, while Jeeva held his head high. The long look he gave Charles and Henry was both proud and candid. It told them he knew what was coming, but he would not surrender his dignity.

Charles helped himself to a sandwich and, chewing, considered Jeeva. "You won't be looking so haughty for much longer, elephant keeper. Bring his wife!"

A soldier came, hauling Anshu with him. Her torn nightdress made only a crude covering for her nakedness. Henry could see how much pain walking caused her. He had not witnessed it, but he knew that she, like all the other women, had been raped.

"She's in pain," he said to Charles. "I'd like to give her some laudanum." He started to his feet, but his guard pushed him back down.

"A bit of bellyache will teach her never to rebel against our rule again," declared Charles.

Henry was so furious, he considered pushing the soldier aside. But he held himself in check. His brother had already shown him who had the upper hand.

Charles finished his sandwich and carefully wiped his hands on his napkin.

"That one first." He pointed at Deepal.

The man, once a distinguished royal minister, now stumbled in front of the veranda, his back bent. He seemed not to notice when a soldier forced him to kneel, pulled back his long, disheveled hair, and cut it off with a knife.

"Very unimpressive," commented Charles and got to his feet. "Deepal Sirisena, I condemn you to death by beheading for high treason."

He beckoned to the corporal. "Carry out your duty."

The man positioned himself behind Deepal at the perfect angle. Within seconds, his saber made contact with Deepal's neck. There was an audible crunch as his head separated from his body.

After Deepal's corpse and head had been removed, Charles gave the order for Jeeva to be brought over. Jeeva, however, shook off the soldiers and turned to Anshu.

"Lives come and go," said Jeeva wistfully. "I would so much have loved more time with you in the bosom of our family, but my time has come. Don't grieve for me, for I am fortunate. The end of this life only brings me closer to eternal release."

Anshu nodded and placed her right hand on her heart.

Then the soldiers forced Jeeva in front of the veranda.

He and Charles shared a long look, but Charles lowered his eyes first. He swiftly masked this moment of defeat with an exaggerated announcement of Jeeva's sentence.

Henry translated, and Jeeva replied calmly. "As sure as a stone thrown into the air falls back to earth, so I shall meet the Buddha. He will release me."

Henry hid a sad smile.

"Arrogant rogue!" shouted Charles. "Tell him we'll do exactly to him what he did to Wilson."

"Do I do your dirty work, then?" Henry yelled back at him.

Charles looked at him with fury, but Jeeva spoke again.

"He is asking for a bowl of water," Henry explained.

When Charles laughed, Henry added, "If you won't do this for him, I will. And you won't stop me."

With the worst grace possible, Charles conceded. A soldier brought a bowl of water and placed it in front of Jeeva. Another soldier loosened the rope around his wrists. Jeeva knelt before the bowl and moistened his hands and face. Then he wound his shoulder-length hair into a bun.

When the corporal stepped behind him and drew his saber, Jeeva's fingers closed around the ivory elephant figurine Vikrama Rajasinha had given him at their final meeting.

Even if this life is now ending and I must leave behind the people I love, I have still done as you bid me, my king.

Behind him the serene voice of his wife began reciting the holy texts of the Enlightened One. He breathed deeply, closed his eyes, and let the words and his wife's voice carry him to the other world.

Henry was listening with equal concentration. He could not understand Pali, the sacred language of Buddhism, but he sensed the significance of Anshu's words.

With a hiss, the saber sliced through the air again. A split second before the blade met Jeeva, he shouted, "Perfect savior, accept me!"

Blood sprayed from the torso as Jeeva's head fell to the ground. From under the veranda came a cry so harrowing that everyone in the clearing shrank in alarm.

Phera had overheard her father taking his farewell of her mother. But her brain had refused to let her understand what was being said.

Now she was faced with her father's staring eyes, his distorted face, his half-open mouth, his blood flowing still at the neck. Her heart broke into a thousand pieces, and she heard herself scream as if at a great remove.

Charles and Henry sprang to their feet simultaneously. Henry knew instantly that the sound came from the creature crouched beneath the veranda. But before he could act, Charles had thrown aside his chair, drawn his reserve pistol, and fired straight through the wooden floor. Splintered wood flew up into the air.

Something shot out from under the veranda, a howling creature covered in mud, and raced across the clearing. The rebel leader's widow screamed her heart out and reached toward the creature as it fled. But it rushed on to the jungle.

Charles felt for his holster, then remembered both pistols were now empty. He was annoyed with himself for not reloading after shooting the Sinhalese girl's husband in the head.

"Your gun!" he barked at one of the soldiers guarding Henry. Before the man could even draw his pistol, Henry had seized the gun himself. He pressed the barrel against Charles's forehead for all to see.

"Anyone fires a shot, he dies." There was a distinct click as he cocked the gun.

Phera spent the whole night and the following morning huddled on the bank of the Badulu Oya, staring in a trance at the fast-flowing brown water.

Three years ago she had waited for her father in the same spot, tucked between the thick roots that fanned out beneath the old fig tree. Back then she had hoped against hope that he and Siddhi would return unscathed from Senkadagala. Now her father was dead.

At dawn the British trumpets had sounded. Soon afterward the soldiers had moved off, leaving behind them the devastated village and its few survivors. Since then a ghostly silence had reigned. And yet Phera did not go back. She was too afraid of what she would find.

On the other side of the river, there was a sudden crackling and rustling in the undergrowth. She jumped up and hid behind the fig tree. This time it was not the British coming out of the jungle, but Siddhi, with Eranga on her back.

"Over here!" Phera called, waving both arms wildly.

Siddhi flapped her ears in excitement and waded into the water. Eranga raised his hand in greeting. Stacked high behind him on Siddhi's strong back were sacks of rice and a small wooden munitions crate.

"Young mistress! Are you well?" As soon as Siddhi's front feet were on the sandy bank, Eranga slid down off her back and stood before Phera, wide-eyed. The girl was filthy. Tears had left tracks down her mud-covered cheeks.

"Oh, Eranga!" Phera buried her face in her hands and broke into desperate sobs.

Eranga knew better than to touch a member of a higher caste, but at that moment she was simply a young girl in need of his comfort. He pushed propriety aside and wrapped his arms around her. "I'm here, I'm here," he murmured, stroking her back. "Stay calm, young mistress, and tell me what has happened."

In a faltering voice, she described the events. Eranga listened in horror. His master, Jeeva, and all the men he had fought alongside against the British were dead, and a whole village razed to the ground.

"I had feared they would take revenge," he said. "I came back as quickly as I could to warn you all, but I'm too late. The British have killed Keppetipola, too."

"What?" Phera pulled away and gaped at him.

The mahout searched for the right words. "The British took him prisoner near our old royal city, Anuradhapura, and executed him."

"But Anuradhapura is far away in the north, and Keppetipola was in Badulla with King Wilbawe!"

Eranga looked at Phera with sad eyes. "Everything I'm telling you I heard in Senkadagala, and it is true. Brownrigg's men are all over Uva Province. Using cannons, they took Badulla. Keppetipola managed to flee, but they caught him at Anuradhapura."

"I hate the British! I will never forgive what they have done to my people and family!" Phera was shouting now. "Why don't they just go away and leave us in peace?"

"Let's go to the village, young mistress," said Eranga. "We can accompany the dead to the other world."

Siddhi grew more and more agitated the nearer to the house they came. The smell of fire, death, and decay frightened her, and Phera and Eranga had to use all their persuasive skills to stop her running back into the jungle.

As Eranga entered the clearing and saw the men still hanging from the Bodhi tree, he snarled, "We should have killed every single one of them in Uva Ravine."

Two boys were standing under the tree, throwing clods of earth at the birds trying to peck at the corpses. Eranga's eyes ranged over the ruined village and fields, and he shook his head in rage and disbelief.

"It's good you've brought some rice," said Phera, "or anyone who survived would starve. They set fire to all the reserves, too."

A few women were dragging the corpses to a spot in front of the manor house, where dozens of dead had already been lined up. Other women had fetched white towels from the house and used them to cover the dead. The few children who'd survived scattered flowers they had picked at the forest's edge, and an old woman distributed palm-oil lights and bowls full of fragrant herbs. Some other older women had torn white towels into narrow strips and were tying them tightly to the veranda railing and to low-growing bushes.

Phera watched two women carrying brushwood to the funeral pyres in the middle of the clearing. Her face lit up. "Mama! Samitha!"

With cries of joy, the two women let go of their bundles as Phera rushed to them and fell into their arms.

"You're alive!" gasped Phera, kissing her mother and her sister. Then she took a good look at Samitha. A purple bruise ran from her left temple all the way to her eye. The eye itself was bloodshot; her cheekbones looked red and sore. Her throat and neck were covered in ugly brown marks.

"Was it the commander?" asked Phera. "I hid under the veranda and heard his voice."

Samitha's face darkened at the mention of the man who had tortured her for hours on end. He had beaten her, kicked her, and choked her so hard, she had lost consciousness more than once. And he had raped her, not only with his penis but also with his pistol. Yet she had never been defeated. She had buried the monstrous pain and absolute terror deep in her soul and sworn she would survive.

"Don't worry about me, dear little sister," she said to Phera. "My body will heal, and he didn't get my soul."

In reality, the stabbing pains and burning around her womb made every movement agonizing. She bravely ignored it and refused to let anything distract her from her memories of her husband, her father, and all the others who had been murdered.

"Where is Mihiri?" asked Phera.

Samitha said nothing and looked at her feet. Anshu took her youngest daughter by the hand and led her to the place where the corpses lay. She stopped by one body, bent down, and pulled the white cloth to one side.

Phera gasped. Anshu put her arm around her and drew her close. "Your poor sister endured the most unspeakable torment. Her body was broken, but her spirit remains in the world on the other side. Your father is there, too, and Kalani."

Anshu gestured toward a shrouded corpse to the right of Mihiri. Phera fell to her knees, drew back the cloth, and gazed dumbly at the face of the faithful servant who had so lovingly been at her side from the moment of her birth.

Her voice trembling, she recited the words of the Buddha: "May you now be happy, free of sorrow, and remain in perfect peace." She covered Kalani again and stood up. "Where is my father?"

Anshu led her to a body near the end of the line. Eranga followed them.

Together the three looked down at the shrouded corpse. It clearly had been decapitated.

Phera struggled to stay on her feet.

"The British took his head with them," said Anshu. "His, and the heads of Psindu, Upali, Deepal, and Tharindu."

"They beheaded them even after they were dead?" cried Phera. "Oh, if only Keppetipola was still alive, he'd take revenge for all of them."

"What do you mean?" Anshu seized her daughter by the arm.

"It's true," Eranga broke in. "Keppetipola is dead." He repeated to Anshu what he had told Phera.

"My father may be dead, and Tharindu, Keppetipola, and all the others, but the fight goes on for our people!" Phera clenched her fists. "The British will pay the price for everything they've done to us. We'll drive them out of Kanda Uda Pas Rata."

But Eranga shook his head. "The British have taken Badulla. Our king has fled with Mahinda, the monk. Nobody knows where they are. They even had to leave the Sacred Tooth behind."

"The Sacred Tooth of the Enlightened One? In the hands of the British?" Phera was appalled.

"That's what people in Senkadagala are saying."

"If the British have the Sacred Tooth, that makes them rightful rulers of Kanda Uda Pas Rata," said Anshu.

"Never," raged Phera. "I will never serve this evil!"

"You will have to, young mistress," Eranga said. "I heard in Senkadagala that they've brought troops from India. Their military is flooding our country. And haven't you yourself seen what they do to us if we don't submit?"

Phera bit her lower lip and said nothing, but defiance still shone in her eyes.

"I keep wondering how the British found out where we were," Anshu murmured.

"I can tell you that, too, mistress." Eranga reached inside his sleeve for some crumpled papers.

"That's my dear husband!" Stunned, she looked at the drawing. The other papers bore portraits of Psindu and Upali. Then she read the Sinhalese text under each picture and went pale. "The British offered money for our men?"

"These notices are all over the city. The British call them 'wanted' posters," Eranga went on. "I took some of them down to show them to my master and warn him. But I was too late."

"Are you saying someone gave away our hiding place?" asked Anshu.

"The British couldn't have found it otherwise," replied Eranga.

Anshu swallowed hard. "So it must have been one of our own."

"Every man has his price," said the mahout. "There was a large sum on my master's head and the others' heads, too. We may never know who did it."

With so many dead and so few survivors, it took until evening to prepare for the traditional burning of corpses. Phera worked with

Anshu and Samitha to gather wood and build the funeral pyres. Eranga recovered the bodies of the twenty hanged men. To do this, he led Siddhi to stand beneath the Bodhi tree, climbed on her back, and cut them down, one by one. The troubled elephant's ears, trunk, and tail twitched constantly, and she kept her friend in sight the whole time.

During the night, the living sat by the dead and kept watch. The smoky fragrance rising from bowls of burning herbs tempered the foul smell of death. As no monks were present, it was Anshu who sang the verses from sacred texts to accompany the dead as they crossed into the other world.

Early the following morning, the funeral pyres were lit and the dead burnt. After Anshu, Samitha, and Phera had carried Jeeva's body to the flames, Eranga asked Anshu, "And what will you do now, my mistress?"

"I don't know," she replied flatly. "It was my husband who guided the family destiny. He was our protector. Now we have nothing left. No caste, no possessions, no home."

Phera held her head high. During the night of the vigil, she had decided that fear and tears achieved nothing. Her father was no longer there, but he had raised her as a boy for the first twelve years of her existence. From now on, she had to be strong and protect her mother and Samitha.

"I will not allow us to live like outcasts, begging every day for a handful of rice," declared Phera. "We're going to leave this place and create a new home for ourselves. I will lead us."

"How can you possibly manage that?" Anshu looked despairing. "You're still practically a child, and a girl at that."

"I'm not a child now. And I am no ordinary girl." Phera planted her hands on her hips. "Eranga, I'd like you to come with us. You can carry on teaching me knife combat and all the other ways of fighting you know. No other member of my family will ever be murdered by an Englishman."

"I am honored, young mistress." Eranga gave a little bow of the head. "If you will permit me to make one suggestion."

He looked from Anshu to Samitha and Phera before going on. "My home village, Mapitigama, is south of Senkadagala, near the Kadugannawa Pass. Before the British came, it was a thriving place with plenty of rice terraces. For generations, the men of my family have been the village leaders. What it's like there now, I don't know—" His voice faded for a moment, but he quickly composed himself and carried on. "In Mapitigama, there is a place for you, Mistress Anshu, and for your daughters. If you wish to come with me, of course."

"But we'll be dependent on the goodwill of your family," said Anshu.

"No, we won't." Phera sprang determinedly to her feet. "We can work. We'll have our own house and our own fields where we'll grow our own rice."

"We can't do that, my child. We're not farmers; we're members of a very high caste."

"We will not become beggars just because our caste forbids us from looking after ourselves," Phera shot back. "We have to do whatever is necessary to survive. Siddhi will help us with the heavy work. And Eranga will help, too, isn't that right?" She looked at the mahout.

He bowed. "It is an honor, my brave young mistress, to play a part in the protection of the family."

"Then so be it," said Anshu.

Phera looked at her sister. "Do you agree as well, Samitha?"

"Upali wouldn't want me to work in the field like a peasant," she replied. "But he'd want me begging for food even less. Let us make a new start in Mapitigama."

Part Two

The Blood Sapphire Road

1822

Chapter Six
Colombo, April 1822

Wielding a windbeaten umbrella, Henry Odell plowed through a muddy puddle, climbed some rickety steps, and stopped outside a narrow door. Torrential rain beat down from the gray skies, streaming off his umbrella and creating a din against the corrugated-iron roofs that lined both sides of Cinnamon Street.

In spite of the weather, the place was bustling. Rickshaw porters charged back and forth in bare feet, chattering and laughing amongst themselves. There was cursing in all sorts of languages, and drunken brawling. It all combined with the rain to create a deafening cacophony.

Henry seemed oblivious to the noise. He stood in front of the plank door, biting his lower lip, his brow furrowed. Eventually, he raised his hand and knocked.

A peephole opened, and a pair of black eyes peered out. "Aah, Mr. Henry! Nice see you! Come, come." Then the peephole shut, and the door opened.

"Good day to you, Chang." Henry closed his umbrella as he stepped into the narrow entrance hall.

The Chinese man bowed, smiling. He was wearing his usual high-necked mandarin jacket of shiny brocade with matching trousers and slippers. He wore his black hair short at the front and braided long down his back. The oil lamp he was holding cast dancing shadows on the walls and closed doors. At the end of the corridor, a curtain of faded pink silk concealed any further view.

Chang snapped his fingers. A small, dark-skinned boy darted out of a little alcove located to the right, just behind the entrance, and took Henry's umbrella, hat, and coat.

"Thank you, Joey." Henry gave him a coin. The boy grinned and slipped back into the alcove.

Chang looked equally pleased. "What can I do for you, Mr. Henry? You want see Molly, then wonderful dream?"

A smile, barely perceptible, played on Henry's lips. "Exactly, Chang. As ever."

"Very well, Mr. Henry." The man hurried down the hallway ahead of his guest. Just before the end, he stopped and opened a door leading into an oblong chamber.

The air here was heavy, shot through with sickly sweet perfume. The walls were covered with red fabric and holders for numerous candles, which cast their flickering light on a bed that took up almost the full width of the room. The only other furniture was a chest of drawers, an oval mirror on a little dressing table with its own chair, and a washbowl and jug on another table.

"Good day, Molly," Henry said.

As Chang quietly closed the door behind him, the young woman brushing her hair at the dressing table turned.

"Good day, Henry," she purred, holding out her hand. He stepped closer, giving her hand a little kiss.

"You're always such a gentleman, dear Henry," she murmured. Of all her clients, she valued Henry the most. He always treated her like a lady, never haggled over the price, and never involved her in anything strange or violent.

Chang claimed Molly was twenty-three, but Henry was convinced she was no more than twenty. She was Eurasian, skin like alabaster, eyes dark and sensual, hair right down to her hips, and an irresistible heart-shaped mouth. Today her body was hiding in a cerise silk dress, black lace trim doing full justice to her cleavage.

"You don't look well," she observed as she ran her index finger down the lines from the sides of his nose to the corners of his mouth. "But you'll feel better soon. Just leave everything to me."

An hour later an exhausted Molly flopped back on the bed, next to Henry. "I've tried everything, and I can tell you like it, but"—she looked at the sturdy erection—"why can't you finish?"

He propped himself up on his elbows and forced a smile. "It's not your fault. Let's just leave it for today."

But Molly shook her head. "If anyone hears that I let you out of here with your manhood that size, my clients will stay away. Come on, lie down again and try to enjoy yourself." She gave his chest a little push. He sighed and let himself fall back in the cushions.

She grasped his erection and massaged it. "That's good, just relax. Do you know that I've never seen a cock as magnificent as yours before?" She slid down, bent herself across his hips, and closed her damp, red lips firmly around his penis.

Henry moaned, pushed her head deeper with both hands, and concentrated hard on the painting that stared down at him from the ceiling. It showed an elegant Chinese man pleasuring three women in a style that would never have occurred to a well-brought-up English girl, even in her naughtiest of dreams. Henry's excitement grew. Then Molly was caressing him with her tongue.

Now, he told himself. *Now, now . . .*

But the painting suddenly disappeared, and all the memories he wanted to escape came crowding in to replace it.

Now he saw only the corpses of twenty men hanging from the boughs of an ancient tree. Their dead eyes seemed to ask, "Why did you let them kill us?"

He groaned in distress, trying to shake off the vision. The image of hanged men disappeared and was replaced with one of a decapitated torso, blood streaming from its neck. The head rolled toward him, the mouth half-open, shouting, "Why did you let me die this horrific death?"

Then this scene faded, too. But the images of dead children, drifting past like ghosts, completed the nightmare. Their mothers' lament came to him: "Why didn't you stop our children being murdered? Why did you watch while our huts and fields burned and our men were butchered? How could you let so many of us die?"

The sights and sounds crowded in on him. All over again, he was looking into the eyes of the mud-covered creature under the veranda. Neither before nor since had he seen so much fear, hurt, and incomprehension in the eyes of a human being, and it was like a knife to his heart.

"Leave it now!" More roughly than he intended, he pushed Molly away and sprang off the bed. He grabbed his pants from the floor and pulled them on. Then he seized his shirt from Molly's dressing table. In his haste, he knocked over her perfume bottle, and it fell to the floor and smashed. The overpowering fragrance of jasmine filled the room, almost taking his breath away.

"Henry!" Molly exclaimed.

"Damn it, I'm sorry!" He knelt to clear up the broken glass.

"Stop, it's all right," she said, more gently now. "Joey can sweep it up."

He got to his feet, pulled his jacket off the hook on the back of the door, and fished out a bundle of cash. "That should be sufficient to compensate you for all this." He placed the money on the table. Then he sat on the edge of the bed to put on his boots.

Molly slid behind him and put her arms around his chest. "It's no big deal, Henry. I often get clients who can't climax. Where there's no obvious injury, it soon rights itself again—"

"That's enough!" He held up his hand to stop her talking.

She rubbed her soft breasts against his back. "I know what you're longing for now, Henry. But it's not a good idea to smoke opium feeling as you do."

He hung his head and stared at his boots. "You're a remarkably talented woman, Molly. But today it's Chang who can help me more."

She breathed a gentle kiss on the back of his neck, then let go of him. "Never hold up a traveler."

"Molly good?" asked Chang as Henry pulled Molly's door closed behind him.

Henry nodded. "Perfect. As ever."

Joey leapt up, ready to bring Henry his things, but Chang shook his head. "Mr. Henry still want wonderful dreams?"

"Very much," replied Henry, and felt his tension easing for the first time in days.

Chang picked up his flickering oil lantern and led Henry farther down the hall. At the end of the corridor, he stopped and drew back the faded pink silk curtain.

On either side of the door were small tables with weighing scales and glowing incense. Opium pipes gave off the heavy, sickly aroma filling the room.

Oil lamps on low shelves cast unsteady shadows over the guests. There were sailors, garrison soldiers, Arab merchants, members of the Sinhalese nobility dressed in western clothes, and a couple of Chinese customers. Most were men, but in the gloom he made out one Chinese woman and two European women.

The guests lay on mattresses on the wood floor. On the walls were prints, yellowed by the smoke, of exotic birds and flowers. A silence hung over the room in spite of the number of people. Only an occasional sigh broke the silence. Two Chinese helpers moved noiselessly around the guests, placing on the low, lacquered tables an array of long-stemmed pipes, bowls filled with lumps of the sticky, brown opium, and lamps for burning it. Some guests were still drawing on pipes, while others had already had their smoke and, their eyes glazed, stared fixedly into the dreamworld conjured by the opium.

"Over here, Mr. Henry." Chang ushered him to a mattress in the corner. "You got nice place here."

Henry nodded. "But I'd like a clean sheet, please."

Chang bowed. "Straightaway." He dispatched one of his helpers.

"Is all right, Mr. Henry?" Chang inquired when the man came back and spread the sheet over the mattress.

"Yes. Now I'll take my pipe. Today I want something good and strong, Chang."

"Did I ever disappoint you, Mr. Henry?" Chang sounded offended. "I make you exquisite pipe with Kokang opium, bought special for good guests like you. Kokang opium take care all worries."

When Chang had gone, Henry sank onto the mattress with a long, low sigh. He took off his boots and placed them next to the low table. Then he loosened his shirt collar.

How he craved that opium. Nothing, not even Molly's charms, it seemed, could deliver him from the suffering he had endured since the attack on the village in Uva.

"You ready for very good drug, Mr. Henry?"

Chang put on the low table a tray bearing a bowl, a small hook, and an oil lamp, then sat on the floor, his legs crossed. Next he took a lump of opium from the bowl, used the *yen hok* hook to break off a tiny piece, and held it over the lamp's flame.

The heat made the drug swell into a hard ball the size of a cherry, which Chang then put inside the pipe bowl. He handed it to Henry. "I wish you wonderful travels."

Henry nudged the lamp to the edge of the table, made himself comfortable on his side, took the bamboo stem in his lips, and held the bowl of the pipe in the flame. It wasn't long before the opium started to vaporize, and he drew the smoke down deep into his lungs.

The images of the hanged men, dead infants, and violated women dissolved; their cries wafted away like the smoke itself, and were replaced by a sense of eternal peace and heavenly happiness.

The following morning, as Henry slipped out of Chang's establishment, the sun was rising above Cinnamon Street. Blinded by its glare, he tripped on the steps and almost fell onto the muddy road. He swore under his breath and pulled the brim of his hat even lower. Real life was intolerable after a dream-filled night in the arms of the opium poppy. He had a dull ache just behind his forehead and felt so nauseous he was afraid he would be spitting bile any minute.

With his head down, he lurched along the street. He wanted to get back as fast as possible to the harbor area and the boardinghouse where he'd taken lodgings for the duration of his regimental leave.

As a trained doctor, Henry knew all too well how destructive opium was. And yet since the Uva massacre, he had been tormented day and night. To calm himself, he had started plundering the regiment's laudanum supplies. But soon the effect of the opium tincture was not enough, and during his leave, his self-control had slipped. Far from his regiment's station in Kandy, he now spent days and nights in Colombo's red-light district. It was crystal clear to him that he was on a path leading straight to hell. To give up opium, however, he needed a reason. He had none.

As the bars and bordellos of Cinnamon Street gradually closed, Arab merchants started to open their shops selling exotic spices, colorful silks, and precious stones from the territory of Kandy's virgin forest. Money changers sat outside their booths, awaiting clients, as did the rickshaw drivers, chewing betel nut as they lounged against the shafts of their rickshaws. Cross-legged in the mud before an eye-catching figurine of the Hindu god Shiva, a half-naked sadhu sat meditating. From tiny food stalls, women preparing rice with spicy vegetables tried to tempt Henry to linger. But he stumbled on, his gaze fixed on the ground in front of him.

After some time he found himself approaching a small square, which was shaded by a makeshift palm roof and next to an Anglican church mission. Fishermen always sold the night's catch here. Baskets of prawns, shrimp, lobsters, and squid were already on display. Huge, silvery tuna lay on the ground, their scales still shining, and white-bellied skates were ready for gutting under the critical eye of local women. Crows and egrets hovered, ready to pounce. Henry had to cross this square to get to his boardinghouse, but the smell was even more pungent than usual. His head still lowered, holding his nose with one hand and waving away flies with the other, he quickened his pace between the dead fish and through slicks of blood and sludge.

"Aargh!" He collided hard with a monk who had been begging with his brothers for their one meal of the day, as was the tradition. A few spoonfuls of rice and vegetables were usually donated by the merchants and street cooks. The monk kept his balance, but Henry slipped on discarded fish innards and fell headlong into the muck.

"Damn!" He picked himself up and looked down at his clothes. His suit was splashed all over with mud and worse. A slimy lump of fish stuck to his knee. He doubled up and vomited. The monks, who had halted at a signal from their leader, watched without emotion as Henry pulled out a handkerchief and attempted to clean himself up.

"Our monastery is very near here." When the senior monk spoke, it was in perfect English. "You can wash yourself there."

Before Henry could reply, a second monk spoke in Sinhalese: "The Englishman needs to see to his cleanliness himself!" His colleagues nodded in agreement.

Their leader gave them all a stern look. "Have you forgotten how the Enlightened One told his pupils to demonstrate empathy at all times?"

He nodded to Henry and set off. The other monks reluctantly followed.

Henry hesitated. But he could not possibly appear before his land-lady in his present state. With a feeling of resignation, he joined the monks.

The monastery was separated from the sea by only a narrow stretch of sand. Henry followed the monks through an archway to a walled area and saw a small, white temple with a tiled roof shaped like a pagoda straight ahead. At its front were two *dvarapala*, mythical warriors made of clay whose task was to keep the Buddha figure inside from harm. As Henry walked past, he caught a fleeting glimpse of the golden statue of the Enlightened One in meditative pose on a stone plinth, surrounded by a host of oil lamps.

Behind the temple was an open space, at its center an open hall around which ranged the monks' cells. A roughly made trestle bearing a bell stood in front of the hall. To its right was a sacred Bodhi tree. Beneath the tree, the temple elephant, the embodiment of the divine Ganesha, stood, tethered. The animal was busy eating a breakfast of palm leaves and fruit and took no notice of the monks' return. To the left of the hall was a pool decorated with lilies, orchids, and dwarf rhododendrons.

The monks went into the hall, sat on the floor, and started their meal in silence. Their leader gestured to Henry.

"Wait here," he said and went off toward the cells. Soon he returned with a clean towel and an orange habit.

"You're giving me your own clothing?" asked Henry in surprise.

"You want to go naked?" replied the abbot. "We have no clothes like those you're accustomed to. Bring the habit back when you are able." He turned to leave, but Henry wanted to talk.

"You speak very good English."

"You British have been in our country so long, it would have been foolish of me not to have learned your language," said the abbot coldly. "When you have cleaned yourself up, go to the hall. There you'll get something to eat and some tea, which will alleviate the effects of the opium."

"How do you know that I—?" Henry felt so ashamed that he could not bring himself to speak the word.

"Look at yourself!" The monk drew Henry toward the pool and pointed at the Englishman's reflection in the water. Henry was shocked at what he saw. Was that really him? This filthy, unkempt, hollow-cheeked specter with lifeless eyes? He quickly turned away again.

"So now you've seen what I've seen," said the abbot. "Do that for two or three more years, and you're dead. I've noticed so many like you around the harbor here. As long as you British go on allowing opium in from India, the suffering will not stop. But you British are ruining not only our people with it, but yourselves, too."

Henry swallowed hard. "You're right," he answered after a pause. "I smoke opium and I deserve your candor." He took a step forward and, in the local tradition, placed his palms over one another and bowed his head. "My name is Henry Odell, surgeon to the Fifteenth Infantry Regiment in Kandy. Would you please tell me your name, venerable hamudru?"

The monk's eyes widened in surprise as Henry switched to Sinhalese. "I am Mahinda Dharmapala, the abbot of this monastery."

◆ ◆ ◆

Meanwhile, a carriage was drawing up outside the residence of the British governor. Henry's brother, Charles, jumped to the pavement. He carried a leather briefcase and a rolled document.

He took a good look at himself. That morning his orderly had polished his boots until they gleamed, and his pants were freshly pressed. As he smoothed down his red jacket, his hand brushed the metal star hanging from his chest on a colored ribbon. After the Uva Rebellion, Governor Brownrigg had awarded him the medal for his commitment in the fight against the rebels. He'd also promoted him to major in the Royal Engineers.

Today Charles had an appointment with Brownrigg's successor, General Edward Paget. Glancing at his pocket watch, he saw it was just after eleven. *And already intolerably hot,* he groaned to himself. Beneath the thick uniform, his skin was hot and clammy. His muscles ached and his eyes were burning. How he loathed this humid heat, which unfailingly hit him like a wall and from which there was no escape even at night. He pulled himself together—no place for feelings here—straightened his bicorn hat, and walked decisively up to the entrance.

The British governor's official residence was an extensive white structure built in Dutch colonial times. It was in the old fortress area of Colombo, not far from the harbor, the markets, and the red-light district. Shielded from the native population, this was where the British resided. There were churches, theaters, garrisons, a cricket pitch, and shops selling everything the British heart desired: from Indian tea and French lavender water to English shotguns. Still, the heat, the palms bordering the avenues, and the airy verandas of the houses were an unmistakable reminder that one was in the tropics, not the cool of England.

Charles walked past the statue of George IV, the reigning monarch, and the horde of small gray monkeys clambering about on it, and bounded up the steps. Soldiers of the Ceylon Rifles stood right and left of the grand double doors and saluted him. Charles let the knocker fall, and the door was opened by a butler in full livery. While Charles was waiting in the pleasantly cool reception hall, he examined the portraits of all the previous governors of Ceylon. The first governor, Patrick Agnew, had come into office twenty-seven years ago in Trincomalee on the east coast. Sir Edward Paget, the eleventh governor, had been in office only a few months. Charles had met him for the first time at his inauguration.

"The governor requests your presence," announced the butler. He opened the office door and bowed as Charles walked through. There was little light in the room, as the windows looking onto the park were covered by shutters against heat and mosquitoes. In spite of a palm fan operated by a servant, the room remained stuffy. Bookcases and filing cabinets covered the walls. The Union Jack hung in the corner, beneath a portrait of the conqueror. Against one wall there was a heavy writing desk piled high with papers. As Charles entered the room, Paget snapped shut the file he had been reading and got to his feet. He was a wiry man in middle age, dressed impeccably in a general's uniform, complete with a medal from the Napoleonic Wars.

"Major Odell! Delighted to see you." He greeted Charles with a handshake. "I'm keen to view what you have brought with you." He pushed a pile of folders to one side. Charles placed his briefcase on the floor against the desk and unrolled the document. Paget bent excitedly to look at it. "A map! Very interesting! Is this to be the new road from Colombo to Kandy?" He tapped at a thick dark line marked with charcoal.

"Quite right, Your Excellency. Here you can see the course of what will be the most important transport route in Ceylon," Charles confirmed. "I have carried out a comprehensive survey. This is the shortest possible route between Colombo and Kandy. When it's ready, we'll be able to move troops and supplies from the coast to the interior faster than has ever been possible."

"If we'd had that road in '17 and '18, it wouldn't have taken so long to subdue the rebels," remarked Paget as he traced the line with his finger. "How many miles?"

"Roughly eighty, and twenty-four feet wide. That way, two goods wagons can pass in comfort. If you will permit me, I'll explain in further detail." Charles smoothed down the map. "The land is extremely difficult and makes considerable demands on our engineering expertise. We shall have to traverse rivers currently not bridged. In the interior, we'll come up against dense jungle, ravines, waterfalls, and steep terrain. The highest point is the Kadugannawa Pass." Charles took a small notebook from his briefcase and leafed through it. "I have been so bold as to list the materials needed. For jungle clearance, I need carts, working elephants, and coolies. We'll recruit men from the surrounding villages and coolies from India for the simple tasks. My Royal Engineers will do the demanding, specialized work, such as bridge construction. The Fifteenth Infantry Regiment will take on supervision of the workers and protection of the British engineers."

"How much should we pay the workers?" asked the general.

"Pay? The coolies?" Charles looked at him in amazement. "I don't believe any payment is necessary. These people are accustomed to forced labor. They had to do it for their own king."

Paget looked doubtful. "The Sinhalese kings were their acknowledged rulers. We're now the unloved masters from Europe."

Charles made a dismissive gesture. "Let me deal with it, Your Excellency. I know how to handle these people. With your permission, I'll explain my plans further."

At Paget's nod of agreement, he carried on. "After the jungle clearance, sand and gravel need to be brought in for the road surfacing. That's the only way to make the road sufficiently resilient. I'll construct it with a fair bit of camber so the monsoon rain has good runoff. To the right and left of the road, there'll be drainage channels—" Charles broke off and gripped the edge of the desk. His face was flushed.

"Are you all right, Odell?"

"Absolutely, Your Excellency. But I could wish for less of this damned heat." He pulled a handkerchief from his trouser pocket and dabbed at his forehead.

The governor nodded and turned back to the map. "This project will be an expensive business, but without a good network of roads, this jungle will never become a modern country. What do you think, Odell? How long before your road is ready?"

"Five years, Your Excellency," replied Charles. "Though it will move that quickly only under my leadership. Nobody knows the terrain as well as I do, and nobody else has worked on the planning with such attention to detail."

Paget raised a quizzical eyebrow. "Five years is an ambitious target."

Charles stood to attention. "I consider ambition a virtue."

"And how will you deal with the villagers living in the path of the road? Isn't there likely to be conflict?"

"I've already given this thought, too, sir. The people will be moved."

"And if they don't want to go?"

"Why shouldn't they want to go? There's any amount of uninhabited jungle they could live in. And besides, I'd like to start the construction work in Kandy, not Colombo."

"What? Isn't that highly impractical? All the material will have to be transported through the jungle to the uplands."

"That's right," said Charles. "I'd prefer to start off with the most difficult part of the route, and it's in the uplands that the terrain is most problematic. It's motivating for my engineers if they deal first with the hardest tasks and then the easier ones."

Paget smiled with satisfaction. "I see you have thought of everything."

"With respect, Your Excellency, you will find no better engineer in our colonies on the Indian subcontinent."

Paget glanced at his pocket watch. "What are you doing now, Odell? Are you staying for luncheon? My wife will be deeply grieved if she can't converse with you again about her petunias."

Charles stood even straighter. "Does that mean I have the commission?"

Paget gave a hearty laugh. "Who else, Odell? You have sold yourself magnificently. But the work will require one hundred percent effort. And you can only manage that if you yourself are one hundred percent fit."

"I certainly am," Charles assured him as he followed the governor to the door.

"I don't doubt it. However, before the work begins, have yourself examined by a doctor."

Charles frowned. "I consider that quite unnecessary, Your Excellency. After all, I've braved the climate here for years now."

Paget held the door open for his guest. "Without that medical examination, I cannot give you the commission. But that's all routine for you, surely?"

"So you're here! I'd already prepared myself for hunting you down in the filthiest doss-house in town." Charles stepped inside Henry's small room at the boardinghouse and paused in surprise. "Packing? Your leave has only just started. Or are you actually going to do something sensible with your free time for once?"

Before Henry could reply, Charles spotted the orange monk's habit on the bed. "What have we here?" He drew closer, grinning broadly, and held up the garment between two fingers.

"A monk lent it to me; that's all there is to it." Henry took a pile of shirts from the cupboard and went over to his trunk, open in the middle of the room.

"Lent? Are you hoping to become one of their dirty beggar monks?"

"Just tell me what you want." Henry went on stacking shirts in his trunk.

"Answer me first. Why are you packing?"

Henry went back to the cupboard and took out a pair of trousers. "I'm going back to Kandy."

Mahinda Dharmapala's words had had a profound effect on him, so profound he had decided to cease his opium use at once. He had seen himself through the monk's eyes and was disgusted when he thought about the kind of person he'd become. If he was ever to regain his self-esteem and any control over his life, he had to leave Colombo and the temptation of the opium dens. However, he had no desire to talk about that with anyone, least of all his brother.

After the Uva massacre, Henry had carried out his threat and reported Charles to Governor Brownrigg for the atrocities and his tyrannical behavior. Yet to Henry's dismay, Charles was not punished but rewarded with a medal and a promotion. By contrast, Henry had been warned to pay attention exclusively to his medical duties in the future and not to involve himself in military strategy.

"You may congratulate me, my dear brother." Charles dropped the monk's robe back onto the bed. "Governor Paget has commissioned me to build the new road from Colombo to Kandy."

"Congratulations! Just the thing for someone with a disease like yours," Henry said sarcastically, and then took a close look at his brother. Charles's face was pale, glistening with sweat; his eyes were glassy and had dark shadows underneath. "Now I understand." He went over to a shelf where he kept his shaving equipment and toothbrush alongside several small brown medicine bottles. He picked one up and tossed it to Charles. "This is why you're here, isn't it?"

Three years earlier, Charles had contracted malaria, but he concealed his condition to avoid it interfering with his career. The first time he had come asking for quinine powder, Henry told him to look for another doctor. However, Charles had caught him stealing laudanum from the medicine cupboard and used this to blackmail him.

Charles unscrewed the bottle, shook out a white powder onto his hand, and licked it up. "Why does this stuff have to be so damned bitter?" He grimaced in revulsion.

Henry didn't answer and went on packing his trunk.

Charles watched him for a while. Then he said, "You've got to certify me fit."

Henry straightened up and stared at him. "Is this a joke?"

"No, unfortunately." Charles took off his hat to fan himself. "Paget wants evidence or he won't let me build the road. He says it's no use to him to have a chief engineer who can't stand the climate."

"I agree with him there," replied Henry. "And that is precisely why my conscience as a doctor will not allow me to lie in this matter."

"Since when has an opium addict had any conscience as a doctor?" said Charles with a superior smile.

Henry's jaw tightened, but he would not change his position. "Go and look for some other idiot to aid your deception."

"As you wish, dear chap," answered Charles. "But you know I'll have some stories to tell your commander about your naughty habits."

Henry brought down the lid of his trunk with a loud bang. "You rotter! Get out of my room and leave me in peace!"

"I'll go as soon as I get the medical certificate. It's up to you."

Henry clenched his fists, and for a moment Charles thought his brother was going to punch him. But then Henry forced out, "You win."

Charles smiled again, satisfied this time. "Very good, little brother. Anyway, I've got even more good news for you. I've asked Paget for your regiment to accompany me as support during the whole construction project."

"Magnificent," said Henry. "I must follow you into the jungle to treat your malaria in secret."

"Don't take it so badly. I want to build this road, Henry, but I need you in order to see it through."

"Fine," declared Henry after some thought. "And I won't be treating only you, but everyone who needs my help as a doctor."

Charles rolled his eyes. "The coolies don't need a doctor. If one of them collapses, we get another one."

"You heard my conditions." Henry turned back to his trunk.

There was silence for a few seconds. Then Charles responded with a sigh. "Suit yourself. If you really want to be saddled with the extra work."

Chapter Seven
Mapitigama, July 1822

"Grandma!"

"Yes, Thambo? What is it, treasure?" Anshu straightened up with some difficulty and tucked a stray lock of silver hair back into her bun. It was almost midday. She had spent the morning planting sweet potatoes in the vegetable garden by the hut which, for almost four years now, had been her home in Mapitigama, together with her daughters and her three-year-old grandson. Now she was spreading cow dung over the vegetable patch to keep away snakes and ants.

"There, Grandma!" The child was pointing excitedly toward the jungle.

Anshu followed his gaze and saw a group of six horsemen in red uniforms trotting toward the village. At the forefront was a young man whose dark hair and features seemed vaguely familiar. As the redcoats drew closer, she was horror-struck. Their leader was the same man who had brutally raped Samitha, whose soldiers had tortured Mihiri to death, who had ordered Jeeva's execution and razed to the ground an entire village.

"Grandma? Who are they?"

Anshu struggled to pick up the child, then ran inside her hut. She set him on the floor and crouched down in front of him.

"Thambo, listen to me very carefully," she said, taking his little hands in hers. "You must stay indoors and be very quiet until I, your mama, or Aunt Phera come for you. Under no circumstances are you to leave this hut. Do you understand me?"

The boy stared at her, his eyes huge, and nodded silently. Anshu held his head in both hands and kissed his silky, dark hair. Then she went outside, pulling the palm-straw door closed tight behind her.

Mapitigama was a settlement of twenty huts a short distance from the Kadugannawa Pass, surrounded almost entirely by virgin forest.

For generations, the village had belonged to the dissava of the royal province of Matale. During the Uva Rebellion, the dissava had joined the insurgency and, like so many, been captured and executed. His family had fled to India, and Mapitigama had been left to itself. The villagers believed their new masters knew nothing of the existence of their village, hidden away in the jungle.

Little huts of mud and straw, animal quarters, and the rice storehouse clustered around a village square, the sacred Bodhi tree at its center. Cinnamon peelers or farmers belonging to the respected caste were permitted to live in the heart of the village. Launderers and palm-wine producers, members of a lower caste, lived toward the edge of the settlement, while those who dealt with the dead resided a little outside the village, as befitted those with no caste.

Anshu's family hut was in the village center, as was appropriate for members of the noblest caste. However, the three women owned nothing more than any other village residents, cultivated their own garden and rice field, and occupied a mud hut with only a single room.

While the young worked out in the rice fields and the cinnamon, nutmeg, and clove plantations, the older people took care of manual jobs close to home, watched over the small children, and tended to their gardens. Here they would grow fruit, vegetables, and herbs for daily use, as well as medicinal plants.

Outsiders strayed into Mapitigama only rarely. The Moorish merchants, who came twice a year and brought fabrics, cooking pots, and the latest city news in exchange for betel, cinnamon, cloves, and nutmeg, had been the only visitors in recent years. The people had not set eyes on British soldiers for the four years since the rebellion, so these arrivals were viewed with fear by the old and bewilderment by the very young.

Meanwhile, the horsemen had reached the village square, its ancient Bodhi tree supported by wooden posts, its canopy of leaves spreading above a small shrine with a reclining Buddha. They pulled up their horses and looked around. The leader dug his spurs into his horse, making the animal rear up, snorting.

"I am Major Charles Odell of the Royal Engineers. Where is the village leader?" His tone was imperious in its arrogance.

Nobody replied. A trace of anger flickered across Charles's face. "Are you mute or just stupid? Haven't you monkeys learned a little English yet?" His eyes flickered as they landed on Anshu.

He's recognized me, she said to herself. Her heart skipped a beat as she imagined what he would do, how he would torture her simply for being Jeeva's widow. Then it occurred to her that the British could be after Eranga. Since the time his elder brother died, he had held the position of *widan*, or village leader. Maybe the British had found out about Eranga's part in the rebellion and wanted to behead him, too.

She winced as Odell stretched out his right arm, pointing straight at her.

"You there, woman! Answer me!"

She opened her mouth, but no words came.

"Make it quick!"

She forced herself to sound calm as she wrapped her mouth around the strange English words. "Widan in rice field."

"Take me to him! Now!"

Anshu ran like a hunted animal. The horsemen followed close behind, frightening away the small, lean cows tugging at the grasses and herbs between the trees. The other women followed at a distance.

Anshu was terrified. Samitha and Phera were in the rice fields, and she was leading the devil incarnate straight to her daughters and the unsuspecting villagers. How could she warn them of the danger? The cruelty of that man, his voice and his satisfied expression while he had tortured and murdered her compatriots, still gave her terrifying nightmares. It seemed that Odell had not recognized her, but she couldn't be certain.

Anshu reached a large pool, swarms of flies darting across its surface. The pool was connected by drainage channels to the rice fields on a terraced slope. This slope was dotted with raised points where children kept watch, shouting and drumming to frighten away wild elephants. Two young men were driving a team of buffalo over the damp soil to break and soften the clods. Behind them fluttered cattle egrets in search of frogs as well as of spiders and other tiny creatures disturbed by the buffalo. In other fields, women stood up to their ankles in water, bearing back panniers full of young rice plants. They moved across the fields, bent low, reaching into the panniers with one hand, taking out a little plant, and placing it in the earth. Samitha and Phera were pulling weeds in their field situated not far from the plantation. They were the first to notice Anshu and the redcoats. Both froze at the sight. Memories of the most terrible hours of their lives threatened to overcome them. The screams and pleas rang once more in Phera's ears, the stink of death and decay returned, and she saw her father's head rolling toward her across the ground. Her stomach heaved. She gagged, close to vomiting.

Samitha clapped her hand over her mouth to stop herself screaming in terror. Pulling a corner of her sari over her head, she turned and ran as if pursued by a pack of leopards.

Phera stared after her, wishing she could flee as well. But under no circumstances could she leave her mother alone with the evil British. She breathed deeply, closed her eyes, and called to mind her oath: never again would she allow an Englishman to murder a member of her family.

She slid her right hand between the folds of her sari to find the small knife she had kept hidden there since that terrible day in Uva. As her hand closed around it, she felt her fear turning into powerful determination. She took her pannier off her back, put it down at the edge of the field, and hurried to her mother. "What do they want, these—"

Anshu cut her off. "Where is Eranga?"

"On the newly cleared field, a bit further down the slope. Why?"

"The British want to speak to him."

"Stop that gossiping! Take us to the widan!" Charles ordered from behind them.

"There." Anshu pointed down the slope.

The soldiers galloped across the rice fields. They showed no regard for the terrified people, who scattered to all sides, or the tender young plants, now trampled down by the horses' hooves.

Anshu grabbed Phera by the wrist. "Go to Samitha," she hissed. "She's bound to have run to Thambo."

"Why?" asked Phera. "Who are these redcoats?"

But Anshu had already taken off running behind the horses. Phera hesitated, then realized that Siddhi was with Eranga, helping him shift roots and undergrowth from the newly cleared field. She decided not to run back to the village but to follow in her mother's wake. All the others working in the field hurried behind the British, too.

Siddhi puffed nervously and tugged against her harness when she noticed the men and their horses rapidly approaching. Eranga, too, looked up in alarm.

Charles pulled up his horse just in front of them. "You the village leader?" he shouted in stilted Sinhalese. He had recently learned enough of the language to make himself understood.

"I am the widan of Mapitigama," replied Eranga. "What do you want from me?" He felt confident these British did not know that he had fought against them during the rebellion.

Charles took a good look at the villagers who had now gathered in a semicircle behind him and his soldiers. "Where are your men?"

"In the fields here," answered Eranga.

Charles cast his eye around. "Where are the rest?"

"You British didn't leave many of our young men alive."

Charles gave Eranga a long and quizzical look, then spoke in a garble of English and Sinhalese. "D'you know you talk like a damned rebel? I'd normally make short work of you. But you're in luck, because I need you. You and all the other men, apart from the old ones. And I need that elephant there, too." He nodded toward Siddhi.

"Never!" Phera gasped.

"Shhh!" Anshu squeezed her daughter's arm. "Why aren't you with Samitha?"

Charles was already urging his horse on toward the two women. "Nest of rebels! I'll teach you all to follow my orders!"

"Leave her! She's still a child." Anshu darted between the horse and her daughter, but Charles skillfully guided the animal around her and reared up right in front of Phera. Once again, Phera felt absolute terror. Yet she also wanted to protect Siddhi, and this gave her the strength to stand up to the tyrant. Her hand floated to the knife in the folds of her sari, fully prepared to kill first the horse and then the man.

Charles stared hard at her face, then at the curve of her breasts beneath her clothing. "A child, did the crone say?" He sneered. "I'd enjoy finding out just how much of a child—"

"What do you need us and the elephant for?" Eranga pushed forward to stand in front of Phera.

As Charles turned his attention to the widan, Anshu pulled Phera behind the other villagers, out of Charles's line of sight.

"What are you doing, Mother? I have to help Siddhi." Phera tried to pull her hand away.

"Stop it! Don't you recognize him?"

"No." Phera took in the desperation on her mother's face. "But you do. Who is he?"

Anshu didn't respond. "Run to the village. Hide at home and don't let anyone see you as long as he's here. Eranga will make sure nothing happens to Siddhi." She nudged her daughter insistently in the back, and Phera stumbled. Why didn't her mother want to say who the man was? Somewhere behind her was his voice.

"I'm building a new road from Kandy to Colombo and need workers and elephants. This one seems to know how to shift heavy weights."

Phera stiffened. Suddenly, she knew why her mother was so upset. It was the voice that had ordered the massacre of her people almost four years ago, had laughed at the death of Tharindu, had organized the execution of her father.

She turned slowly and looked protectively at her elephant. Siddhi was standing quietly, flapping her ears, always a sign she was taking careful note of everything going on around her.

Unrest had broken out amongst the villagers on hearing Charles's announcement. That the British were building a road near Mapitigama had been reported by the Moorish merchants on their last visit. However, they had said nothing about men being enslaved to do the work.

"You want a road, then get your own people to build it!" called out one young man.

"We're not doing any *rajakariya* service for you people," added another, sparking murmurs of agreement. "You're not our beloved king!"

Rajakariya was the labor service they had done for their kings in olden times. They had cleaned the irrigation pools and temples and maintained the jungle paths. However, in stark contrast to laboring for the British masters, carrying out work for the king had been an honor.

Eranga raised his hand. "I can give you neither men nor elephant. We are in the middle of the planting season."

"That was not a request. It was an order!" roared Charles. He took out his watch, studied it, and then said, "You and your men have thirty minutes to say good-bye to your families. Anyone not coming of his own volition will be manacled and taken away by force."

The grumbling started again, louder this time. Some of the young men pointedly picked up stones. The soldiers immediately drew their sabers and positioned their horses alongside their commander. Charles had drawn his pistol, and now he aimed straight at Eranga's head.

"Call your people off, Mr. Widan."

Several seconds of tense silence passed.

"We agree to your conditions," said Eranga, his expression grim. He gestured to his men, and they let the stones drop to the ground.

With a smug smile, Charles returned his pistol to its holster. "Your village square in thirty minutes. The clock's ticking." Turning his horse, he galloped off. His soldiers followed him, sabers swishing menacingly as they went.

The villagers stood there in shock.

"Run home, pack whatever you need, and bid farewell to your families," Eranga urged the young men. "Hurry! You heard what the demon said."

They shuffled away in bewilderment.

Phera rushed back down the slope toward her elephant.

"You can't give him Siddhi, Eranga!" She grabbed the rope on Siddhi's harness.

"I could have killed the commander, but his men wouldn't have left any of us alive," he said. "Forgive me, my young mistress, I had no choice."

"I'd rather drive Siddhi into the jungle than leave her to this evil man!"

"I can't prevent you from doing that, young mistress," he replied. "But then they'll take revenge on the villagers. You know what these British are capable of."

Phera's head fell, and she rested her forehead against Siddhi. She wondered whether she should tell Eranga who the man was. But if she did, Eranga might decide to avenge Jeeva's death. He would kill the Briton, and he, and many others, would pay for it with their lives.

I can't say anything, she thought, fear clutching at her heart. *Forgive me, Siddhi, for not being able to protect you better.*

The elephant lifted her trunk and gently touched her friend's cheek with its tip. She gave soothing snorts as if to say, "Don't worry about me."

Phera took a deep breath and looked at Eranga. "Swear to me that you will look after Siddhi."

He nodded solemnly. "I'll protect her as I would my own eyes."

Charles guided his horse across the construction site and stopped at a point that gave him a good view in all directions. Three months had passed since they first broke ground, and the work had progressed well.

Behind him, the new road wound in generous curves through the narrow valley below the Kadugannawa Pass. Only a half-mile stretch, a good foot in depth, still needed to be filled in with gravel, brought with extreme difficulty all the way from the coast to the uplands. At the edge of the site, a group of laborers was breaking down a cartload of gravel that had arrived too bulky for use. The rhythmic hammering echoed around the steep, wooded hills, which had for centuries shielded the ancient royal city of Kandy against invaders. Where the roadbed had already been filled, elephants were dragging heavy boulders over the gravel to make a strong, resilient surface.

Charles had divided the workers into columns, each under the direction of a soldier from the Royal Engineers. Work started at sunrise, after a meager breakfast of flatbread and rice. Then Charles would announce the workload for the day. This was usually so great that the men had to work until evening with only a short break for another small scoop of rice. At the beginning, the workers had protested the conditions. A number had fled. But Charles had sent soldiers after them and captured every single man. On Charles's orders, each was flogged, then hanged for all the others to see.

Now he turned his attention to the most recently built section, stretching a good mile ahead of him, to the edge of the jungle. Somewhere in that dark-green mass, the Nanu Oya flowed. Charles heard the rush of water tumbling in waterfalls to the valley bottom. In the distance, a huge granite mass rose out of the green jungle, its peak half-veiled in wispy white cloud. To the local people, this was Bathalegala, but Charles, like all the British, knew it as Bible Rock.

On the section of road in front of Charles, workers were excavating the roadbed and digging side channels for the rain runoff. Charles watched a small group doing a second gravel pour where the last heavy rain shower had washed away the first. The frequent changes in weather were an annoyance. Storms brewed up quickly in this country and caused considerable damage.

Rocks of different dimensions also presented problems, but these could be overcome. Those the size of a coconut were dug out. Medium-sized obstructions were heated, then doused in cold water to make them shatter. A boulder the size of two elephants protruded from the ground at the end of this section. Rocks this large had to be blown up. To this end, workers had drilled a number of holes in its sides, and an engineer now placed leather tubes filled with black gunpowder inside the holes. Another engineer set the fuses. They were made of black gunpowder and reeds soaked in alcohol.

Someone was guiding his horse over the uneven ground, slowly moving in Charles's direction. He sighed when he saw the rider was none other than his brother, Henry. Charles already knew what the bore wanted: better food for the workers, longer breaks, more medicine and dressings.

"Good day, Charles," said Henry, pulling up his horse next to his brother's. "You look pleased."

"We've made such good progress in the last few weeks that we're three miles ahead of schedule," explained Charles.

"I hope you know such speed comes at the workers' expense. If you don't want to risk more injuries, they need rest, and urgently." Henry pulled his hat farther down against the glare of the sun. "It isn't even midday yet, and I've put splints on three broken legs, dealt with various fractures and countless compressions to fingers. One worker's lost a thumb, another has been rolled over by a tree trunk. The number of fever cases is back up. I won't even start with the bad nutrition, which weakens them even further."

"Why d'you bother, then?" interrupted Charles. "I told you at the start that sick coolies will be replaced. If you want to pamper and fuss over them, that's your personal delight."

"You're treating them worse than slaves," Henry retorted.

"Slaves are worth something to their owners. Coolies aren't," Charles shot back.

"It's bad enough they don't get a single penny in return. The least we can do is look after them properly. They need suitable clothing and shoes. And they can't do this hard, physical work on rice alone. They must eat meat."

Charles gave a shout of laughter. "Has it escaped your esteemed attention that their absurd religion forbids it?"

"As is so often the case, you are inadequately informed about this country and its people, dear Charles," countered Henry. "Only some Buddhists abstain from consuming meat. If you give these workers decent food, you'll see how much stronger and more resilient they become."

Henry thought of the book of the teachings of Buddha that he had bought at a Kandy market. Every night, when he lay awake under his mosquito net and longed for opium, he read this book. When the craving grew almost too great to bear, he would call to mind the words of the abbot, Mahinda Dharmapala, and swear to himself that he would never again be that broken-down addict whose vice could be spotted at first sight.

He cleared his throat, took a scrap of paper from his jacket pocket, and passed it to Charles. "I've made a list of all the medicines I need. Dressings running low again, too. And I want the workers to have reasonable overnight accommodations."

"If people pitch in hard enough during the day, they should be so tired at night, they can sleep anywhere." Charles put the list in his pocket without giving it a glance.

For the British engineers and soldiers, there were tented accommodations the full length of the construction site. This included living and dining areas, a huge field hospital, and a tent especially for meetings. Even the horses had their own tent for the night.

For the Sinhalese and Indian workers, there was nothing remotely approaching this. They slept in makeshift huts rigged up from a few palm branches. Soldiers were on guard to ensure nobody fled and nobody fought. The Indians were Hindu while the Sinhalese were Buddhist. Over and above this, the Indian laborers were "untouchables." For the Sinhalese, who came from castes of farmers and tradesmen, it was unthinkable to sleep side by side with these people or to eat anything cooked in the same pot. However, Charles disregarded all this. If news of disagreements reached his ears, punishment was swift and severe.

"As far as the accommodations are concerned—" Henry started to speak, but Charles had moved on.

"Here comes Brooks. Now we can get on with the blasting."

"We are ready, Major," confirmed the engineer, Charles's second-in-command. "The soldiers are clearing the construction site."

"Superb!" Charles exclaimed. "Gather the engineers. Before the explosion takes place, I want one final camp meeting." He trotted away on his horse without paying any further attention to his brother.

"This road would be a great achievement if only you could build it without destroying so many people in the process," murmured Henry.

Eranga stood with Siddhi at the edge of the blast area and looked at the enormous boulder. He wanted to see as much as possible of the explosion. Over the weeks spent on the construction site, he had witnessed one or two lesser blasts. It fascinated him to see how a handful of black dust and a flame could shatter huge rocks to smithereens, and he wanted to know everything about this magical phenomenon.

If we'd had this gunpowder in Uva, we'd have won the battle and Kanda Uda Pas Rata would be a free kingdom today, he thought. He wondered whether he should try to steal some. But he swiftly dismissed that thought from his mind. The British guarded their munitions aggressively, and he would only expose the village and its inhabitants to danger if the theft came to light. The old Kanda Uda Pas Rata had perished and would never rise again, even if he stole a whole barrel of explosives.

The piercing warning bugle sounded, first once, then twice. Engineers lit the fuses. Eranga smiled to himself as they ran like rabbits.

Siddhi snorted in agitation. She knew to associate the sound of the bugle with a huge bang. As all the elephants on the site were afraid of explosions, the mahouts had to secure their front and back legs to stop them fleeing in panic. During the explosion, they always stood close by their animals to calm them.

From the folds of his sarong, Eranga took a piece of flatbread, saved from breakfast, and offered it to Siddhi. The elephant, however, ignored this tasty tidbit and tossed her head back and forth restlessly. Eranga saw the fear in her eyes and hummed soothingly as the fuses hissed and burned. The flame arrived at the blast holes. There was a deafening crack and bang as the gunpowder caught. The enormous boulder shattered into countless pieces, and a mighty dust cloud rose, splinters of stone flying in all directions.

The elephants let out piercing sounds as their mahouts struggled to soothe them. Siddhi ripped up chunks of undergrowth and tossed them in the air. Eranga placed the flats of his hands across her broad chest to pacify her and hummed a gentle melody.

Once the dust had subsided, Charles went first to one engineer, then the other, thanking them with a handshake. The bugle sounded again, signaling the end of the danger. The mahouts and elephants were now to drag the biggest and heaviest pieces of broken rock out of the roadbed. Eranga loosened Siddhi's foot bindings and checked that her harness was sitting properly. Then he led her to the crater created by the explosion. Intrigued, he peered down into the pit, as deep as a man is tall. The sides dropped down steeply. Its base was covered with gravel and rocks that had broken away. The gravel shone with moisture, showing that the groundwater here was close to the surface. A hefty boulder rested on an angular granite ledge which, before the explosion, had been hidden in the ground, and its other end projected above the edge of the hole. Eranga studied the boulder. It was big and heavy, but Siddhi would be able to drag it out of the hole. He decided to run a rope along the length of the boulder and create a strap. But first he needed help raising the stone with poles so that he could run the rope beneath it. He called over two men from the village, and together they set to work. Just as he had fixed the rope to Siddhi's harness, Charles sauntered over.

"Time to show us what your elephant can really do, widan," he said in the mix of languages Eranga had learned to follow. "I'm going to watch the show from down below." He squatted, then slid down the crater wall.

Eranga positioned himself by Siddhi's head and rubbed the ankus against her shoulder. "Daha! Forward!"

Siddhi's muscles tensed as she bent her powerful body forward, her back curving with the effort. She took one small step, leaned into the harness again, and took the next. The boulder shifted and started slowly to slide forward.

"You're doing well," Eranga encouraged the elephant. "Daha, daha. You're nearly there!"

Just then Charles shouted, "Stop!"

"Ho, ho," Eranga ordered Siddhi reluctantly.

The elephant shook her head in frustration. She could feel the weight of the stone and knew she hadn't completed her task. Eranga praised her and stroked her trunk. Then he went to the edge of the pit and looked at the Englishman.

Charles's head and shoulders were hidden behind the huge rock linked to Siddhi's harness, so only his body was visible. Odell's hands appeared to be scratching at the ground. Eranga could hear scraping noises, and small stones and lumps of earth came flying over the crater edge. Then Charles's head came into view. "Give me that elephant stick of yours!"

Eranga handed him the ankus. Charles vanished once more behind the rock, and Eranga heard scraping sounds.

"How long will your investigation take, sir?" he asked. "It is tiring for Siddhi to sustain the weight of the stone all this time."

Charles's head popped up once more. "Loosen the strap. No further work is to be done here." He threw the ankus over the edge of the crater and clambered up behind it.

Eranga stared at him.

"Did you hear?" snorted Charles. "Disappear with your elephant. The work here is over." He hurried away.

Eranga shook his head in annoyance that Siddhi had been made to work so hard for naught. On top of this, he had to use a knife to cut through the rope attached to her harness, because it had been pulled so tight, he couldn't undo the knot. Once the huge rock at last slid back onto its granite ledge, the elephant fell forward with a little puff of relief. Eranga turned and saw Charles giving orders all over the site for work to cease. He then called all his engineers together. When the British had gone inside their meeting tent, Eranga went to the edge of the crater and squinted. What on earth had Odell seen down there?

Two weeks later the construction work was running at full capacity again. The sound of axes echoed through the jungle, interspersed with agonizing cracks and crunches as yet another giant of the primeval forest toppled. Eranga watched as the trunk of an ancient tamarind split and snapped. The moment the tree hit the ground, the workers started hacking off the boughs, and Eranga helped drag them to the side of the forest path.

When only the stripped trunk was left on the ground, Eranga guided Siddhi to its end and got the harness ropes into position. He wondered yet again why Odell had decided to change the course of the road after the blasting of that huge boulder. The abandoned section was nearly a mile long, and as useless and ugly as a scar. The new route no longer went west to Colombo but through the jungle, a good way northwest of the original plan.

This change worried Eranga deeply. As the work progressed, it became ever clearer to him that the road would lead straight to Mapitigama. He knew the major would give no consideration to a small Sinhalese village in the path of his road.

As he placed the rope around the end of the tree trunk and secured it to Siddhi's harness, Eranga thought about Charles's justification for the change. He'd claimed that the ground revealed by the blast had turned out to be predominantly granite and, consequently, was far too hard for excavation and leveling.

On the same day, the engineers had marked out the first section of the new route. Then clearance work had started and was now speeding toward Mapitigama. Eranga calculated that in a week, ten days at the most, they would reach his ancestral village.

When he had harnessed Siddhi, he noticed Charles was riding along the pathway.

On impulse, Eranga hurried to meet him, waving his arms to attract attention. "A word with you, sir?"

"What do you want, man?" Charles rode right up to Eranga, reining in only at the last moment.

But Eranga did not flinch, and his voice was steady when he spoke. "The new road, sir. If it takes this course, it will pass straight through our village."

"What's your village to do with me?"

"These people live there; it is our home. If you continue to build in this direction, we'll lose everything: our houses, our fields, our spice trees."

"For heaven's sake. You'll just have to build your houses and dig your fields somewhere else. Now get out of my way. I have no time for such nonsense." Charles brought his heels to his horse's flanks.

But Eranga swiftly stepped in, grabbing the reins.

"Are you insane?" Foaming with rage, Charles raised his riding crop, but Eranga stood firm.

"At least think of our Bodhi tree, living residence of souls and gods. To chop it down would bring bad karma on us all, on you!"

"Do you know how little I care about your stupid tree?" Charles jerked at the reins, but Eranga held them with an iron grip.

"You cannot build the new road through Mapitigama, sir. It will bring great misfortune."

"Go away and take your superstitions with you," growled Charles. "And get back to work or I'll cut your rations." He dug his heels in, and the horse shot forward, its shoulder knocking Eranga to the ground.

Stunned, he lay there for several seconds. Then he struggled to his feet. He would defend his village and its sacred tree. He'd seen granite blasted with gunpowder time and again. The Englishman was lying; it wasn't too hard. If Eranga wanted to save his village and the tree, then he had to find out why the road was being rerouted.

That night Eranga lay awake on his makeshift bed of palm leaves and listened to the sounds around him in the darkness. He heard the snorts of elephants tethered nearby, the breaths of sleeping men, the gentle scurrying of rodents in the undergrowth, and, in the distance, the muted voices of two British soldiers on watch.

When the moon, looking like a great golden fruit, rose out of the jungle, Eranga sat up cautiously. For a moment his thoughts drifted longingly to his village, where the remaining women and elders would be celebrating tonight beneath the Bodhi tree. Binara Poya was the celebration of the full moon in the seventh month of their calendar, the ninth month of the British calendar. It was likely that a monk had come from a hidden forest monastery and was there, telling stories from the life of the Enlightened One. The villagers would be sitting before him on the ground, listening attentively, praying, and meditating.

Eranga put his palms flat against his forehead, closed his eyes, and breathed deeply. If he wanted the people of his village to celebrate Binara Poya beneath the Bodhi tree in the years to come, then he needed to reflect hard on his plan.

He reached for his oil lamp and an earthenware bowl in which he had concealed, under some dried moss, a piece of glowing charcoal stolen from the cooking fire. When he stood up, his muscles were stiff, and his bones ached from the relentless daily labor. He suppressed the pain and slipped silently away. When he reached the chatting guards, he snuck past unnoticed.

Without making a sound, Eranga moved parallel to the new course of the road, through the jungle, guided only by the fractured light of the moon through the trees. When he eventually stepped out of the forest, he saw before him the junction leading to Odell's new route. He looked around carefully, then bent low and moved swiftly to the blast crater. He looked over his shoulder to check that nobody had followed. Then he squatted down and slid into the black hole itself. Water had accumulated in the bottom, so Eranga splashed in up to his calves. Using the piece of charcoal, he lit his lamp's cocoa-fiber wick, and soon a small but bright light illuminated the crater. Eranga shone the light around the pit but saw nothing unusual. He bent down, scooped a handful of gravel out of the water, and held it to the lamp. In the light of the flame, the little stones glinted. Eranga placed the lamp on the protruding granite slab and let the little stones run through his fingers. Sometimes he would hold on to one, look at it hard, and then let it drop back into the water. Then he took another small stone, scrutinized it, and put it in a little bag he had concealed in the folds of his sarong. What he saw in the dancing lantern light transformed his suspicion into certainty. Now it was clear to him why the major had altered the course of the road. But how should he use that knowledge to save the village and the Bodhi tree?

Some small rocks gently clattered behind Eranga as they rolled down the crater wall and softly plunked into the water. He whipped around, knocking over the lamp. With every muscle tensed, he curled like a wild cat ready to strike its prey and listened hard in the impenetrable black of night.

Chapter Eight
September 1822

"Higher, Grandma, higher!"

Little Thambo giggled on the swing Eranga had hung from the mango tree in Anshu's garden. His playmates hopped about with excitement as they eagerly awaited their turn. Anshu did as he asked, and she smiled as her grandson shrieked delightedly and waved his little feet with glee.

That smile faded the moment she saw the horseman. He was an Englishman, just like the rider who, more than two full moons ago, had taken away all the men from the village. But this man was not a solider. He wore jodhpurs and boots, a dark jacket, and a broad-brimmed hat pulled low over his eyes. Anshu looked frantically for a weapon but saw nothing. She stopped the swing, lifted her grandson off, and transferred the child to her hip. With her free hand, she shooed the other children.

"Run home now! Quickly, quickly!"

With reluctance, the children toddled away but not far, as they did not want to miss anything.

The Englishman reined in his horse. "Ayubowan," he said in greeting.

"Ayubowan, stranger," replied Anshu hesitantly. No Englishman had ever greeted her with courtesy, not in his own language and certainly never in her own.

The stranger looked at her for some time. Then he bowed and said, "I didn't expect us to meet again."

Anshu studied the Englishman, and slowly his face brought back images of the day that changed everything forever. Here in front of her was the man who had saved her youngest daughter's life. But did that mean she could trust him? An Englishman?

"What do you want?" she said, her voice flat.

He smiled kindly. "How are you and your children?"

He must mean Samitha and Mihiri. The commander had ordered his removal before the soldiers had raped Mihiri to death. And he couldn't have known Phera was her daughter. Anshu was relieved that Samitha and Phera were out pulling weeds in the rice field.

"Is that your grandson?" continued the Englishman. He winked at Thambo, who was gazing wide-eyed at the horse.

Anshu nodded warily and held the child closer.

Henry sighed. "You do not wish to speak to me. I fully understand. I ought to introduce myself: My name is Henry Odell. I am surgeon to the Fifteenth Infantry Regiment and am the doctor accompanying the new-road construction work." He paused to remove his hat. His voice took on a solemn tone. "What happened then, in Uva, was appalling. My brother should never have incited his soldiers to such barbaric behavior. And the execution of your husband and the other man was a crime."

Anshu listened in shock. His brother? Was the only Englishman who had objected to the atrocities against her people really the brother of the monster who had given the orders?

How can two people as different as day from night be born to the same mother? she thought, shaken to the core.

"Grandma?" Thambo's little voice pulled her from this numbness. "What's that?" He was pointing at Henry's mount. Instinct made her put her hand on the back of his head, and she drew his face protectively toward her chest.

"A 'horse,'" she replied, setting him down. "Now go on with your friends." But the little boy clung to her sari and whined, pointing at the fascinating animal.

"Be a good boy, Thambo." She nudged him gently away. Reluctantly, he stomped off, his face crumpling, near to tears.

Henry watched him go. "How old is the boy?"

She ignored this, too, and asked again, "What do you want, stranger?"

Henry turned his attention back to Anshu. "Where can I find the village leader's family?"

She hesitated again, then said, "You can talk to me. Our widan was associated with my husband all his life."

"Well, in that case—" Henry took a deep breath. "Sadly, I do not bring good news. Your village leader is dead."

Anshu's face showed only disbelief. "Dead? How—?"

"This morning he was found lifeless at his elephant's feet. Numerous wounds cover his head and body. It seems the animal was restless overnight, and he went to calm it. The elephant must have attacked him."

Anshu narrowed her eyes. Elephants did occasionally kill humans, but it was usually a bull in the rutting season or an animal previously beaten and maltreated. For Eranga, elephants were divine creatures worthy of the utmost respect. And Siddhi loved him almost as much as she did Phera. That the cow elephant had attacked Eranga was, in Anshu's eyes, out of the question. But why should she explain that to an Englishman who understood nothing of elephants and the significance they held for her people? So all she said was: "I shall arrange for the widan and the elephant to be brought home. He must be cremated."

"It's not as simple as that," responded Henry. "The animal won't let anybody near it or the body. Even though it's tethered, it tries to attack anyone who gets close enough. I need a mahout who knows the animal and how to deal with it. My brother has given me until this evening to find one, or he will shoot the elephant."

"No!" Anshu cried. "Do you British murder everything that goes against your wishes?"

"Not in my case," said Henry. "Would I be here looking for a mahout if I didn't want the elephant to live?"

Anshu's head spun. There was one mahout: Phera. But the thought of her daughter being anywhere near the evil commander made her stomach clench. On the other hand, Phera would never forgive her mother if she didn't have the chance to save Siddhi.

"Perhaps I know someone," she replied hesitantly. "But I can't promise anything."

"We have only until tonight." Henry put his hat back on and rode off.

"Why did you send for us, Mother?" Samitha stepped inside the hut, followed by Phera. Her little boy left his playmates and ran over to her, clacking together two coconut shells as he went.

"Horse!" he shouted, proud of his new word.

Samitha scooped him up into her arms and kissed him.

As always, it was like twilight inside the windowless hut. A little daylight shone through the open door.

Stacked on the shelf along the wall were storage baskets, food bowls, and cooking equipment. On the other side were a clothes chest and a spinning wheel with a little three-legged stool, and in the corner were sleeping mats, rolled and stored during the day. The family cooked outside, beneath the canopy. On the hut's back wall there was an altar. Every morning Anshu's first walk of the day was to the garden, where she picked fresh flowers for the altar. Then she lit the oil lamps, prayed, and thought of her dead husband and her dead daughter.

She sat before the altar now and turned her eyes toward the small golden Buddha. Her mind was focused on the two Britons and the strange way their paths had crossed again with her family's. She was repelled by the idea that the brothers' destiny could be intertwined with theirs. But she knew that she, too, had to follow the eternal law of cause and effect. If the scales of justice became imbalanced, they would seek equilibrium.

"Is everything all right, Mama?" asked Phera. It was unusual for her mother to be praying in the middle of the day instead of working in the garden.

Anshu stood up and went over to her daughter. "Something terrible has happened."

"To Siddhi?" asked Phera, horrified. Ever since she had consented to the elephant being used on construction of the new road, she had found no peace. Every day she regretted her decision but had no idea what else she could have done.

"An Englishman was in the village," began Anshu. "He brought the news that Eranga is dead. He—" The rest of the sentence was drowned out by a scream of horror.

Anshu gestured for her daughter to be quiet. "They say Siddhi killed Eranga."

"Siddhi would never hurt Eranga," Phera wailed.

"She always obeyed Eranga," chimed in Samitha.

"I share your opinion, my daughters," Anshu responded. "But the British think otherwise. They want to shoot Siddhi because she won't let anyone near Eranga's body. They are asking for a mahout who can calm her."

"I will not allow that to happen!" Phera rushed over to the clothes trunk, flung open the lid, and rooted around inside. Right at the bottom, she found her old baggy trousers and looked at them carefully. They might be a bit short now, but with luck they would still just about fit her. She bent over the trunk again and took out a linen cloth and shirt of her father's.

Anshu looked at her in some irritation. "What do you want with those?"

Phera clutched the bundle of garments to her chest. "The British are asking for a mahout for Siddhi. They'll get one."

"Oh, my child! These British are dangerous." Anshu hugged her daughter tight.

But Phera gave a decisive shake of her head. "Siddhi is my friend. I'll help her. And I'll bring Eranga home." When she saw the fear in her mother's face, she spoke more gently. "Mama, please don't worry. I can look after myself. Eranga trained me well. And we all know that Siddhi didn't kill him, so perhaps I can figure out what really happened."

Anshu thought of the day when the monk, Mahinda, had revealed the contradictions in Phera's birth horoscope: sensitive Cancer, poisonous Scorpio, the sentimental Moon, and the aggressive Mars.

"Phera's mind is as sharp as a newly whetted blade. But if it is not used wisely, it can turn dangerous and deadly, like an untamed elephant," the monk had said.

Anshu would have liked more than anything to lock Phera up to keep her away from the British. But she could not stand in the way of destiny.

"After Father's death, Eranga gave us a new home," said Samitha. "Without him, we'd have been outcasts and would have had to do the work of the lowest of the low. It is honorable and good for Phera to bring him back home." She put Thambo down and held her hand out to Phera. "Let me have that linen, Phera. I'll help you to bind your breasts flat."

Phera stripped off her sari and slipped into the baggy pants. Samitha wound the linen tightly around her sister's upper body.

"I still haven't told you everything," said Anshu. "The Englishman who brought me the news of Eranga's death—we know him."

Samitha lowered her hands, still clutching the end of the linen. "Was he there, too, when—?" Her voice broke.

Anshu nodded. "He was the one who tried to hold back his countrymen. He wanted to help Mihiri and Father and Tharindu. And you, Phera, he saved your life when the commander wanted to shoot you." She swallowed hard and took a long look at her daughter. "That same commander is his brother."

Phera stared at her mother without seeing her. She saw instead that horrific day when Tharindu had died before her eyes. She saw the Englishman's face as he bent down to try and help Tharindu. She saw him discover her hiding place and look into her eyes.

"My child." Anshu carefully touched Phera on the arm. "Please stay here."

Phera brushed the memories aside and looked at her mother with determination. "What would happen to Eranga's body, Mother? And Siddhi? No, I'll go." She tied the ends of the linen binding, which Samitha had now finished wrapping. Then she put on her father's old shirt and tied her hair up into a bun at the back of her head, like their men did.

"You're so brave, Phera. Aren't you afraid?" asked Samitha. She was standing next to Thambo with her hand on the child's head.

"Yes, I am. But I'm going to act as if the fear isn't there." She reached for her knife. As she started to secure it in her belt, Anshu held her again.

"Wait."

She went to the altar, took a long, flat object from behind the shrine, and solemnly handed it to her youngest daughter.

Phera's eyes widened. "Father's dagger."

"It will give you strength and will protect you."

Phera's fingers closed around the silver handle. She felt its weight in her hand and executed a few rapid movements through the air. Her face showed fierce concentration.

"The dagger is for you to use in self-defense only," warned Anshu.

Phera returned the weapon to its sheath and attached it to her belt. "Doesn't the man guilty of killing Father and Mihiri, and of causing Samitha unspeakable pain, deserve retaliation?"

Anshu held her daughter's face with both hands and looked into her eyes. "You know what you are taking on if you put out fire with fire."

Phera broke away from her mother without a word and left.

Siddhi scented her friend from afar and trumpeted so loudly that Phera heard it over the din of the construction site. The desperate sound went right through her. She hurried on and soon discovered Siddhi in a small clearing. A British soldier was guarding her from a safe distance, his rifle at the ready. It appeared that Eranga had secured Siddhi to a tree trunk by means of a rope looped around her left foreleg. He had then attached a second rope from that same foreleg to the left hind leg so that she could take only small steps if she got free. Now the elephant was pulling at the rope with all her might and stamping her feet in anger.

The soldier saw Phera and bellowed something in English. She took no notice, concentrating only on Siddhi.

"Ho, ho. It's me."

Siddhi let out a puff and immediately stopped stamping. She stretched out her trunk, touching her friend's neck, hair, and face. Phera stroked her soothingly while looking down nervously. Eranga lay on his back between the elephant's legs. His dark skin had taken on a gray pallor; his now-lifeless eyes stared out of his motionless face.

His sarong was torn, pushed up high, his half-naked body covered in wounds and filth. Phera saw that his rib cage was crushed. And one leg was twisted into an unnatural position.

She fought back the nausea and crept slowly beneath Siddhi's belly. All the while, she spoke soothingly to the distressed elephant. Once she was close enough, she lifted Eranga under the arms and, little by little, eased his body out from under Siddhi. The corpse was heavy, and it took all her strength to move it. On top of that, rigor mortis had set in, and Eranga's body was as stiff and hard as an ironwood tree.

"Wait!" someone called out in Sinhalese behind her. "I'll help you, boy!"

She turned and saw an Englishman hurrying toward her. Her heart raced as she recognized the man who had spared her life. But he looked weary and far thinner than she remembered. Perhaps he had been sick. She knew that foreigners did not fare well with the climate in her country.

Siddhi lifted her trunk and trumpeted menacingly.

"Stay back!" Without waiting for the man to reply, Phera turned away and got hold of Eranga again, struggling to drag him out of reach of Siddhi's feet.

The Englishman told the soldier to keep his distance. Then he placed his crossed hands flat against his chest and gave a little bow. "I am Henry Odell, surgeon to the Fifteenth Infantry Regiment. I care for the sick here on the construction site."

Phera stared at him, as shocked as Anshu had been to hear an Englishman use the greeting a local would. "My name is Phera. I am a mahout. I'm taking Eranga home."

Phera watched for signs of recognition, but his face revealed nothing.

"Hello there. I would like to examine Eranga before you take him away."

"Why?"

He looked first at Siddhi, then at the dead man. "I often saw how Eranga worked with the elephant. He was always careful to ensure the animal didn't overexert herself. Every evening he would seek out a water hole so the elephant could bathe, and would put fresh greenery where she liked to take her rest. I am unsure why an elephant would kill anyone who looked after it so well."

Phera's eyes lit up. "Siddhi would never have done Eranga any harm. He brought her into the world and taught her everything she knows."

"But whatever happened here, she was clearly ready to use force against anyone threatening Eranga," Henry said. He turned and knelt down. "I shall now start the examination."

Phera crouched down near him, watching intently as the British doctor assessed the injuries on the front of Eranga's body.

"You're very young, lad," said Henry, as he carefully palpated Eranga's broken leg. "Are you already a fully trained mahout?"

"I'm nineteen, actually. My training started when I was only five."

He turned and looked at the mahout. For a nineteen-year-old, Phera's face was strangely smooth, with no sign of stubble. The eyes were velvety and dark, framed with long lashes.

A pretty boy, Henry thought. He felt himself getting aroused. What was happening to him? He cleared his throat and concentrated on examining the corpse. "Was Eranga the man who trained you?"

The lump in Phera's throat stopped any words from coming out.

"Was he your father?"

"No." A shake of the head. "But I knew him from the day I was born. He was with my family for years."

"May he rest in peace." Henry reached out and closed the dead man's eyes.

"Just like you did before, sir!" exclaimed Phera, recalling Tharindu. Startled by her own words, she clapped her hand to her mouth.

153

But Henry, deep in the examination of Eranga's wounds, replied absently, "A doctor, especially an army doctor, has to close the eyes of many dead."

"How is the soul supposed to leave the body if you close off the gates?"

He looked up with concern on his face. "Have I done something wrong?"

"Probably not," Phera said after some thought. "Eranga has been dead for many hours. His soul will already have arrived in the world beyond this one. Have you found out yet why he died?"

Henry grasped the dead man by the hip and the shoulder and gently turned him over so he could examine the back of his body. "I know only this: the broken bones and the wounds to his belly occurred after death."

Phera's eyes were wide. "How can you tell?"

"It's not sorcery, my boy." He smiled. "I have noted that those wounds barely bled. That is a sign that they came about after death, because the blood stops flowing then."

Phera swallowed hard. "I think Siddhi made those wounds. She was so agitated, she injured his dead body where it lay, between her feet. But she didn't mean to. She wanted to protect her friend."

Henry nodded. "I think you're right."

"So someone dragged Eranga between Siddhi's feet after he died, to make everyone think she killed him!"

Henry thought about this. "But she attacks every stranger who comes near."

"Perhaps someone pushed Eranga between her legs using a stick. Then she wouldn't have been able to reach them."

Henry looked around but didn't see any such implement. Still, the culprit could have easily hidden it a short way off. He nodded. "But that would also mean that someone had a motive for killing Eranga."

"I can only speak for the people of Mapitigama. Eranga was our village leader and held in high esteem by everyone. There was no ill will toward him from any quarter."

Henry turned back to the dead man. He looked over the whole body, noting the dark bruises where blood had pooled since death. Then he looked long and hard at the head. His breath caught in his throat and he leaned closer. He tried carefully to part the matted hair. The long, graying strands were stuck together with a dark substance.

"Blood," said Phera. "A lot of it. So it must have flowed before Eranga died."

"Yes. From this wound." Henry moved aside slightly so that Phera could see better.

The wound was not large, but it was deep. Its edges were lightly encrusted with dried blood and traces of gray.

"That's where brain has seeped out," explained Henry. "There are a few splinters of bone in the wound. So Eranga either fell, hitting his head on something extremely long and sharp, or he was hit over the head with a sharp rock or an iron hook."

"Someone killed him!" whispered Phera. Her stomach churned, and she swiftly turned her head away.

Henry frowned. "All we can say for sure is that it can't have happened here. The ground is soft. And there are no traces of blood." He patted the forest floor.

Siddhi gave a loud snort.

"If she could talk, she'd tell us what happened."

The elephant looked long and hard at the two humans. A clear liquid was running from her eyes and leaving dark streaks on her gray cheeks.

"She's weeping," said Phera softly.

"You're allowed to weep for your tutor, too, you know." Henry touched the young mahout on the shoulder.

Phera half-turned and looked at him with those huge, dark eyes. Hastily, he withdrew his hand, as if he'd been scalded.

"Whoever succumbs to grief harms himself. And it would distress the souls of the dead in the other world. I want to know how Eranga died. If you can find out, will you tell me?"

"I promise, my boy." He held out his right hand.

Hesitantly, Phera accepted it. "My thanks to you."

Henry took a deep breath. "I'm going to turn Eranga on his back again. After that you can take him home. Will you be carrying him on the elephant?"

"Yes."

Phera grasped the dead man's shoulders and Henry the legs. Then they carefully turned him over.

"Look! Look at this!" exclaimed Phera.

His sarong had shifted as they turned him. They now saw it had been concealing a little cloth bag, one or two objects clearly still inside. Henry hesitated but then carefully took hold of the bag between two fingers. Out slipped a tiny wooden Buddha, followed by a small stone. Without a word, he gave Phera the Buddha. Then they both stood looking at the stone. The size of a cherry, it looked as if two small pyramids were stuck to its base. It was dark in color, somewhere between gray and black. He examined the stone, turning it this way and that, running his finger over its sharp edges and smooth surfaces.

"Do you know what kind of stone this is?" he asked, holding it out.

"No. What an unusual shape. I've never seen anything like that."

Henry's fingers slowly closed around the fragment, and he slipped it into his pocket. "I wonder whether I should show this to my brother. He's an engineer and knows about rocks."

"Your brother doesn't know anything!" Phera's face twisted into a scowl. "He has only contempt for my land and its people."

Henry looked somber and nodded. Perhaps it was best to keep this to himself for now, see what he could find out.

Just then Siddhi let out a shrill cry. Phera jumped up and ran to her, but the elephant was beyond soothing. She tossed her head and strained at her ropes.

"Is the beast still pretending to be crazed?" Charles stepped into the small clearing. His face was red and perspiring. Unusually for him, his uniform jacket was open and his shirt collar loosened. He took off his bicorn, revealing hair damp with sweat.

A fever, thought Henry. *Probably another malaria attack.*

Siddhi stamped angrily, and her trunk whipped at the air. Henry feared what would happen if she managed to break free. It annoyed him a little that the young mahout was no longer making even the smallest effort to subdue her.

"Keep that beast in check or it'll kill someone else!" Charles yelled. He pulled his pistol from its holster and tried to take aim. But his hand was trembling too much.

At the same moment, Phera drew Jeeva's dagger. "Don't you dare, Englishman!"

"Stop, immediately!" Henry ran over to his brother and placed himself in front of him.

"Please go back to camp," he said to Charles, beseechingly. "You need medicine and must rest."

Charles reluctantly lowered the gun. "I should have put a bullet between that beast's eyes long ago," he snarled.

Henry reached out, pried the pistol from his brother's grip, and stowed it in the belt of his own trousers.

Slowly, Phera lowered the dagger, then used it to cut through the bindings around Siddhi's feet. *Siddhi will never work for you British again; I'll see to that.* At a tap on the right foreleg, the elephant obediently raised her leg. Phera clambered onto her back and sat up straight.

"Bring me Eranga, would you, so I can get him on Siddhi's back?" she said to Henry.

He hesitated, unsure what this powerful animal would do when he approached. The elephant, however, remained still and placid as he carried the corpse over his shoulder and then raised it high. Phera took hold of Eranga's arm and pulled him right across Siddhi's neck, giving the cold body a sad embrace.

When Phera looked at Henry again, those eyes were brimming with tears. "Please remember what you have promised me. Find out the truth."

Then the mahout and the elephant vanished into the forest.

Chapter Nine
September 1822

At sunrise the next morning, the villagers committed the body of their deceased widan to the fire. A long procession followed Siddhi as she bore the corpse, wrapped in white linen, to the banks of the Nanu Oya. Nobody spoke. Only rhythmic drums and bells echoed in the stillness. As the flames shot up, Phera threw in the little wooden Buddha.

Once the fire had died down, the funeral helper brushed the deceased's ashes into an earthenware pitcher and handed it to Anshu. She gently placed the pitcher in the shallow waters near the riverbank.

The crowd watched in reverence as it coasted toward the middle of the river, and Siddhi lifted her trunk and made her sad puffing sounds. Like a tiny ship, the pitcher danced on the rippling waves, gradually tipping as it took in water. Eranga's ashes were carried away with the current.

"His old life is now finally over," said Anshu. "Cleansed of all the evil of the past, his soul is ready for a new life."

The crowd slowly dispersed. Anshu, her daughters, and Siddhi stayed on the bank and stared at the water, while little Thambo dug in the sand around the elephant's feet.

The women looked up as a group of six women drew near to them. They were all members of the most highly regarded families in Mapitigama and owned the biggest rice fields and most of the valuable cinnamon trees. They stopped in front of Anshu.

"Most esteemed lady." The oldest woman in the group crossed the flat of her hands against her chest and bowed. "We need a new widan for Mapitigama."

Anshu nodded solemnly. "Who do you have in mind?"

"You, ma'am." The oldest woman bowed again, and the other five nodded in support.

Samitha's and Phera's eyes widened, but Anshu's face was impassive. "I decline," she said firmly. "Find another village leader."

The six women exchanged dismayed looks.

"But who?" one lamented. "Eranga's family is gone, and none of the men we have left can take on the office."

"There are still men in the village," argued Anshu.

"Only old men who are either too fragile or can't think straight!"

The oldest of the women gestured for silence, then turned back to Anshu. "Allow me to explain, ma'am. Of all the people in the village, you have the greatest experience with the British. We need a widan who knows how they think, how they work. Ma'am, you are clever and courageous. You bear your destiny with dignity and without complaint. Who other than you will the British meet with any respect?"

People who have stolen our king and our land from us, who have violated our women and murdered our men, respect nobody. They strive only for domination at any price, thought Anshu. She understood the women's reasoning, but her memories of Uva were too painful for her to imagine voluntarily interacting with the barbarians.

"I shall not be your widan," she repeated. "Don't press me any further."

In stunned silence, the six women bowed. Disappointment covered their faces as they turned and walked back toward the village.

Phera watched them go. "They trust you, Mother. You could at least have given some thought to their request."

"It's right that she turned it down," said Samitha. "Have you forgotten what the British did to our family?"

"Forgotten?" shrieked Phera. "No, sister, I have not. But we have a duty to the people of Mapitigama. If they hadn't taken us in, we'd have become beggars."

"Stop it!" Anshu held her hands up defensively. "I have nothing left to say on the matter."

A few days later, Anshu was resting in the doorway to her hut, contemplating the jungle in front of her. It seemed impenetrable, but its appearance was deceptive. Deep in the dense greenery, there was humming, rumbling, grinding, pounding, hammering. And this din was getting closer and closer, louder and louder.

All the villagers were uneasy and had called a meeting to talk over the alarming events. Old and young came from hut and field alike, gathering together at the shrine to Buddha under the Bodhi tree. When Anshu saw her daughters, she called Thambo in from the garden and went to join them.

Waiting in front of the shrine was the oldest man in the village. He had been born in the days when only the peaceful Dutch had arrived on the coast of Lanka, not the greedy British. His daughter-in-law, the oldest of the women who had asked Anshu to be widan, stood at his side and supported him. The elder was looking hard at the gathering, chewing on betel nut all the while.

"Ayubowan," he said eventually. "We have gathered together because—"

Boom! An explosion rang out from the construction site. The startled villagers clung to one another, while the younger children burst into tears.

The elder raised a scrawny arm, pointing accusingly in the direction of the noise. "That is why we have gathered together! Because the British are threatening us with their road."

"Soon they'll reach our village," added his daughter-in-law.

Everyone murmured in agreement. A young mother, her baby fussing in her arms, called, "And they're frightening the children!"

The elder spat a stream of red betel juice onto the ground. "We must find out what the British are planning."

"But how?" objected another old man. "That horrible commander can barely speak our language. Besides, he would sooner kill us than consent to a meeting."

"Their doctor, he speaks our language well," Phera announced. "And I believe he has kindness in him. I can ride Siddhi to the building site and ask him."

"No!" shouted Anshu. "Absolutely not."

She grabbed Phera by the wrist, but the young woman angrily shook her off.

"Phera, you know why I want you to stay away."

But the woman with the baby said, "That's a good plan, young mistress."

Once again came murmured agreement from the crowd.

Phera gave her mother a defiant look. "I'll fetch Siddhi straightaway."

"You'll put all of us in danger just because you have to do everything your own way," Samitha said angrily.

"I want to help Mapitigama, and I'm not putting anyone in danger—the British won't recognize me, especially when I'm dressed up as a man," Phera told her.

"You are very honorable in your concern for the well-being of the village, young mistress," broke in the elder. "This task, however, is for a widan. Sadly, we have none." His rheumy eyes looked straight at Anshu. She lowered her head. In the last few days, she had repeatedly asked herself if she had made the right decision. She knew she was indebted to the people still giving her family sanctuary, but everything within her fought against this dangerous task. Now she sensed everyone watching her.

"We need a widan who can talk to the British." The village elder's daughter-in-law spoke straight to Anshu. "Mistress, I beseech you once more to be our widan. You belong to Mapitigama now, and the people of Mapitigama need you."

Anshu looked at the sea of faces and saw concern, but hope, too. *What would Jeeva have done?* She already knew the answer.

Her husband had fought for the people of Senkadagala and had died for their freedom. Had he still been alive, he would not have hesitated to bear this burden as well. What right did she have to shirk this duty? She straightened her shoulders and took a deep breath. "I accept."

There was loud cheering. The elder bowed his head before Anshu. "We place the destiny of our community in your hands, widan."

"I'll fetch Siddhi," said Phera, "and we'll ride to the building site together."

When the two women were ready to set off, the villagers solemnly assembled under the Bodhi tree to watch the departure of their new widan. They knew how much depended on Anshu's conversation with the British doctor.

Phera was already seated on her elephant. She had put her hair up like a Sinhalese man, was wearing her baggy pants, and had hidden her father's dagger inside her shirt. She told Siddhi to kneel so that Anshu could comfortably climb aboard.

Anshu's face shone with determination. Now that she had taken on the role of village leader, she would represent the people's interests as well as she could. She had put on her best sari and the little gold jewelry she still had. Gold was the Enlightened One's color, and she hoped his wisdom would guide her through the difficult task ahead.

She was just hitching up her sari to climb onto Siddhi's left foreleg when the elephant suddenly gave a nervous shake of her head.

Hoofbeats rang out, and four redcoats came charging into the clearing.

The commander's contemptuous gaze roved over the assembled villagers. Anshu shuddered. She had recognized the group's leader straightaway as Charles Odell.

She stole a discreet glance at her eldest daughter. Samitha was partially concealed amongst the crowd of villagers. She had lowered her head and was attempting to hide Thambo. But just then the little boy whispered loudly, "Mama, horsey!"

All four Englishmen turned toward the child who, half in fear, half in curiosity, peeped out from behind his mother. While the three other soldiers were smiling at the little boy, Charles's attention was on Samitha.

He looked her up and down lasciviously. "You!" he shouted in his pidgin Sinhalese. "Blue sari. Come here!"

Samitha quickly passed Thambo to a woman nearby. Then she held her sari veil across her face so that only her eyes were visible and hesitantly obeyed. She stopped at a safe distance from Odell.

"What's a beauty like you doing in this godforsaken dump?" he asked, a greedy smile on his lips.

Samitha stood calmly and gave no reply.

"Speak, woman!" Full of impatience, he brought his whip down against his own boot.

"I live here," she said quietly. "Mapitigama is my home." Her hand shook as it held the veil in place.

Charles looked at her long and hard. Something about her bearing, those dark eyes, stirred up memories. If he had seen her before, it must have been the day they had recruited the laborers. Anyhow, he found her extremely attractive. For a moment he thought about having her brought to his tent, but knew the most recent bout of malaria would stop him performing. *You won't get away from me*, he thought. *Next time I'll really give you a good seeing-to.*

"Where is your husband?" he asked. "At work on the road?"

Samitha remained silent.

"Answer, damn you! And uncover your face!"

Samitha did not move, and a tense silence pervaded the square. Then there was a mighty snort. It came from Siddhi as she slowly pulled herself to her full height. It was as if a huge gray boulder had come to life. Charles's horse shied and almost reared.

Charles turned and saw Phera looking down at him disdainfully from Siddhi's back. Phera smiled, pleased with the successful diversion.

Charles, however, was anything but pleased. He did not like having to strain his neck to look up at this insolent young mahout.

"Well, well, it's the little monkey who stole an elephant from my construction site. Where did you creep off to when I was recruiting workers?" His whip hissed as he swiped it through the air.

Phera's dismissive smile broadened. "You simply couldn't see me."

This threw Charles into a rage, and he turned on the frightened villagers. "Where did you hide this able-bodied lad from me? What else are you conspirators hiding?"

The villagers stared in amazement. Anshu was the one to reply. "We hid no one from you. The boy was in Colombo making purchases for the village when you took our men away."

Charles gave her a hard look. "Presumably, you're this good-for-nothing's mother!"

Anshu blanched but went on bravely. "I am the new village leader of Mapitigama."

Charles gave a shout of laughter. "A woman leader? That's the best joke I've heard in years. Answer my question, oh leader. Are you his mother?"

Anshu lowered her head and nodded.

"If you want to keep the boy alive, then teach him how to behave in front of an Englishman. He is to report to the construction site with his elephant—today."

Anshu was about to object, but Phera gestured for her to be silent.

Charles turned to look at the villagers. "Enough nonsense. I am here because your huts have to go. The tree as well." He pointed his whip at the Bodhi tree and gauged its strength. "The elephant can just push it over."

Gasps and cries of outrage ran through the crowd. The villagers, in spite of their fear, banded together around their sacred tree and the shrine to the Enlightened One.

"My new road will go right through it," said Charles cheerfully. "Your tree is in the way, and so are all of you." He turned to Phera. "Go on! Use the elephant to knock the tree over. Now."

But Phera just glared at him and did not move.

"So you want to act the rebel, do you? I'll show you all how to fell a tree!" Charles jammed his spurs hard into his horse. The animal reared, then raced toward the villagers, who were forced to dive for the ground. Charles drew his saber, leaned forward in the saddle, and took a swipe at one of the wooden props supporting the heavy boughs. The tree creaked and groaned; the bough cracked and fell. Charles grinned. "I'll take care of the tree, mahout. You can just drag it off when I'm done."

Phera's face darkened and froze. But then a powerful cry rose up from deep within: "Daha!"

The elephant let out a deafening trumpeting and began to move forward, picking up speed like an unstoppable avalanche. She rushed Charles and his soldiers at full tilt.

"Stop!" Charles held his whip high.

But his horse panicked at the sight of the charging giant. It bucked wildly and threw Charles out of the saddle, leaving him dazed on the ground. His horse did an about-face and galloped off into the jungle. The soldiers drew pistols, but their mounts reared and bucked, too, so all three men were thrown, and their horses fled into the primeval forest. Two of the soldiers stayed on the ground, groaning. The third leapt up and shot at the elephant but missed. Siddhi would have trampled Charles to death, but he managed to roll to one side at the last second. Charles struggled to his feet and aimed at Siddhi's hindquarters. The shot rang out just as Phera looked back. Siddhi gave a piercing shriek, but she carried on running as Phera drove her onward into the safety of the jungle.

"I ordered a dozen lashes, good and hard." Charles's voice sounded above the din of the building site. "What're you stroking him for? D'you want me to demonstrate on your own fair body what I mean by 'good'?"

Henry, who was examining patients in the field hospital, frowned. He had ordered complete bed rest for his brother's fever, shivers, and cramps. And yet at dawn Charles had ridden off with three soldiers and, judging by the noises, was now back and in the foulest of moods. Henry beckoned an assistant to take over bandaging his patient's crushed foot and hurried out of the tent.

The construction site was its usual hive of activity.

Henry went to a nearby overseer. "Where is my brother?"

"There, Doctor." The man pointed.

Henry looked where the man was indicating, and his blood ran cold. Not far from the field hospital, ten halberds had been rammed into the ground. Tied to each halberd was a worker from Mapitigama, naked but for a loincloth, fully exposed to the merciless sun. Charles paced up and down behind the bound men. He looked crazed, his uniform filthy and his hair unkempt. He was gesticulating furiously at the corporal standing by, a whip with nine strands of braided, knotted rope in the man's hand—a cat-o'-nine-tails. It was the same corporal who had carried out the beheadings in Uva.

He had already flogged the first victim to the limit. The beaten man's back was covered with a lattice of open wounds. Blood dripped to the ground. The man had lost consciousness and now hung help-lessly by his wrists. The corporal had already started on the next. Charles, however, seemed dissatisfied. He seized the instrument of tor-ture from the corporal. The nine tails hissed through the air, landing a sickening crack on the back of the Sinhalese man, who screamed out and struggled against the ties that bound him.

"Now he knows he's being punished!" snorted Charles. Seconds later the "cat" hissed again and cracked on the man's raw back.

Thoughts crowded in on Henry. Flogging was permitted as a form of punishment for only the gravest of offenses. It seemed highly improb-able that the men tied to the halberds had committed any wrongdoing that could justify this degree of force. All the men feared his brother like the devil incarnate and did everything they could to avoid provok-ing him. As Charles prepared to administer the third stroke, Henry hurried forward.

"Halt! Stop this immediately!"

Charles whipped around. "What the devil—"

The brothers stared at each other for several long seconds.

"Get out of here!" roared Charles, raising the whip once more. "That's an order!"

"Just what have these men done?" Henry demanded. He seized his brother by the arm.

Charles put up a fight, but when he could not break free, he burst out angrily, "Four wounded and four horses gone! There's something the brown monkeys will live to regret."

Henry shook his head. Extreme fever must have clouded Charles's mind.

"You need your medication," he said, trying to pacify him. "And I have ordered bed rest for you, in any case."

"Leave me! I have to teach him a lesson, this, this—"

"Not now," said Henry, determinedly pulling him away.

Fifteen minutes later Charles was in his tent, slumped in a camp chair, hardly able to keep his eyes open.

"He'll sleep for a couple of hours," said Henry to Charles's orderly. "Put him to bed, but stay close. Do frequent checks to see if his temperature's coming down." He went over to the washstand behind a folding screen, dipped his hands in water, soaped them, and carried on. "I've given him quinine powder in laudanum. Watch his breathing; check it stays regular. If his condition deteriorates, send for me immediately."

The young man nodded, got down in front of Charles's chair, and started to remove his superior's boots for him.

Henry came out from behind the screen and looked at his brother, already snoring on the camp bed the orderly had dragged him over to. This was the worst malaria attack yet. Henry thought it highly likely that the Sinhalese men had committed no wrongdoing whatsoever. On the construction site, Charles was feared for his cruelty, yet Henry feared that his excesses would eventually lead to an uprising. And Henry could imagine only too well how Charles would react to that.

He stowed the medicine in his bag, nodded to the orderly, and left the tent. Now to tend to the workers.

The ten men were still tied to the halberds. The corporal paced up and down behind them, obviously unsure whether to carry on with the floggings. Other workers, digging a drainage channel nearby, stole surreptitious looks at the shocking scene. When they saw Henry, relief glimmered in their eyes. As much as Charles was a source of fear, so his brother had become a source of relative hope.

Henry beckoned to the corporal. "Help me untie them." He took his knife from his pocket, but the corporal blocked his way.

"Has Major Odell ordered this, sir?"

Henry looked at him in disgust. "You've got eyes in your head, haven't you? Humanity alone orders these men be set free."

"I'm sorry, Dr. Odell," the corporal said. "I take my orders from the major. If I go against his instructions, there'll be consequences."

Henry angrily pushed him aside. "If you get in my way, that'll bring consequences, too." He went to the unconscious worker and sliced through his bindings with one swift movement. The man slumped to the ground and lay there, motionless.

Henry knelt and glared accusingly at the corporal as he felt for a pulse. At last the soldier dropped his whip and helped release the men.

Henry examined the wrists and ankles of those who had escaped the beating, then sent them back to work. Finally, he turned to the two men who had been flogged.

"We're taking these two to the field hospital. We'll carry one each."

Orderlies and patients alike gave the doctor and corporal odd looks when they dragged the beaten men into the tent. It was not customary for sick or injured natives to be treated in the same place as the British. But Henry ignored the looks, set down his wounded man on a vacant wooden bed, and gestured to the corporal to do likewise.

"What was their offense?"

The corporal was at a loss. "When Major Odell and his escorting party returned from the village, they had no horses and the major was very angry. He demanded ten men from Mapitigama, told me to tie them to halberds and then discipline each with one dozen lashes."

"You brought him ten men chosen at random?"

The corporal swallowed hard. "That's right, sir."

Henry went to the medicine cupboard and took out a bottle of alcohol and a handful of the cotton fiber scraps they used for dressing wounds. "Did Major Odell say anything about what had happened in the village?"

"He mentioned a conspiracy, sir."

Henry turned to look at him in alarm. "A conspiracy?"

"Yes, sir."

Henry sat on the bed of the more worryingly injured man, soaked some cotton with alcohol, and carefully dabbed the man's flayed skin. "And have you any idea what this conspiracy is supposed to be about?"

The corporal shook his head. "It is simply my task to carry out prescribed punishments."

Definitely easier than worrying about what's right and what's wrong, thought Henry. Then he said, "Thank you for your help. You can go now."

The corporal moved off, relieved. Henry tended to the other man and gave both of them a sleeping draught of diluted laudanum.

As he was putting the bottles of alcohol and laudanum back into the medicine cupboard, he asked himself yet again what had turned his brother into such a brutal man. Charles had not always been like this. When they were children, Charles, the elder by three years, had shown him how to climb trees and balance on the roof of the shed behind their parents' home. But that Charles was gone, and Henry knew he would never find him again.

This country has changed us both, thought Henry.

He looked at the laudanum bottle in the cupboard. More than anything else, this poppy juice had the power to dispel all his painful memories. With every fiber of his being, he craved the release and oblivion only it could bring.

Just one mouthful, he thought, *and I'll feel better.*

He immediately pulled himself together. After the rapture, there was always disillusionment, the hard landing back in reality, and the dispiriting sense of failure. At all costs, he had to stay strong.

And yet the hideous events of the day crowded in on him. The more he tried to quash them, the stronger they became. His eyes feasted on the brown glass of the bottle. He knew he ought to lock up the cupboard straightaway and run. But he there stayed, rooted to the spot.

Since leaving Colombo, he had not taken any more opium. And he'd had not so much as one complete night's sleep. He was exhausted. He was in urgent need of peace and a few hours' rest.

He raised his hand, fondled the brown glass, and curled his fingers around the bottle. Then he took a cautious look over his shoulder and, when he was sure there was nobody watching, slipped it into his jacket pocket.

Henry sank into the soft, enveloping warmth of the cloud as it drifted languidly across the heavens. He was at ease, filled with only pleasurable feelings and surrounded by peace. The balmy air caressed his skin; the sun's rays played on his eyelids. He breathed deeply, opened his eyes, and gazed in wonder at the endless azure skies above. Never before had he seen such a superb blue. If he blinked, he could even make out the individual color particles and set them dancing. This made some of them change color, turning to purple, red, orange, and yellow and becoming a new shape—a rainbow.

At first the rainbow was small and distant, but it gradually floated toward Henry. On the arc of the rainbow was a tiny figure, childlike in stature. When the figure slid down the rainbow toward him, he realized this was no child, but Phera. His heart skipped a beat, not in fear, but in joy.

With one bound, Phera jumped from the rainbow and lay next to him, stretched out on the cloud. Henry looked at that body, delicate but supple. His gaze drifted to Phera's mouth. He had never seen such beautifully shaped lips before. They were slightly parted, showing teeth like little pearls nestling in a mussel shell.

"Why are you here?" he asked.

"Because you want me to be," replied Phera.

That's it, he thought in astonishment. *That's what I want.*

He looked upward and met Phera's huge almond eyes with their lustrous lashes. How he longed to dive into the dark eyes and lose himself as in an eternal ocean. He wanted to touch Phera's skin, breathe in its sweet smell and—

Stop! The desire shocked him. *This isn't you!* But his body was telling him something very different.

Phera moved those beautiful lips and said something. But Henry was so confused by his feelings that he couldn't make it out.

Now someone was digging their fingers hard into his shoulder. He sat up too quickly and hit his forehead on something.

"Ow!"

"Wake up already! You've got to get up!" Phera shook him.

He rubbed his aching forehead. His head whirled. Was Phera really here in his tent, or was it still a dream?

Suddenly, his dream came back to him, that longing for Phera, and he went cold. He let himself fall back on the mattress with a crash.

"Don't you dare go back to sleep!"

"Go away," growled Henry. He turned to face the wall. "Leave me alone."

"What the hell is wrong with you? Have you had too much palm wine?"

Henry heard footsteps tapping across the wooden boards covering the floor of his tent. There was clattering and then water running. The footsteps came toward him, and seconds later cold water splashed over his head.

"Damn it! What do you think you're doing?" He shook himself like a wet dog and leapt unsteadily off the bed. His feet brushed against the laudanum bottle he had left open on the floor. With a gentle clink, it tipped over, and his patients' entire supply of laudanum poured out. The numbing poppy fragrance wafted up.

"That's a strange smell." Phera made a face. "What is it?"

"Just something for headaches." Burning with shame, Henry kicked the bottle under the bed.

Phera took a hand towel off the rack by the washstand and threw it to him. "Pull yourself together, will you?"

He scratched his head. "How long have you been here? And what do you want, anyway?"

"Hours! I kept trying and trying, but you just wouldn't wake up!" The mahout looked exhausted. "You must come with me, Dr. Odell. I need your help."

"What's happened?" He put the towel aside.

"Your brother shot Siddhi." Her voice had become timid, desperate.

"Who's Siddhi?" asked Henry, still befuddled.

"What on earth is wrong with you? Have you really forgotten my elephant?" Phera was beside herself now. "We've got to hurry."

Thin blue streaks in the sky heralded the new day, but it was still dark enough for them to slip away unnoticed. Keeping low, Henry and Phera hurried between the tents, crept past guard posts, and plunged into the jungle. Henry stumbled along behind Phera on the muddy track.

The ground was wet after the usual night rain; but the heat had hardly let up, and it increased now as the sun began to rise. Sweat ran down Henry's back, a dull ache pounded at his head, and the musty scent rising from the damp earth made him feel nauseated. He heard creatures rustling in the dense greenery all around him, and he sup-pressed images of the snakes, scorpions, and poisonous beasts that might be making these noises. Whenever he trod through pools, he felt leeches around his ankles and calves and cursed himself for not think-ing to put on boots.

At least Phera seems to know the way, he thought as he watched the boy running ahead with feline agility and speed. Henry tightened his grip on his doctor's bag and hurried in the wake of the mahout, deeper and deeper into the jungle.

Just as he wanted to ask how much farther they had to go, a sunlit clearing opened up before his eyes. Colorful birds, butterflies, and drag-onflies flew up in front of him, and an emerald lizard flashed behind a stone. He heard the rush and gurgle of water and then saw a sheer rock face, a waterfall tumbling down it into a natural stone pool. In places the water foamed and fell from a great height; in others its descent was slowed by rocky ledges. Trees and bushes hung over the rock, and liana clung to it down as far as the water.

On the edge of the clearing, shaded by tall, luxuriant tree canopies, he saw a simple hut built of branches and leaves. It was obviously the mahout's shelter.

Henry observed the elephant wading in the pool. She had stretched her trunk as far as she possibly could over her back and was spraying her right hind leg with water. He could see she must be in pain from the wound, the size of a man's palm, high on her hip joint.

As Phera and Henry drew near to her, Siddhi turned with difficulty and limped out of the water. The powerful animal looked first at Phera, then took the measure of Henry with her solemn amber eyes. She walked slowly to him, then lifted her trunk, felt his head with it, and puffed her warm breath in his face. Henry looked at Phera, unsure how to react.

"She's welcoming you." Phera placed her hand on the elephant's trunk. "She knows you're a friend and that you'll help her. You will, won't you?"

"I'm not a veterinary surgeon," replied Henry hesitantly. But when he saw Phera's desperate look, he added, "But I'll do everything in my power, of course."

First Henry cleansed his hands with alcohol. Then he touched the wound with the greatest of care. It was red and swollen inside, septic around the edge. The tip of the bullet stuck out of its center.

"I'm going to remove the bullet," Henry said. "It'll probably hurt a little. Please make sure she stays still." One false step from those legs like pillars and he'd be crushed.

He selected a scalpel from his medicine bag and began carefully to cut away the bullet from the infected flesh. While he was doing this, Phera whispered to Siddhi and fed her bananas pulled from her trouser pockets. Siddhi allowed the operation to proceed in complete calm. Only her leg muscles betrayed a little twitch.

"That should be it," said Henry, dropping the bullet on the ground. "Now I need to disinfect the wound." He took some iodine solution from his bag and sprinkled a few drops on the raw flesh. "My brother was in your village yesterday. What did he want, and why did he shoot the elephant?"

"He said he's going to build his road through our village. He tried to make Siddhi desecrate the tree of the Enlightened One," Phera told him. "So I instructed her to chase him off. It's partly my fault she got shot." She fell silent, contrite.

"Did Siddhi try to attack my brother, giving him cause to act in self-defense?"

"No." Siddhi hadn't intended to hurt him, that was true, but Phera wasn't sure what would have happened if the Englishman hadn't rolled out of her way. "The horse took fright and your brother fell. When I was escaping into the jungle with Siddhi, he shot at her."

"Don't blame yourself," said Henry. "My brother has done Siddhi an injustice. Now tell me everything in detail."

As the words tumbled out, Phera wondered how she could trust the young doctor so. Although he had never been cruel, he was nonetheless one of the hated British, aiding and abetting their misdeeds. And yet he had helped her against his brother several times now. It was confusing.

After she had related everything there was to tell, Henry murmured dejectedly, "The alleged conspiracy. Now I see."

"What do you see?" she asked hopefully.

But he just shook his head and cleared his throat. "Siddhi's wound should heal nicely. I'll leave you the iodine and alcohol to clean it with in case." He placed the bottles on a flat stone and then added a handful of cotton.

"Thank you." A little disappointed, Phera bowed her head. But what had she been expecting? That he would haul his brother off to Colombo and put him on the next ship to England?

When Phera looked up again, those lovely eyes were wet with tears, a sight that cut Henry to the quick. "Will you take a look at her again tomorrow?"

Absolutely not! said his reason. *Keep your distance from this boy.* But his mouth said, "I'll try."

They made the return journey in silence, each lost in thought. Just short of the camp, Phera stopped. "You'll have to go on alone now. Your brother best not see me. 'Good-bye,' Dr. Odell. Isn't that how you say it in your language?" She held out her hand.

He nodded without a word. When his large hand closed around Phera's small one, he was filled with a joy so intense, it frightened him. He turned swiftly and fled.

Moments later Henry crashed out of the jungle and into the construction site. It was swarming with engineers, soldiers, and laborers. No women anywhere.

No wonder, he thought, hugely relieved. *I just need a woman.*

Many of his countrymen, his brother included, regularly had women brought to them from the surrounding villages. For Henry, that was out of the question. Yet he could not deny he had urgent physical needs.

Molly. He would go see Molly. Why on earth hadn't it occurred to him sooner?

Because she couldn't satisfy you the last time you were together, observed a spiteful little voice in his head. On top of that, Molly was in Colombo, several days' ride away.

But did he have any choice? Anyway, there was another reason to go to Colombo—he had to replace the laudanum.

He decided briefly to let Charles know he was going and then to set off. The construction site invalids would have to manage without him for a couple of days.

"Charles!" He pushed aside the tarpaulin at the entrance to his brother's tent and stepped inside. "Charles, I—" He stopped dead.

"Dr. Odell!" Charles's orderly stepped out from behind the corner screen. "I've been looking for you everywhere!"

Henry shot him a stern look. "Where is my brother? I ordered bed rest. You were supposed to be watching him."

"I tried, Dr. Odell. But the major wouldn't be held back."

"Held back?"

The boy nodded miserably. "As soon as he woke up, he demanded I get him dressed. Then he ordered me to pack his saddlebags and bring a horse. He said he had to go to Colombo, to the governor."

Chapter Ten
October 1822

Molly straddled Henry as she moved rhythmically, hypnotically back and forth. He lay flat on the bed between her spread thighs, unable to take his eyes off her. Molly's gorgeous, full breasts were pushed up by the corset, and her erect nipples, artfully painted red, made him so excited he struggled to hold back.

She leaned forward, took one of his hands, and pressed it against her breasts. Her breathing quickened. "Harder! That's it. Just how I like it."

"I'm nearly there, nearly there, Molly," he said, moaning.

She threw her head back with laughter. "And I can feel you, Henry. You don't know how much I can feel you."

Henry laughed, too. He felt stupendous. He sensed that today he would find the release he needed to make his strange feelings for the young mahout a distant memory.

He clutched Molly's hips, pushed her down hard onto his pelvis, and then, with a great roar, he climaxed. But at this most intense moment of their coupling, soft, bouncing Molly faded, and the image of someone else stood before his eyes—Phera, sweet and enticing, like in his opium dream.

The shock was like a knife in his gut. The moment he had so longed for was destroyed. He covered his face with his arm. He wanted to vanish.

"You were magnificent, Henry." Molly's soothing fingers stroked his ribs.

"Please stop." He pushed her hand away.

She looked at him in surprise. "What's wrong? Wasn't it nice for you? You exploded like fireworks!"

He grunted unintelligibly.

"It was good for me," she went on. "It's always good with you, Henry, and that's not something I can say about all my clients."

He turned away. "There's no need for flattery."

She shrugged, now at a loss as to what to say. She slid off the bed and went over to the washstand. He watched silently as she stooped and removed from her vagina the lemon-juice-soaked sponge intended to prevent conception and threw it in a tin bucket. Then she got a clean washcloth and dunked it in the water.

"Why are you in such a bad mood?" she asked as she wrung out the cloth and washed between her legs. "If you'd had problems, like last time, I could understand it. But you didn't!" She glanced at him over her shoulder with a little smile. "You had so much egg-fry. I'm full of it."

"The opposite of last time," he muttered.

She threw the cloth in the bucket, then took a silk dressing gown from a hook on the wall. Now she went to her dressing table. Next to pots of cream, hairbrushes, and powder puffs were a carafe and two tiny china cups. She picked up the carafe, poured a clear liquid into each cup, and, smiling playfully, sashayed back to Henry. "Drink!" She handed him one of the cups and sat on the side of the bed.

"What's this?" he asked suspiciously.

"Baijiu, Chinese liquor. It'll do you good."

He raised the cup to his lips very hesitantly but downed it in one gulp. "Whoa!" The burning effect made his eyes water.

She topped up his cup. "This is better for you than opium."

"At least opium doesn't taste so awful," he grumbled.

She took the cup from him and put it on the floor near the bed. "Tell me, what is it that's upsetting you so?"

He stared past her to the mirror on the wall and his pale, unshaven face. "I—" He shook his head.

Molly poked him in the ribs. "Out with it!"

"I—" He tried to find the courage. "I don't understand myself these days. Here." He pointed to his head. "And here." He pointed to his penis.

For a while she stared at him blankly, then threw back her head and gave a hearty laugh. "I can't believe that."

He edged away from her a little, irritated. "I'm afraid you don't understand what I'm trying to say to you. Have you had clients, long-standing, coming to you and then suddenly realizing that they're"—he nearly choked on the word—"that they no longer feel the same way about women?" He felt his face flush with shame.

"Yes, of course, but—aaah, now I understand." Molly took him by the chin and gently, but firmly, turned his head so that he was forced to look straight at her. "You think you lust after men?"

He managed a sheepish smile. "I didn't really want to hear it quite like that. Will it pass?"

She thought hard. "It hasn't amongst my clients. They would come here only to prove to themselves that they didn't have needs like that. But it didn't work."

He groaned and covered his face with his hands.

"Henry! Look at me." Gently, she pulled his hands away. "Whatever happens, you mustn't be beaten."

"Yes," he said flatly. "You're right, I know." And yet as he got dressed, he felt more beaten now than ever before.

◆ ◆ ◆

"Mr. Henry, wonderful good morning! I got good tea, special for you. Best tea in Cathay." Chang set the tray on a low table near Henry's mattress.

"Thank you, Chang. And good morning to you, too." Henry sat cross-legged on the edge of the mattress and ran his fingers through his disheveled hair.

"I must look like a vagrant," he muttered as he reached for his shoes.

Chang flashed a broad smile. "After you saw Molly, you smoked lot opium pipes. Give you plenty nice dreams."

Henry held the steaming bowl with both hands and took a mouthful. He looked at the other guests, still stupefied on their mattresses. In the gray half-light of the room, their faces looked pale, drawn, their cheeks sunken.

Had the opium turned him into a specter like that, too? He rubbed furtively at the stubble on his chin and face. He suspected he would frighten off small children, at least. After swallowing another mouthful of tea, he took his watch from his vest pocket and glanced at the time. Nearly noon. He had wasted half the day.

I'll get the new laudanum and then set off, he decided. He knew if he stayed any longer in Colombo, he would only smoke more opium and wallow in remorse about his feelings for the mahout. At least on the construction site he had a meaningful occupation, and if he pulled himself together, he could hopefully manage not to dip into his patients' supply of laudanum again.

He placed the empty teabowl on the table and reached across the mattress for his now-crumpled jacket, but Chang was there first. "I help you, Mr. Henry. Hey! What's this?"

A small stone that looked as if two tiny pyramids had been stuck to its base had fallen from his pocket.

"I forgot about that." Henry bent to pick up the stone he'd found on Eranga's body. Yet again, Chang got there first.

"If you allow me, Mr. Henry, I take a look." Holding the stone between thumb and forefinger, he scrutinized it. "Beautiful. Where you find it?"

Henry gave him a quizzical look. "Why should that interest you?"

Chang looked up. "Because could be precious stone. Where you found, could be many more."

"Do you know about precious stones, then?"

"Little bit, Mr. Henry. Here plenty precious-stone dealers. Many my clients. I listen good when they talking."

Henry examined the crystal. "But it could just be a simple quartz." In the twilight of the room, the stone looked dark and unremarkable.

By way of reply, Chang placed the stone on the flat of his hand. Then he took Henry's teacup and tipped some dregs over the stone. Small, globular drops formed and rolled off without losing their shape. "When water go like that is good sign of precious stone."

"Are you sure?"

"To be absolute sure, more investigation needed," replied Chang. "If you want, I can arrange."

Henry thought for a moment. "I'd be much obliged."

Chang nodded. "One good client jewel trader. I give him stone for polish. Next day you know more."

"Agreed." Henry put on his jacket.

A short while later, Henry was in a rickshaw on the way to the Fifteenth Infantry Regiment barracks. He planned to get a few bottles of laudanum from the regiment's pharmacy and stock up on quinine and dressing materials.

The barracks bordered the red-light district, and the rickshaw puller sped through crowded alleys bustling with traders. But Henry paid no attention to either the colorful displays or the tempting blandishments of the stallholders.

If Chang were to be proven right about the crystal, that would raise many questions—for example, whether it explained Eranga's fatal head injury. If so, that would mean someone else knew about the find.

The rickshaw stopped unexpectedly, jolting Henry from his musings. He could see they had not yet reached the barracks but were stuck fast in a crush of rickshaws and passersby. When an elephant trumpeted nearby, he turned and was surprised to see they were outside the little monastery where the abbot had helped him several months ago. Through the open gate, he could see the temple elephant tethered beneath the spreading canopy of the Bodhi tree. A monk stood with the elephant, feeding it fruit. At that moment the monk turned his head and looked at Henry. It was Mahinda Dharmapala, and he smiled at Henry so calmly, it was as if he had been expecting him.

Without thinking, Henry sprang out of the rickshaw and pushed a few coins at the startled puller. Then he hurried through the monastery gate.

"Ayubowan, venerable hamudru." He put his hands together in front of his forehead and bowed.

Mahinda Dharmapala returned his bow. "So, Henry Odell, you are here." He turned and went toward the open hall in the middle of the courtyard.

Henry followed him with a furrowed brow.

In the hall was an older monk, sitting alone on the floor and meditating, and a group of novices listening attentively to their teacher reading from the wisdom of the Enlightened One. Mahinda sat cross-legged in one corner of the hall and indicated Henry should join him.

There was a short silence. Then Mahinda said, "I read of this meeting in the stars some time ago."

Henry let slip a small laugh of disbelief. He knew that astrology, horoscopes, and the prophecies deriving from them played an important role in the native population's faith. But he himself thought it sheer hocus-pocus. He almost regretted his sentimental, impulsive decision to come in.

Mahinda was looking at him indulgently. "You Europeans think your way of looking at the world is the one right way. In fact, it is one of many and—pardon my candor—it often seems like looking into a narrow tunnel."

"It's simply hard for me to see what the stars in the sky have to do with our chance meeting here on Earth," retorted Henry.

"Astrology is an ancient science. The Enlightened One knew early on that it holds knowledge and understanding. Its secrets are revealed only to those who understand the language of the stars," Mahinda explained patiently, as if telling a child the sun does not drown in the sea at night, even though it has vanished into the water.

Henry frowned, but before he could say anything, Mahinda raised his hand. "I know you don't share my faith. But didn't you come here today because you cannot give up opium?"

Henry dropped his eyes. It was extraordinary that a stranger he had met only once before could see through him as if he were made of glass.

"I abstained for a few months," he admitted with reluctance. "It wasn't easy. Every day I had to fight against it all over again, and in a moment of weakness, it beat me." Furious and ashamed, he clenched his right hand into a fist. "I have worries that drive me to the drug, but they shouldn't be used as an excuse." He looked into Mahinda's tranquil eyes. "I have seen terrible injustice meted out by someone close to me, and then rewarded by those who should stop it. And, as if that isn't bad enough, I've begun to doubt my own mind. When I look in a mirror, I see someone I no longer recognize." He broke off. He hadn't envisaged speaking to a stranger about his brother's violence or his own feelings for Phera.

Mahinda placed a hand on his arm. The touch was only momentary, but it gave Henry some consolation.

"Don't worry. Your mind is in good working order, but there are obstacles in every human life. Many are small and we overcome them with ease. But others seem insurmountable, and we fear never overcoming them. We bring the most difficult obstacles with us from our earlier existences. Perhaps we did someone an injustice. Perhaps we made a promise and did not keep it. Whatever it is, equilibrium has to be maintained, even if it takes us many lives to reach it."

"You talk of karma. I've read some of the writings of your Siddhartha Gautama," said Henry. "At the moment it seems like I'm not righting previous wrongs but actually creating new ones. Perhaps I'm just making sure I don't get bored in my future existences," he added with a wry smile.

"First of all, you must learn to conquer your craving for opium," said Mahinda. "Everything else will follow. Your craving exists only in your spirit. So you must learn to control your spirit."

"Sadly, I have no idea how to manage that." Henry spoke as if resigned to failure.

"You must practice the art of meditation."

Henry looked over at the lone monk. He was still sitting on the hard ground, his legs crossed. His hands lay intertwined in his lap. His back was straight and his eyes closed. His face showed concentration and yet also relaxation.

"During meditation our spirit is calmed, and we understand that quiet is an eternal space for freedom and wisdom," said Mahinda. "If you practice daily, you will learn that what we see as our worries can neither oppress us nor break us."

"I fear just that posture would finish me off," said Henry. "And it's hard to believe that crossing the legs and closing the eyes is enough to beat opium."

Mahinda laughed. "Masters don't fall from the sky. Is that how you say it, too? Just as water will seep into a house with a poor roof, so desires will insinuate themselves into the spirit that does not practice meditation. This is the teaching of the Enlightened One. By retreating into quiet, you will find the endless source of strength concealed within you. Whether you use it is your decision."

Henry sighed. "It sounds like the art of sitting around and doing nothing takes plenty of practice."

Mahinda thought for a while, then said, "It's easier to learn under the guidance of a teacher. If you wish, you may come here to the monastery every day and meditate with us."

"That's so generous of you, venerable hamudru. But tomorrow I'm leaving Colombo to ride back to the Kadugannawa Pass. As a doctor, it is my job to tend to the workers building the new road from Kandy to Colombo. If I still have a bit of time left after straightening fractured limbs, fitting splints on broken bones, dealing with crush wounds, and caring for malaria victims, I'll try and have a go at meditation." He stood up. "I thank you for your kindness and your advice, venerable hamudru."

Mahinda got up, too. "You will be too busy caring for your patients, and you will neglect your own welfare—to their ultimate detriment as well. If you will allow me to, I'd like to help you. I am not bound to this one monastery. We monks often follow the example of the Enlightened One and travel through the country, teaching and preaching. I shall accompany you and, during the journey, will teach you to meditate and conquer your craving for opium."

"You would really do all that for an Englishman?" Henry marveled.

"Our paths have not crossed by chance, Henry Odell," said the abbot. "I don't know why, but it seems we are meant to walk some of the path through life together."

◆ ◆ ◆

During the journey to the Kadugannawa Pass, the Sinhalese monk and the British doctor grew slowly to trust one another. To cover more ground, they rode together on Henry's horse, Henry in front, Mahinda behind. They quickly fell into conversation.

Mahinda talked about the caste he was born into, Bamunu, and how priests and monks traditionally came from this group. His parents had committed him at a very early age to a monastery where, on his twentieth birthday, he had received Usampada, the highest level of Buddhist ordainment. When Henry asked him which monastery he had grown up in, and when he had come to Colombo, the abbot became evasive and asked instead how people lived in Great Britain. He wanted to know everything about the distant island empire, from the weather and landscape to the food and styles of dress—even what the royal palace and London itself looked like. When Henry talked about his medical studies at the Royal College of Surgeons, and his subsequent service in India and Ceylon as staff doctor, Mahinda listened with particular interest because he himself was trained in the healing art of Ayurveda. The two men enjoyed exchanging ideas on different methods of treatment and compared medicines, their administration and effects. Henry, however, was mistrustful of any system which maintained that human health depended on the balance of energies in the body.

"Whether such energies even exist needs to be proven using scientific methods, and I can't imagine how one would do that," he said as the two men prepared to set up camp at dusk on the fourth day of travel.

Mahinda slid down off the horse. "It's easy. Don't you feel energies in your belly?"

Henry shook his head, baffled.

"These energies are what cause your incessant tossing and turning at night. During the day I feel them in your tense voice and nervous movements as your thoughts revolve around the temptation of opium. Please permit me to give you a medicine which will bring your body's energies back into equilibrium. It will make you more relaxed during the day and will give you the gift of sleep at night."

Henry dismounted, too, undid his horse's girth, and then took off the saddle. "I doubt there's anything other than willpower that can beat opium," he said, surprised at how accurately the monk had once again recognized the state of his soul.

He led the horse to a little river. While the animal was drinking, Mahinda collected dry wood and small branches, lit a fire, and took out two earthenware bowls.

"This must be the Nanu Oya River," Henry said. "That means we'll reach the construction site sometime tomorrow."

Mahinda now took dried herbs from the leather pouch he wore, and dropped them into one of the little bowls. Then he sprinkled into the other bowl a handful of ground roots, also taken from the pouch.

"This is root of hathawariya. I use it to prepare a drink that will bring you rest tonight. If you take this medicine every night, it will help you regain your equilibrium."

"What are your plans, once we've reached our destination?" Henry asked, watching the monk retie his pouch.

"If you want me to, I'll stay near you," replied Mahinda.

"Thank you," said Henry quietly.

He took two tin pots out of his saddlebag, went to the river, and filled them with fresh water. Back at camp, he took from their luggage a small bag of beans and another of rice, put a handful of both in one of the pots, and set it on the fire. Mahinda put the other pot next to it and, when the water was boiling, poured the liquid into both earthenware bowls.

"Are you hungry?" Henry asked Mahinda as the aroma rose from the rice and beans. He asked this every evening. And, every night, the abbot would shake his head with a smile. He ate his only meal of the day early in the morning, a little steamed rice with herbs from his leather pouch.

"Your drink is ready." He handed Henry the bowl of root stock. Henry emptied it in a few mouthfuls. The stock was almost clear and tasted not unpleasant, a little like spinach.

"How did it begin with you and the opium, my friend?" asked the monk, sounding less formal than before.

"It's not so easy to explain."

Henry picked up the pot of beans and rice, stirred it with a metal spoon, and started to eat.

"I imagine you're carrying someone else's burden on your shoulders, would that be it?"

Henry's throat tightened. He lowered the spoon and sat for some long moments.

"It began after the Uva Rebellion."

Mahinda's body stiffened, but Henry did not notice because he was staring into the dancing flames of the campfire.

"Our regiment was ambushed by the rebels. Almost all of my colleagues were killed. Afterward the governor at the time, Brownrigg, ordered retaliation attacks throughout Uva. I was present at one such attack and watched as an officer and his soldiers massacred a whole village. Nobody was spared. The men were murdered, the surviving women brutally raped, and every last rice plant burnt."

"Did you yourself murder, rape, and pillage?"

"No. As a doctor, I took a solemn oath to save life, not to destroy it. I wanted to prevent the massacre and I failed—" Henry buried his face in his hands.

Mahinda made an abrupt movement. But he checked himself and regained his serenity.

Henry let out a deep breath and let his hands drop from his face. "After two years we had the rebellion under control. Calm returned to the country, but not to my head. The memories of the brutality I saw still haunt me." He wiped his forehead with the back of his hand. "I can only forget them when I'm smoking opium."

He stopped talking and stared into the flames. Mahinda was silent, too.

The only noises were the crackling of the fire and the calls of the night birds. After some time Mahinda said, "My friend, you must report these events to the governor."

"That's what I did!" Henry's fists were clenched. "I reported the whole thing to Governor Brownrigg. Without the slightest success. All that mattered to him was that the rebellion had been subdued."

"Were the lives of my brothers and sisters worth nothing?" asked Mahinda.

Henry shook his head slowly. "Apparently not." He closed his eyes, realizing how desperately he needed to talk openly about the atrocities. It would slightly reduce his own burden, and bring some small sense of justice for the Sinhalese, the violated and the dead.

"My own brother instigated that massacre. He had an entire village sent up in flames because five rebel leaders had hidden away there. Three of them died when he captured the village. He forced the remaining two to watch while he tortured their families. Then he had them beheaded."

"Are the families dead, too?"

"I don't know anything about the family of the one whose name was Deepal Sirisena. But the other was Jeeva Maha Nuvara. His widow actually lives with her two children not far from here. I saw them again quite by chance, when a mahout—"

"Only two children?" Mahinda's eyes flashed. "Are you sure?"

"Very sure," answered Henry. "She has a daughter and a son, and the daughter has a little boy."

Mahinda stared into the fire. The dancing flames reflected in his eyes and made them glow like hot coals. His posture was so still it reminded Henry of the statues of Buddha he had seen in the temple. The monk's face, however, no longer radiated serenity and peace but looked stiff with shock and anger. Then a shudder ran through him as if he was trying to shake off inner demons.

"You must feel like a grain of rice between two millstones whenever you think about your brother," said Mahinda, his voice raw. "In spite of that pain, you will one day have to make a choice: your brother or justice. Now finish your food and then let's meditate."

Henry ate his food down in silence. When he had finished, and had washed up his bowl and spoon, he sat down again before the fire, straightened his back, and crossed his legs. The position was still uncomfortable. But, like Mahinda, he placed his hands low, beneath his navel, closed his eyes, and tried to concentrate on his breath. It often took a while for his thoughts to calm, but today he could not manage it at all.

The ostensible benefits of meditation seemed further out of reach than ever. All the unresolved crises still echoed through his thoughts. Charles and his violent outbursts, the young mahout who triggered his worrying cravings and dreams, and Eranga, who had likely been murdered over the stone Henry now knew to be a sapphire. He slipped his right hand into the pocket where he had stowed it.

On the morning of his departure, he had gone back to Chang and could not believe his eyes when the man handed him, instead of a hunk of gravel, a jewel, its deep blue like an ocean without end. Chang told him how the jeweler who polished the stone had wanted to pay a lot of money for it. Chang himself had already offered Henry an astounding sum in return for the stone and information about where it had been found. But Henry wasn't interested in the money. He wanted to find out how, and why, Eranga had died. Once Chang had understood that Henry would not sell him the stone, he gave his guest a warning.

"Mr. Henry, you good man, so I give good advice. This sapphire very valuable. Not show everyone. People killed for much less."

People like Eranga, Henry thought once again. He shivered in spite of the warm night air.

The cacophony of frogs' mating calls coming from the river broke his train of thought. Somewhere in the branches above, an owl was hooting, and Henry's horse stamped impatiently. Although Mahinda had not yet said the meditation was over, Henry opened his eyes. The forest surrounded him, black as pitch, impenetrable. The orange light of the campfire played over Mahinda's face, motionless, as if sculpted in stone.

What secrets are you hiding? wondered Henry, looking at him keenly.

He called to mind all the conversations he had so far had with the monk. A picture gradually took shape in his mind's eye.

"You were a rebel," he said softly in the darkness. "Once the rebellion was put down, you went underground."

Mahinda opened his eyes.

"You're hiding in that little monastery in Colombo, right? Are you being hunted by the British?"

"I was the personal astrologist to Sri Vikrama Rajasinha," replied Mahinda. "Before making important decisions, the king would always seek my advice. I drew up horoscopes for him and served faithfully for years. After we lost him, I supported the rebellion under Wilbawe. I took the Sacred Tooth of the Enlightened One to Badulla so that the people could acknowledge Wilbawe as king. You British never knew about me. You are now the first."

A burning branch snapped on the fire, and a glowing length of wood rolled from the flames. Mahinda picked up another small branch and threw it in. "I heard about the massacre when Jeeva and Deepal died. I realized that we'd lost, so I helped Wilbawe to flee."

"It is my duty to hand you over," said Henry, his voice subdued. "In my government's view, you're a criminal."

"You will no more hand me over," said Mahinda calmly, "than I will slit your throat tonight while you sleep."

"Are you threatening me, friend?"

"Don't be afraid, Henry Odell," said the abbot. He leaned forward. "The Enlightened One says, 'Enmity gives rise to enmity; friendship puts it to rest.'"

Chapter Eleven
October 1822

"I don't hear anything." Henry reined in his horse. But the jungle was never silent. All around was buzzing, squawking, chirping, screeching, and whistling.

"How can you say that?" asked Mahinda from behind him in the saddle.

"What I mean is no construction noise."

It unsettled him not to hear hammering or sawing, the crack of splintering timber, the roar from gigantic trees as they fell to the ground. He listened for the overseer's signal horn and the piercing bursts of trumpeting from the working elephants. The building site could not have been more than half a mile away.

"Hold on tightly!" he told the abbot, and urged his horse into a gallop along the narrow jungle path.

Thin branches whipped painfully at their faces, and Mahinda bounced in the saddle like a sack of rice, clinging to Henry for dear life. Fortunately, it was not long before they saw the new road, winding down from the Kadugannawa Pass like a huge, rust-colored snake.

"Something's not right." Henry pulled up his horse so sharply that Mahinda flopped hard against his back.

"It looks very quiet," his travel companion agreed, trying to regain his balance.

An almost-deserted construction site lay before the two men. A small group of Indian workers dozed beneath the broad canopy of a jacaranda tree. In a water hole a short distance from the road, two elephants were bathing, their mahouts grooming them with coconut shells. A few Sinhalese workers squatted around a small fire, cooking what looked like a pot of rice. There was not one Englishman to be seen.

"Hey, you!" Henry trotted his horse over to the men.

They woke in alarm. When they saw Mahinda, they bowed their heads respectfully. Though Hindu, they wanted to show their respect for the monk. The Sinhalese around the cooking fire also greeted Mahinda.

"What's going on here?" asked Henry. "Why aren't you working? And where are the soldiers, the engineers, and all the other British?"

The workers looked uncertainly at one another.

"All the white men are sick," said one of them.

"What do you mean, sick?" asked Henry.

The man looked helplessly back at him. "They're sick."

Henry was seized by guilt. It was his responsibility to care for everyone at the site. Instead, he had been in Colombo for reasons he could not explain without heaping trouble upon himself. Maybe an epidemic had broken out and men had actually died. If so, then he had utterly failed in his duty as a doctor.

Just then Henry heard pathetic gasping in the undergrowth close by. He jumped down from his horse and hurried toward the noise. He almost tripped over the corporal, crouched behind some tall ferns with his trousers down.

"Good God, man, what are you doing?"

"Dr. Odell!" Red in the face, the corporal quickly stood up. But he had forgotten his trousers, still around his ankles, and he stood naked from the waist down.

"Heavens above!" Henry turned away. "This place stinks like a cesspit. Have you got diarrhea?"

"I'm afraid I do. Sincere apologies." Grimacing with pain, the corporal bent to pull up his trousers. "Just as you'd left, it all started—vomiting, shitting, the lot. None of our men escaped. Only the coolies didn't go down with it. But they're used to the food and this hellish climate." Sighing wearily, he fastened his pants. "Since everyone got the runs, it's been chaos. With all the white men sick, the Sinhalese and coolies have been able to disappear bit by bit."

"Sorry?"

"They've cleared off, gone to ground somewhere in the jungle. Every day just a couple here and there, so it wasn't noticeable at first. But we've all been too sick to have stopped them, in any case. Meanwhile, there's only a handful of workers left."

"So my brother isn't back from Colombo?" asked Henry, hardly able to believe what he was hearing.

"If the major had been here, none of this would've happened. He'd have cracked down hard, that one. Damn!" The corporal, seized by more stomach cramps, hurried back to squat behind the ferns again.

Henry turned on his heel and made his way back to Mahinda, waiting near the Sinhalese workers, still patiently holding the horse by its bridle.

"I must get to the field hospital. An epidemic's broken out," Henry told him.

"I'll come with you." Mahinda swiftly handed the reins to one of the workers.

"There's vomiting and diarrhea through the entire camp," Henry explained. "I fear it could be typhus."

A strange, ghostly atmosphere hung over the narrow paths between the rows of British tents. Occasional groans and violent retching came from inside.

Prepared for the worst, Henry pushed back the tarpaulins at the entrance to the hospital tent. The nauseating smell of disease, unemptied chamber pots, and unwashed bodies hit them. In this heat, the stink was almost unbearable.

The tent was packed. Men lay in twos on the narrow, makeshift cots. Blankets had been spread on the floor to create even more bed space. The faces of the sick were drawn, their cheeks sunken. Some tossed and turned, moaning. Others vomited. Henry and Mahinda clambered over arms, legs, and heads, but had to watch out for brimming pots and sick bowls, too. Henry stopped at one bed and spoke to the soldier.

"Tell me how you are."

"Got pains," groaned the man, clutching at his belly.

"Diarrhea? Vomiting?"

The soldier gave a feeble nod.

While Henry questioned him about what he had eaten and drunk, he felt the patient's forehead and was relieved to find it cool. He lifted the man's undershirt to examine his torso for the purple rash typical of typhus and palpated the area around the spleen. Eventually, he said, "Try to get some sleep. Then drink some tea with plenty of sugar. That'll help you get strength back."

He carried out the same examination of several other patients. All had the same severe pains, but none showed any symptoms of the feared disease.

"It looks like we are not dealing with a typhus epidemic, at least," he told Mahinda, who'd followed silently at his side.

"No rash and no swelling of the spleen," agreed Mahinda. "But if the toxins in the gut multiply, typhus can still develop."

"What action would you advise?" asked Henry, impressed that Mahinda had made the same diagnosis.

"A meat-free diet, because meat rots inside the gut," the abbot answered. "Give them tea made from the bark of the *kumbuk* tree. And get them to gargle with salt water. On top of that, they must rest until they are well."

"I'd thought of something similar," said Henry. "But I'm not familiar with this tree."

"There are a few on the banks of the Nanu Oya. I'll go and collect some bark for you. Then later I'll show you how to prepare the tea."

"Doctor! God, it's good to see you back!" One of Henry's assistants lurched toward him from the back of the tent. He looked exhausted, his weary face unshaven, his once-white apron heavily stained. Two more assistants appeared behind him, carrying chamber pots for emptying outside.

"We don't know how to carry on, Doctor," conceded one of them. "I've given them peppermint tea and mustard plasters, enemas and hot poultices, but nothing helps. Then, the men suffering most, I wanted to give them laudanum. But there isn't any. I could have sworn there was another full bottle." He wiped his perspiring face with his filthy sleeve.

"You've done well," Henry reassured him, inwardly berating himself. "The laudanum was finished, but I've brought more from Colombo." Prepared for the worst, he looked around them and asked, "How many dead?"

"None, thank God. But there're a few who won't last much longer. The epidemic set in soon after you left."

"Have you boiled all water, as instructed?"

"Yes, sir. We've made sure all the food was thoroughly cooked." The assistant rubbed at his eyes, red and sore.

Henry placed a hand on the man's shoulder. "When did you last get any sleep?"

The man smiled weakly. "The day before yesterday, I think."

"Go and put your head down for a couple of hours. I'll take care of the patients now."

Henry left the field hospital. He wanted a good look at the kitchen. There could, after all, be infected foodstuffs there, incorrectly prepared and the cause of the enteritis outbreak. Mahinda, who had already returned from the river with some strips of fresh bark, accompanied him.

The field kitchen was nothing more than a sturdy cart, the back half of which consisted of a roughly crafted cupboard. The doors stood open, revealing wooden shelves of bowls, little packs of spice, bottles, jugs, and cooking utensils. Food supplies, principally rusk and sacks of rice, dried peas, and beans, were stored in the cart itself. The work surface was composed of a folding table under a tarpaulin stretched between the top of the cupboard and two posts rammed into the ground. The stove consisted of a hole in the ground for a fire, on which an iron cauldron was simmering gently.

A Sinhalese kitchen worker was gathering together cooking equipment on the worktable. He had stacked the dirty crockery and cutlery in a pot ready for scouring with sand down by the river. As Henry and Mahinda got closer, he hurriedly put the little spice packs and a couple of earthenware bowls in the cupboard and closed the doors.

"Where's the regimental cook?"

"He's sick," replied the man. His gaze followed Mahinda, who had gone over to the cupboard and opened it again. "Are you looking for something, venerable hamudru?"

"Only somewhere to keep the bark," answered the monk. Without turning his head, he stuffed the rolled strips of bark into an empty container and began inspecting the cupboard.

The kitchen helper started to say something, but Henry interrupted him. "What are you cooking there?" He nodded toward the heavy cauldron.

The Sinhalese man gave a start. "Rice, sir," he replied, recovering in a flash. "Rice is good for the sick and makes them well again. Come,

I'll show you." He hurried over and lifted the lid. "Come and see, look, look." He beckoned eagerly to Henry.

While Henry peered into the cauldron in which rice, and only rice, was indeed simmering, Mahinda was opening all sorts of containers, sniffing at the contents and, now and again, having a taste. Then he took the stopper out of the little bottle that the helper had just put away in the cupboard, and sniffed it. He frowned, let a drop of the viscous liquid drip onto his palm, then tasted it. He turned to look at Henry, still standing at the cauldron. But Henry had his back to him and was stirring the rice. The Sinhalese man, however, stared unflinchingly back at Mahinda. Mahinda pursed his lips and gave a slight shake of the head. Then he closed the bottle and tucked it into his own leather pouch.

"You really don't want to stay in the camp?" asked Henry after Mahinda had told him how to make the kumbuk-bark tea. "You could use my bed. I'll be up all night working, anyway."

Mahinda shook his head. "I'll ask the people in Mapitigama for shelter, but I'll come to see you every day so we can still meditate together."

"Today's not going to be any good for that," responded Henry. "I have to take care of my patients."

Mahinda nodded in understanding. "But at least have some hathawariya tea." He took a handful of the roots from his pouch, wrapped it up in leaves he had torn from a bush, and gave Henry the little bundle.

"Don't worry about the epidemic," said Mahinda. "It might seem frightening, but they'll soon recover."

"Did you read that in the stars, too?" Henry teased.

The monk bowed with a smile. "Ayubowan, Henry Odell." He turned and vanished between the rows of tents.

◆ ◆ ◆

Mahinda followed the jungle trail that the workers had shown him, and in half an hour he was at Mapitigama.

He looked pensively at the simple huts with their small gardens. A few women were working outside, children were playing, and chickens clucked as they scratched here and there. In the village center was an old Bodhi tree, so fragile the villagers had propped it up with wooden posts. The shrine to the Enlightened One was lovingly decorated with flowers. A large branch had broken off and lay beneath the tree, leaving a gaping wound on the trunk.

If the widow of Jeeva Maha Nuvara really had taken refuge here, then her life must be very different from her life at the royal court of Vikrama Rajasinha.

A very lean old man was sitting on a bench in front of one of the huts, chewing betel nut and enjoying the sun on his bones. Mahinda went up to him.

"Ayubowan, wise one," he said. "Are you the widan, and can you tell me where I'll find Anshu Maha Nuvara?"

The old man squinted up at him. "Ayubowan, venerable hamudru. I am not the widan. You'll find our leader there." He pointed to a hut near the Bodhi tree.

"And where does Anshu Maha Nuvara live?"

The old man gave a giggle, showing teeth stained red with betel-nut juice. "There. She is our widan. I am happy that the Enlightened One has sent you to us, hamudru."

"I thank you." Astonished, Mahinda walked to the hut.

The carefully tended garden was deserted. The banana palms and mango tree bowed under the weight of their fruit. Jasmine and cardamom twined around bamboo poles, and beans, okra, and chili pods thrived in perfect raised beds. Mahinda also noticed various medicinal plants and an abundance of colorful flowers that pleased his eye.

The hut door stood open, and he went in. In the dim light, he made out the silhouette of a woman sitting on a stool, cleaning beans piled in a basket at her side. A little boy crouched at her feet, passing her more beans when she was ready.

When Mahinda's shadow darkened the doorway, the woman started. Her grip on the knife tightened.

Mahinda placed the flat of his hands across his chest. "My greetings, Anshu Maha Nuvara."

She stared at him for a moment. Then, very slowly, she relaxed her grip on the knife. "Mahinda Dharmapala?"

He nodded. "Yes, it's me."

She stood up, placed the knife on a shelf out of the child's reach, and greeted the visitor. "Ayubowan, venerable hamudru. Forgive me for not recognizing you."

"It has been a long time," he replied.

"How did you know—" Her voice failed her. The unexpected reappearance of the abbot stirred up painful memories of happy times that were now so long past.

"I met the British doctor, Henry Odell, in Colombo, and came back with him. He told me about you." Mahinda's eyes wandered over the simply decorated hut, took in the house altar with its fresh flowers, the spinning wheel, and then lingered on the little boy who was staring at the visitor with a mixture of mistrust and curiosity. "Is this your grandson?"

She nodded. "Thambo is Samitha's son. She's out in the rice field, working."

Mahinda bent toward the child, gently took him by the chin, and looked at him for a long time. "Does he know about his father?"

Anshu's face hardened. "He has no father!"

Mahinda straightened up. "The day will come for him to learn."

"May the gods protect him!" Anshu turned brusquely away and went over to the shelf on the wall. She took down a jug of water, poured some into a beaker, and offered it to the monk. "You must be thirsty."

"I thank you." Mahinda drank it quickly and handed back the beaker. "Your daughter Mihiri is dead?"

Anshu almost dropped the beaker. "You know about that, too?"

"Who's Mihiri, Grandma?" piped up Thambo.

Anshu gave no answer. She put the beaker back on the shelf, took Thambo by the shoulders, and steered him toward the door. "Go outside now, my little one, and play with your friends."

Thambo resisted, asking again, "Who's Mihiri, Grandma?"

She sighed. "I'll tell you later. Now go and play. Quick, quick!" She pushed the boy outside and watched him as he ran off. Behind her, she heard Mahinda's voice.

"The British doctor mentioned only two of your children, a daughter and a son. So I knew either Samitha or Mihiri must be dead. And the doctor said Jeeva was executed."

Anshu turned away without a word, and went to the altar. While she tidied up fading blooms here and there, she told him quietly how Jeeva and Mihiri had met their ends. For the last four years, she had tried to come to terms with the horrific deaths of her husband and her child, but the pain would not subside, no matter how often she told herself the two of them had exchanged this life for a happier existence in the other world.

Mahinda listened carefully without interrupting her. He already knew how merciless the British had been toward his countrymen during the rebellion, but to hear it from Anshu herself made him burn with rage. When she fell silent, he said in very subdued tones, "Sometimes it's very hard not to follow the path of revenge."

"That's exactly what I try to explain to my children," she acknowledged. "But it's very hard. Especially for Phera."

Mahinda's face lit up. "Where is Phera?"

"With Siddhi. Do you remember the king's gift?"

Mahinda nodded. "I do indeed. Your youngest child has a special destiny."

Anshu thought back to the day of Phera's birth and the years her youngest had spent as a boy, her father's heir. "It was I who sealed Phera's fate," she said, downcast. "If I hadn't—"

Mahinda raised his hand. "You made a lapse of judgement, but your circumstances were not easy. Do not torment or reproach yourself any further. Your youngest daughter's destiny was already written at her birth. You couldn't have changed it."

Anshu's eyes widened. "You know?" she whispered. "You know that Phera isn't a boy?"

"I've known since I drew up her horoscope. Humans cannot keep secrets from the stars. Now tell me about how you came to live here and how you are getting on."

Anshu prepared a tea using the dried herbs she kept in earthenware pots, sat down with the monk in the shade of the mango tree, and began her story. "We lived in peace for almost four years," she concluded later. "But destiny caught up with us a few months ago."

"You mean the two British brothers?"

Anshu nodded and pulled her sari more snugly around her shoulders.

Mahinda leaned forward and looked straight into her eyes. "Tell me everything you know about them."

"One of them, the doctor, seems a good man, in spite of being English," Anshu began, her voice hesitant. "He wishes no harm to our people and has actually helped us. But the other is so wicked in every thought and deed that he could be Mara incarnate, the demon bringer of death. He should have an entire village on his conscience, men who were brave fighters. My own husband. From Samitha and Phera, he stole all peace, and from Mihiri, her life." Her voice trembled so much that she stopped speaking. Once she had collected herself, she pressed on. "He dragged the village men from Mapitigama and made them his slaves. He plans to drive us out from our homes for his road, and even to chop down the tree of the Enlightened One. Only Phera and Siddhi prevented him from doing it already. That's why they must hide in the jungle."

"Perhaps you already know that the building work has been delayed? The British have all got diarrhea, while the workers remain well."

Anshu looked at him nervously, but when she saw Mahinda wink at her, she could not help a mischievous smile herself. "I heard, yes. And I hope the plague stays a long time."

The monk reached into his leather pouch and set the small bottle on the bench between himself and Anshu. "I found this in the British kitchen. It contains oil pressed from the seeds of the miracle tree."

Anshu's smile broadened. "I am the widan here, and a widan must, after all, take care of the community. I sought advice from the women, and together we came up with the idea of miracle-tree oil. One of us is married to the cook working for the British. She met with him in the forest and gave him the bottle. He stirs a bit into the Britons' food every day. That's the only thing keeping our village safe for the time being. And the women have their menfolk back."

Mahinda laughed. "I've seen only one very elderly man here. Where have you hidden all the others?"

"There are plenty of places in the jungle the British can never find."

"But what'll happen next?" Mahinda was serious again. "You need to defend yourselves against being driven out of the village, but you'll put yourselves in worse danger if the British ever find out what you've done. Your idea was a good one, but I beg you not to continue with it. That's why I took the bottle, so that nobody finds any evidence that the mysterious epidemic started with all of you."

Anshu lowered her head. "You're right. It's too risky. Venerable hamudru, do you know some other way of keeping this devil, Charles Odell, away from our village?"

The abbot leaned toward her and gently touched Anshu's arm. "At this moment I don't know, but stay calm and trust in the power of poetic justice. Remember what Buddha said: 'Sit by the river and wait for your enemy's corpse to float by'!"

Chapter Twelve

October 1822

Almost immediately after Henry's return, the diarrhea and vomiting began to abate and the men gradually recovered. Henry put this down to his treatment of diet, rest, and Mahinda's kumbuk-bark tea. He was enormously relieved that the epidemic had not claimed any lives. When he looked for causes, however, there were no clear answers. He had questioned his orderlies and the cook, and been assured that all hygiene procedures had been adhered to during his absence. It was, of course, obvious to him that the climate of Ceylon fostered a lot of harmful miasmas: vapors thought to spread disease through the air. In addition, he'd recently learned of miniscule bacteria and parasites in the ground and water.

Henry observed how nobody asked about Charles or when he was coming back from Colombo. Not a soul, not even the engineers and soldiers, missed him. And amongst the few workers left, there was a relaxed, almost cheerful atmosphere.

"Do you think it possible that the workers are responsible for the outbreak?" Henry asked Mahinda before one of their daily meditation sessions.

"How could they be?"

"Not a single one of them was affected by the epidemic, and while the British were confined, they could run off without fear of being hunted down and recaptured. Isn't it possible that one of the kitchen assistants slipped something in the food?"

"Everything is possible," replied Mahinda casually.

Henry gave him a hard look. "Why do I feel that you know more about this than you're prepared to say?"

Mahinda smiled. "If you have a problem, try to solve it. If you can't solve it, then don't make a problem out of that." Before Henry could reply, the monk took up his meditation pose and closed his eyes.

But there were no more outbreaks, so Henry let the matter drop. One week after his return, he could leave his patients unattended for a few hours and do so with a clear conscience. He had decided to check on Phera and Siddhi. The mere thought filled him with joy and unease.

He set off early and, after hunting around for a bit, found once more the little path to the waterfall. His spirits were the highest they'd been in a long time, and he whistled a tune as he hurried through the jungle. The difficulties with his brother and the mysterious epidemic faded into the background. Even his craving for opium, still gnawing away at him in spite of the meditation, softened. He felt alive, yes, happy, even if Phera was at its root.

Since his return to the construction site, he had watched himself carefully to see whether men stirred him sexually. Amongst the soldiers were quite a few who were handsome and well built. During medical examinations, he had to see them undressed and touch them in the most private of places. And yet doing this stirred up no excitement or feelings of desire. Thus his feelings toward Phera must be something unique, extraordinary.

Today I'm going to allow myself my feelings, he decided as he pushed aside some branches and stepped into the little clearing. *I'm not going to run away from them, nor will I behave as if they are not there. But they'll remain my secret, and nobody will find out about them. Not even Phera.*

The roar of the waterfall mingled with the multitude of other forest noises. He looked toward the rock face. Water tumbled over the ridge between trees and bushes, here a foaming white force, there a gently shimmering curtain of pearls. He could not see the pool as Siddhi was blocking his view.

The elephant maneuvered her huge body in his direction and greeted him with a deep rumbling sound.

Henry glanced around the clearing but could not see Phera. He tried to skirt the elephant, but with a few astonishingly quick steps, she blocked his way. Then she turned her hindquarters to show Henry her wound. Cautiously, he leaned forward to inspect the bullet's point of entry and was pleased to see the wound was healing and now nearly closed. With the greatest of care, he touched the flesh around its edge and found the swelling had reduced. During this examination, Siddhi was looking behind her as her short neck permitted, watching Henry. Encouraged by her trust, he went to her head and stroked the sides of her gray face. She puffed softly, rifling through his jacket pockets with her trunk in search of treats.

"Whoa there!" Henry laughed, stumbling backward. As he did so, he stepped on a small pile of clothes, heaped carelessly on the grass. He picked them up and recognized Phera's shirt and baggy pants. Just then he heard singing, muffled by the roaring waterfall. The voice was smooth and feminine.

Henry let go the clothes and peered past Siddhi's head to the waterfall. In the bright sunlight, the millions of droplets conjured all the colors of the rainbow, like in his dream. Then he saw the woman. She was standing on a broad ledge partway up the rock face, her back toward him, letting her body revel in the water. Her singing turned to laughter as she arched her spine, lifted her arms, and threw back her head, taking uninhibited pleasure in the gushing water as it caressed her. It trickled from the tips of her long, dark hair onto her shapely bottom, and glistened on her amber skin.

Henry was transfixed, his mind suddenly a void, his heart pounding. Bewitched, he stared at the woman, at her graceful shoulders, her slender waist, broadening into the soft curve of her hips and leading to her long legs. As she turned slightly, Henry saw her face and was dumbstruck. Had he slipped back into some opium-induced fantasy? He shut his eyes and counted silently to three. But when he opened his eyes and still saw the woman beneath the waterfall, he realized this was the real world. And this world was better than any opium dream.

"Phera," he whispered. The happiness flooding him was beyond description. "Phera."

He wanted to go to her, take her in his arms. As a sigh of longing escaped him, he realized he was behaving like a lascivious voyeur. He had to be a gentleman, however difficult that might be. Once he had moved back behind Siddhi's mass, he allowed himself time to think through his discovery.

So Phera was not a young man, but a beautiful woman who dressed as a man for the outside world. She must have had sound reasons for doing this and so would not want her secret to come to light, particularly not in front of an Englishman and in her naked and vulnerable state.

If she sees me here, she'll never forgive me, Henry rapidly calculated, finding the mere thought unbearable.

As he withdrew silently into the forest, he thought how he would have to put aside his own desires and longings to win Phera's affection. Her secret needed to be safe with him until she herself chose to disclose it. Until then, he had to learn patience, cherish the newfound joy in his heart, and have faith that the hope he harbored deep inside could become a reality.

When Mahinda came in search of him just before dawn for their meditation practice, he gave Henry a searching look. "You are happy."

"Yes, my friend," said Henry. "I am happy because some of my difficulties are resolving themselves."

When Charles arrived at the construction site the following day, he couldn't believe his eyes. During his three-week absence, the work had moved no further forward. He dug in the spurs, and his horse shot down the rubble track.

"What's going on here? Have you already packed up for the day?" he bellowed.

The few remaining workers fled into nearby undergrowth at the sight of the raging commander.

Charles urged his horse on toward his tent and pulled up sharply outside. "Boy! Where are you hiding?"

"Here, sir!" The frightened orderly came running out.

Charles jumped down from his horse and threw the young man the reins. "Unsaddle, water, feed! Where is everybody? Why is nobody at work here?"

"We've had an epidemic, Major," the orderly told him. "We've all been sick."

"Sick? Everyone?" Charles's jaw dropped. "What's that supposed to mean?"

"A plague broke out. The most awful diarrhea. A lot of men didn't think they'd make it."

Charles frowned. "What am I paying a doctor for if he can't prevent an outbreak of disease?"

"Permission to speak, Major. But Dr. Odell wasn't here."

"Come again?"

"He left for Colombo right after you did. And while all of us were flat out, the coolies made off."

Charles was incandescent. "This is unacceptable! I leave for a couple of days and everything goes completely haywire! Has Dr. Odell come back?"

"Yes, sir. A week ago, sir. He is in the field hospital at this very moment."

Charles gave the boy a disgusted look and stormed off toward the sick tent. "Henry!" he roared, frightening the sick men on their cots. "Where the devil are you?"

Henry soon appeared from the back of the tent, a medicine bottle in one hand and a spoon in the other. "You're back, brother dear."

"Report to my tent. Immediately!"

Henry looked thunderstruck. Then he turned and went back to the patient he had been treating. Only after that was complete did he set off to see Charles. When Henry stepped into the tent, his brother was pacing like a caged leopard. "How frightfully kind of you to appear at last!"

"And a very good day to you, too. You look full of energy. Your malaria attack seems to have subsided."

"Stop that bootlicking. I want to know why you neglected your duties. A doctor who takes off on a whim is one I can do without!"

Henry stiffened. "You abandoned the site as well, in spite of being chief engineer!"

"Don't blame me for what happened! If you hadn't absconded, my men wouldn't have fallen ill and the coolies wouldn't have buggered off. Have you even the slightest idea how much this delay will cost us?"

"Not a great deal, I'd have thought, as the coolies don't get paid, anyway," said Henry. "But it's true that I regret my absence. I do share the guilt."

"What did you want in Colombo?"

"That's got nothing to do with you."

"That's where you're very much mistaken. You deserted, and I can make you formally accountable for that. How about running the gauntlet? Or would you prefer branding?"

"I'd be very careful with hasty punishments—your own excursion leaves you equally guilty of desertion," retorted Henry. "In any case, I am not subject to your authority. The construction of this road is not a military deployment, and I am, as you so often remind me, a civilian, not a soldier."

Charles was taken aback by Henry's newfound self-assurance. Irritated, he hissed, "Anyway, I know what you wanted in Colombo. Whores and opium."

Henry shrugged. He had no interest in what Charles thought of him. Since he had found out that Phera was a woman, he felt full of an unshakable inner strength.

"And what was the reason for your own hurried journey?" he inquired calmly. "It must have been very important for you to have left the site without so much as a by-your-leave."

Charles gave a nasty smile. "I got permission from Paget to take military action against that nest of rebel vipers in Mapitigama. When I tried to come to an amicable arrangement with the people there, that monkey on an elephant tried to kill me. But I'm not going to be tyrannized by a bunch of savages."

"You did what?" Henry blanched. "You need written orders from the governor for that."

"And so I got them." With a triumphant gesture, Charles pulled a folded sheet of paper from his inside pocket and waved it about.

"Show me!" Henry tried to grab it, but Charles skillfully whipped it away again.

"What's this? You're doubting my word now?" Swiftly, he stuck the paper back in his jacket pocket. Henry stepped toward him again, but Charles pushed him back roughly. "Get out of here. In fact, go to hell. I need to work out how to get hold of new workers."

Henry grabbed his brother by the collar. "You're a damnable bastard, and it's time someone put a stop to it." He stormed out of the tent.

Burning with hatred, Charles watched him go. His resentment, however, was directed not only at Henry but also at all the malingering soldiers and engineers, all the coolies who had been so disrespectful as to run off, and all the people of Mapitigama, those old men, women, and children who had dared to stand up to him. When he thought of how they had humiliated him, particularly that boy with his elephant, he felt like a steam boiler about to burst.

Now was the time to bend every soul in that unruly village to his will, to make every single one of them beg for mercy. And he would shoot that brute of an elephant right off its feet and have them made into a nice stool or two. He stomped out of the tent.

"A horse and six-man mounted escort—now!"

Henry heard the shouting from the farthest corner of the hospital tent. Concerned, he hurried to the entrance and peered outside. If his brother was shouting for horses and men, it could only mean one thing—he was planning to take revenge on Mapitigama immediately. Henry rushed to head them off at the stable tent. When Charles's orderly led his superior's horse out of the tent, Henry pushed aside the astonished young man and seized the bridle.

"Wait!" he shouted as his brother made to put his foot in the stirrup. "Let me negotiate with the people first. We can find a peaceful solution." He looked at the soldiers, who watched with unease but dared not get involved.

"Enough out of you!" Charles got hold of the pommel, ready to mount, but Henry pulled him back.

"Be fair for once in your life, Charles! I beg you."

Charles raised his riding crop. For a split second, Henry braced himself to be struck in the face, but at the last minute, Charles remembered that they had an audience.

"Very well, then," he snarled, lowering his arm. "You get one chance. You'll only make a fool of yourself, in any case."

"We'll see about that!" Henry pushed Charles out of his way, swung himself into the saddle, and galloped off.

◆ ◆ ◆

"Would you all like another story?"

Mahinda was seated beneath the Bodhi tree, looking at the village children gathered around him. The oldest of the menfolk, together with some mothers and grandmothers, including Anshu and Samitha, had joined them. Phera was also there. She had left Siddhi safely in their hiding place.

The children cheered at the prospect of another tale in the life of the Enlightened One. Only Thambo grumbled. "No story. I want to play!"

The grown-ups laughed. Samitha, full of a mother's pride, kissed her son, and Phera leaned over to tickle him until he squealed with delight.

Mahinda just smiled. His gaze rested on Phera's graceful form. He had not seen Jeeva Maha Nuvara's daughter since the night the British had marched into Senkadagala. The child may have grown, but he'd recognize her anywhere.

She was wearing men's clothing, but her body language, her voice, and her laughter made it clear she was a woman. He knew that the conflicting strengths of her birth horoscope had not dealt her an easy destiny. It seemed to him as if she was still living in two worlds, and he wondered how she managed.

Mahinda cleared his throat. "I'll tell you a very short one; then you can go and play. Ready? Once a man asked the Enlightened One, 'Are you a god?' And Buddha replied—" He looked at the children, waiting for the answer.

"No!" they chorused.

Mahinda, laughing, carried on. "Then the man asked Buddha, 'Are you an angel?' And Buddha replied—"

"No!" came the joyful cry.

"The man asked a third time," Mahinda continued, leaning forward, his eyes wide. "'Are you a—'"

Hoofbeats drummed in the distance, rapidly getting louder and closer. The villagers shrank together with fear. Mothers held their children close.

They braced themselves for bloodthirsty Charles Odell and soldiers, come to take revenge for being chased off several weeks prior. And yet today just one horseman raced into the village square. They all relaxed a little when they realized it was not Major Odell.

Mahinda stood up. "Ayubowan, Henry Odell. What brings you here, friend?"

Henry pulled up his foaming horse and leapt from the saddle. "You are all in danger! The whole village! We must call a meeting. Gather everyone together, including the men. They're hiding close by, is that right?"

The women looked at one another, shocked and uncertain. What was all this about? Could they trust this Englishman, or was it a trap to drag their men back to the building site, where they would doubtless be severely punished?

But Mahinda calmed them. "We can trust him. Send the children to fetch the men."

"What happened?" he asked Henry.

"My brother is back from Colombo—with worrying news."

Mahinda nodded solemnly in reply. "For as long as he's there, I won't be able to come to the camp for our meditation practice."

"Of course," answered Henry. "I wouldn't have you risk it."

Half an hour later, all the villagers were seated beneath the Bodhi tree. The escaped workers had left their jungle hideout and joined the group, all except a few watchmen who kept a close eye on the jungle in the direction of the building site.

In just a few words, Henry reported that Charles had acquired written orders from the governor to take armed action against the residents of Mapitigama.

"My brother thinks I've come to persuade you to abandon your village, but"—he raised his hand in response to angry murmurs—"in truth, I have come to try and find, with you, a way out."

Anshu, Samitha, and Phera exchanged looks. They knew better than anyone what Charles's "armed action" really meant.

Then Anshu felt all eyes turn to her and was seized by panic. The people expected their widan to protect them, to make a wise decision. But she had not the slightest idea what tiny, defenseless Mapitigama could do when faced with the devil incarnate. The only defense against Charles Odell was to run as far away as possible.

While she racked her brains for words to convey to the people hope and confidence that she herself did not feel, she heard Mahinda's voice.

"What exactly did this order say?" he asked. "We need the details."

"I didn't read the document," Henry replied. "I wanted to, but Charles wouldn't let me."

"So there could have been anything on that piece of paper."

Henry's eyes widened, and he felt a fool for believing his brother's claim. On reflection, he realized it may well have been a lie. Paget was reputed to be a prudent man who avoided armed conflict where possible.

"I'll look at the document myself," he said, getting to his feet.

Phera jumped up, too. "No matter what it is, Charles Odell will never stop tormenting us, because he has no wish to live in peace with us. He doesn't know the meaning of the word." She slipped her hand inside her shirt and, to Henry's amazement, produced a dagger. "There's only one way of protecting ourselves!" She brandished the weapon. "Charles Odell must die!"

"But not by your hand!" Anshu was on her feet now, too.

Angrily, Phera looked back at her. "Have you forgotten what he did to us, Mother? Mihiri's blood is on his hands, and Father's. And the blood of Psindu, Upali, of Deepal, Tharindu, and Kalani. He did appalling things to Samitha, who—"

"Stop it!" Samitha screamed. "Never speak the words!"

Henry stood mute, as if rooted to the spot. In the oppressive silence which now hung over the gathering, he slowly understood what he had just heard. Phera, a daughter of Anshu and Jeeva Maha Nuvara, must have been present at the massacre. But he could not remember seeing her. Where had she been when Charles and his soldiers had savaged her family? Suddenly, the image of the mud-covered creature under the veranda came back to him, the creature that had fled, screaming, from Jeeva's execution. How could she ever love him, the brother of her family's torturer? Until a few minutes ago, he had been happy from head to foot. Now his exhilaration collapsed in on itself.

As if from afar, he heard Phera's voice.

"We don't need to know what's on the piece of paper. We just need to kill Charles Odell."

"Be quiet!" Anshu rounded on her daughter. "Do you have any idea what you're saying? You think the British will let any of us live if we murder one of their own?" She looked fearfully at Henry.

He cleared his throat to speak. "Have no concerns, Anshu Maha Nuvara. I am here to assist." He looked at Phera. "But I don't want you to murder my brother. Your mother is right. My countrymen would hunt you down."

Phera's grip on the dagger was so fierce that her knuckles showed white. "I'll just flee to India afterward." Her voice shook a little. "The British will never find me."

"You're mistaken. India is full of Britons—especially soldiers." He was desperate. He wanted to put his arms around her, to comfort her until the hatred melted from her eyes. He wanted to beg her to love him, even though his brother was a monster. How could he ever find a way to her heart?

"Get this vengeful murder out of your head once and for all," said Anshu, her voice stern. "Doing anything like that will give you a burden of guilt throughout your future lives."

"Why should I care about my future lives?" hissed Phera. "I want back the peace of mind that he has robbed from me in this life! Surely you can't have stopped missing Father."

"Phera! You are forgetting yourself!" snapped Anshu.

Mahinda stepped in. "Your mother's words are wise, Phera. Revenge won't bring you peace of mind."

Phera was silent, torn between desperation and the knowledge that the monk was right.

Nobody spoke. For a long time, the soft weeping of a child, frightened by Phera's shouting, was the only sound.

Anshu turned to Henry. "Your brother could come with his soldiers anytime. Before you even have the chance to see the document. How do we escape his violence?"

Henry's thoughts were frantic. "Surround the village with guards, and take them food so they can be on duty day and night. Be prepared to leave at any time."

"Abandon our village? So the British get everything they want?" one of the men shouted.

"Not entirely," said Henry. "Construction is at a standstill because my brother has hardly any workers left. But your lives are in immediate danger. I fear that my brother will punish you for your resistance, and cruelly so."

"But what will happen to our Bodhi tree?" asked the oldest of the men. "Who will protect our sacred tree if we all flee?"

"Nobody. But your lives are more precious than the tree."

Angry murmurs got louder.

"You should not give your lives for the tree," Mahinda announced. "It is a very old, fragile tree, which will soon die."

The village elder spat a disdainful stream of betel juice. "And I'm very old, and very fragile, too. I'm staying with our tree."

"What about taking a cutting with us?" suggested Anshu. "The tree will live on through the cutting."

There were a lot of furrowed brows, but nobody could come up with anything better, so the villagers were forced to accept Henry's and Anshu's suggestions. Soon the meeting broke up.

Henry had just mounted his horse to ride back to the camp when Phera stepped in his path. The rage and hatred that he had earlier seen in her face was gone. She smiled and stroked the horse's nose.

"I'd like to come part of the way with you. I've never ridden a horse."

He held out his hand. "Climb aboard."

She grabbed hold and put one foot in the stirrup. He pulled her up and helped her settle in the saddle in front of him. This meant touching her arms and hips, and he thought how he had never been so close to her before. He breathed in the scent of her skin and had to stop himself kissing the back of her neck.

Charles be damned. He could not deny his feelings for Phera. He could not give her up before they had even started.

He let go of her supple body with reluctance and slid his hands under her arms, first right, then left, to take the reins. She wriggled a bit to find a comfortable position in the saddle. The curve of her buttocks pressed against the very top of his thighs. He longed to drop the reins and wrap his arms around her. But he managed to stifle his desire, gently squeezing his heels in his horse's sides.

Once the animal had set off, she looked at him over her shoulder. "You've helped my people yet again. You may be an Englishman, but you're a good Englishman." She gave an impish smile, and he yearned to kiss her beautiful mouth.

At a further squeeze, the horse broke into a trot. Phera let out a little shriek of surprise. Sitting astride Siddhi's broad neck felt very different from sitting on this animal, its back narrow and in constant movement. Henry quickly placed an arm around her and held her close.

"Don't worry. I'll hold you," he whispered in her ear, his voice husky.

Soon her body was rocking in rhythm with the horse, and she reveled in the animal's speed. She wondered why Henry had not visited her since treating Siddhi's bullet wound. Day after day she had waited for him to return, but he had not. She had started to invent reasons to ride to the construction site so she could catch a glimpse of him. Only the thought of Charles Odell, doubtless waiting for any opportunity to get his hands on her, had held her back.

When Henry had galloped into the village today, so unexpectedly, the sight of him had set her heart pounding. His lithe body had sat deep in the saddle as he'd guided his horse; and like a lover's hand, the breeze had gently tousled his hair. Now she let herself sink back onto his chest, listened to the regular hoofbeats, and enjoyed feeling his strong arm around her. An exciting tingling was making itself felt in her lower belly. It was like years ago, when she had been in love with Tharindu, only even stronger. She shook herself out of this dream. Was she really in love with an Englishman? How could that be?

Then she thought how this Englishman had saved her, not once but twice, and how their paths had repeatedly crossed, as if they were bound together by an unknown destiny. A shiver ran down her spine.

But she held herself in check. Henry Odell could not possibly imagine a future with her. He certainly was not the slightest bit interested, and for one simple reason: he believed she was a man.

You must tell him the truth, an inner voice whispered. But did she actually want that? Was it not easier to let the Englishman move on and for her simply to live her life? She slid away from him a tiny bit, and straightened up.

"Stop!" she cried.

Taken by surprise, Henry halted the horse, and Phera jumped down.

"Phera! What on earth's wrong?" He, too, slid down from the saddle.

She wanted to run, disappear into the jungle, but her feet would not move, and she was amazed to hear herself saying, "Why have you stopped visiting me and Siddhi? Don't you care how she is?"

"I do care! I care how Siddhi is, and I care how you are!"

Now she was looking at him with a mixture of uncertainty and expectation.

Encouraged by this, he went on. "In fact, I visited Siddhi yesterday. I'm satisfied the wound is healing and that she is well. And yet I did not actually see her keeper." He put special feeling into his words, intently awaiting her reaction.

"Go on," she said.

"I did not actually see her keeper," he repeated. "But I heard singing, and when I looked to see who it was—"

"Don't say it!"

He fell silent a moment.

"What I saw brought me the happiest moment of my life," he whispered gently, hoping upon hope to persuade her to forget his brother and to see him as he was, Henry Odell, a man who loved her with all his heart.

Her lovely mouth made a silent "oh." Her face gave away a host of conflicting emotions. Henry let go of his horse, stepped close to her, and, with the greatest of care, took hold of her hands. His eyes held hers, and he saw reflected in her steady gaze his own feelings—excitement, desire, and longing. He stayed completely still, held her hands tight, and waited to see what she would do.

Her fleeting inner battle was over the moment she saw that he knew who she was, and that he loved her. She wanted to know how it would feel to lie on his broad chest, to be held tightly in his arms, to taste his lips. She pushed aside the voices telling her he was an Englishman with a monster for a brother. She closed her eyes and sensed how his mouth met hers, and she felt everything she had longed for.

Chapter Thirteen
October 1822

It was pouring when Henry got back to the construction site in the afternoon, but rain could not dampen his joy. That Phera returned his love was a gift that made him feel strong and self-assured. For the first time in his life, he had the confidence to face his troubles.

He went into the hospital tent and busied himself with his rapidly improving patients, feverishly wondering how to get his hands on the document with the alleged order against Mapitigama. During the day, Charles surely kept it on him, in his uniform jacket. At night he probably stowed it in the small lockbox in his tent.

After the evening meal, Henry went to his tent for meditation. He had come to rely on this daily practice, and afterward he felt much calmer and more assured. When he opened his eyes, he had a plan.

The rain had stopped, and mosquito swarms danced in the pale moonlight. The moist, warm night air seeped through his clothing. It smelt of damp earth and of the smoke coming from the herb fires burning all over the camp to keep the mosquitoes at bay. As Henry reached Charles's lair, he noticed light shining through the pale canvas.

He pushed aside the tarpaulin and stepped inside. Charles was sitting at his writing desk, his back to the door. His lockbox stood open before him.

Henry took a deep breath. "Good evening, Charles. Isn't this the perfect weather for a nightcap? I picked up some fine Scottish whisky in Colombo and really don't want to drink it alone." He held out his drinking flask. Two tin beakers stuck out of his pocket.

Charles slammed shut the box and graced his brother with a contemptuous smile. "So you want to tell me all about your nice little goodwill visit to the village, do you? Spare yourself the trouble. My decision stands: either the brown monkeys disappear of their own accord, or I'll make them disappear."

He pulled out from his inside pocket a key, always kept on a long chain attached to his clothing, and locked the box. The sodden tent was letting in the recent rain, and a drop plinked down noisily on the box's iron lid.

"God, how I loathe this weather," he snarled.

Henry pulled up a stool next to his brother's chair. "My tent leaks, too. I reckon a good slug of this will help."

"If you think a drop of whisky is going to save your precious natives, you are very much mistaken," retorted Charles. "Your negotiations have failed, haven't they?"

Henry feigned a meaningful sigh. He moved aside a couple of rolled-up building plans, set out the flask and tin beakers on the desk, and poured two generous measures. Then he toasted his brother and put his own beaker to his lips. But he only pretended to drink.

"Run out of opium, have you, so you'll settle for alcohol?" asked Charles before taking a huge gulp.

Henry ignored the remark and talked instead about his negotiations. His report was a complete invention from start to finish, but he masterfully embellished his supposed failure in order to keep his brother amused. And Charles listened with growing schadenfreude, slapping his thigh with laughter. He emptied his beaker and wiped his sleeve across his mouth.

"It makes the philanthropic heart bleed, eh, when you think how those brown monkeys didn't want your well-meaning advice?"

Henry refilled his brother's beaker. "Wouldn't it have saved us a lot of trouble, though, if you'd stuck to the original route?"

Charles's mood changed. "What right have you got to question my decisions? You have no idea what it means, building a road in this country!"

"For God's sake, I'm thinking of the strain on your health. Your last attack wasn't so long ago."

Charles looked at him with suspicion. "Wouldn't you rather see this bloody disease finish me off?"

Henry noted with satisfaction that his brother's speech was already a bit slurred. "I'd never wish that on you. And I'm speaking both as a brother and a doctor." He raised his beaker again. "To the best engineer in the British army!"

Suitably flattered, Charles clinked beakers. He was already so tipsy that a good part of the whisky sloshed over the edge. He knocked back the remainder. "Then let it be said, Henry, old boy—when I want something—I get it!" He banged his right fist clumsily on the desk. "I'll get the road, and the other thing, I'll get it all."

"Sorry?" asked Henry. "What do you mean?"

Charles was swaying in his seat. He waved one of his hands around to no effect. "Everything. You know, don't you? When I want something—" His eyes closed. His body slumped forward. With a deep sigh, he stretched his arms across the desk, settled his head on the iron box, and fell fast asleep.

Henry put his beaker on the desk, waited for a minute or two, and then prodded Charles in the side. The sleeping man grumbled softly but did not wake. Whisky and laudanum really were a stunning combination.

Henry stared at the iron box. Not only was it locked, but it now served as his brother's pillow.

He gently lifted Charles's head, moved the box aside with his other hand, then lowered his brother's head onto the desk. The only reaction was loud snoring, even when Henry felt inside Charles's jacket for the key. Fortunately, the chain was easily long enough. With the greatest of care, he opened the box. As well as various documents and letters, it contained several bundles of bank notes, bags of coins, and a munitions pouch full of bullets. The document Henry wanted was underneath a little leather pouch. Henry pushed the pouch aside, took out the document, and unfolded it. It was covered in closely written text and adorned with the official seal of the governor. He brought it close to the oil lamp on the desk and started to read.

"Damn it," he muttered after only a few sentences. "What's all this about?"

The document was, as Mahinda had suspected, not an order for military action. Perhaps the governor had refused to give one. Perhaps Charles hadn't even raised the matter. The text of the document suggested the latter. It was a title deed for a considerable piece of land awarded to Charles by Paget. And at a laughably low price, at that. If Charles finished the new road before the contractually agreed date, Paget would refund his purchase price, giving him the land for free.

Now Henry understood why Charles was in such a rush to obliterate Mapitigama and its people. To get the land for effectively nothing, he would have to meet a tight schedule. He could afford no delays. To be on the safe side, Henry searched the lockbox for any order from the governor but found none.

As he skimmed over the title deed again, he wondered why Charles had never mentioned this land acquisition. After all, it was not unusual for the Crown to reward its subjects with land in the colonies. Henry looked for the land's parcel number, first on the deed and then on the site drawings he had pushed aside earlier. He found the plot and realized it was quite nearby, on the abandoned stretch of road that Charles had claimed could not be excavated.

Still at a loss, Henry placed the deed back in the box. Just as he went to close the lid, he noticed the little leather pouch. He picked it up, curious now, and felt the small, sharp-edged object inside. He hesitated, undid the lacing, and tipped the contents into his hand. He gasped.

"Henry! How lovely to see you here!"

Phera had just finished checking Siddhi's wound, now fully closed and nicely scabbed over. Gathering up her sari, she ran toward him. Her long hair streamed behind her as if competing with the lightly billowing veil of her sari, and he looked appreciatively at her figure, usually hidden under men's clothing. Full of smiles, he enveloped her in his arms.

"You look wonderful dressed like that."

She gave him a mischievous look. "I put it on for you. It's not as practical as pants, but I knew you were coming and I wanted to please you."

"How on earth did you know I was coming?"

"I sent out a powerful message of desire to entice you here!"

He bent and kissed her. "I just can't resist you." He kissed her again. Before he could kiss her a third time, Siddhi brushed his face with her trunk.

"Whoa there!" Henry gently shook her off. "Are you jealous, or did you smell the treat I've brought you?" He took from his pocket the mango he had picked on the way and held it out to Siddhi. The elephant skillfully wrapped her trunk around the fruit and placed it in her mouth.

Phera stroked the huge animal's trunk. "Siddhi and I were born on the same day, you know, her in the king's stable and me in my father's house on the palace grounds."

"Your father held high office at the court of Vikrama Rajasinha, is that right?"

Phera nodded proudly. "My family served the kings of Kanda Uda Pas Rata for generations. They were Gajanayake Nilame, which means they oversaw the royal elephant stables. After you British drove out our king, my father and Eranga gave the elephants their freedom."

"Wait, that was your father and Eranga?"

Phera nodded again. "He was my father's senior mahout."

Henry worked to piece the story together. "The king's elephants were supposed to be shipped to Europe. I was assigned the job of checking if they were fit for travel. But before they could be sent away, they vanished without a trace."

Phera looked at him with new eyes. "It was you, then!"

"What do you mean?"

"Now I know where we first met!" she exclaimed. "It was outside the elephant stable. You told the guards to let me inside."

Henry's eyes widened. "You were the boy wanting to get to his elephant? And Eranga was teaching you?" He hesitated. "So you'd presented yourself as the son of the Gajanayake Nilame, not his daughter."

She nodded and snuggled against him. "For the first twelve years of my life, I was my father's son and heir. He only had daughters. My parents decided to make me the male heir so that my father could pass on his office. Nobody outside the family knew, not even the king. After you British drove out Sri Vikrama Rajasinha, the office of Gajanayake Nilame no longer existed, and I didn't have to be a boy anymore."

"What an extraordinary life!" Henry put his arm around Phera. "Was being a boy difficult?"

"No, actually it wasn't, because I had all sorts of freedom my sisters didn't." She raised her head and looked deep into his eyes. "But now that I know you, I'm so glad I don't have to be either a boy or a man any longer. I only disguise myself as a man now if it's going to be to my advantage."

Henry thought of the torment his feelings for Phera had stirred up inside him. He bent and kissed the parting of her sleek, dark hair. "I'm so glad I found out what an enchanting young woman you are." He looked over at the waterfall where she had bathed naked, and desire filled him all over again.

"Would you like to have been under the waterfall with me yesterday?" teased Phera.

He laughed, embarrassed. "I can't deny it. Although it was very difficult, I wanted to be discreet."

Phera thought this over. Then she took him by the hand and led him to the pool. When they reached the edge, her right hand reached across to her left shoulder and stripped off her sari. Instead of wearing the traditional blouse underneath, she had wound only the full length of the sari around her body. As the bright-yellow cloth fluttered down around her feet, she stood naked before Henry. She turned to him, laughing.

"What are you waiting for, Henry Odell?"

With one bound, she was in the pool.

He was mesmerized as she glided through the clear water. She surfaced at the waterfall and tossed back her long hair, making drops of water cascade around her like a silver veil. He was still standing at the edge, enraptured by her beauty and easy nudity, hardly believing his good fortune that she returned his feelings.

He thought about her age, only nineteen, making her eight years his junior. She was probably a virgin. The knowledge that she trusted him, even though her family had suffered so much at the hands of his own brother, made him feel at once admiring and tender toward this young woman.

"Henry Odell!" she called out. "How long do you want to go on being so discreet?"

Stripping off his clothes, he dove headfirst into the pool. He broke the surface near the plateau of rock to find her there, sitting on its smooth face. With one hand, she splashed water in Henry's face, then squealed with delight at her own playfulness. He ran his hands over her thighs, gently pushing them apart as he stood in front of her. Then he held her head to kiss her, tentatively at first, then with growing passion as he tasted the sweetness of her mouth. The waterfall coursed down on them, pouring over their heads and shoulders, over Phera's breasts and Henry's back.

He stroked back her hair and whispered, "I feel as if I'm in paradise."

"What's 'paradise'?" She was curious to find out.

He kissed the droplets away from her neck. "It's a place like this, a wonderful place, where the first two people created by my god experienced perfect happiness."

"Then let's experience that same perfect happiness, too." She took hold of his sex and guided Henry inside her. He felt her wince as he slid himself into her warm, wet body. Swiftly, he put his arms around her, drew her close, and looked into her eyes.

"Is this all right?" he asked softly. "Do you want me to carry on?"

She nodded. "Come closer. I want to feel you even more."

He began gently to rock back and forth inside. She wrapped her legs around his hips and moved in time with him, experiencing excitement and pleasure more delicious and enchanting than anything she had ever known. She wanted this perfection to last forever. They moved in harmony, letting their mutual passion lift them higher and higher until they climaxed and collapsed together in perfect peace.

◆ ◆ ◆

A little later they lay together on the grass, letting their bodies dry in the warmth of the sun and watching Siddhi spray herself in the shallows. The birds sang and the frogs croaked. Henry caressed Phera's body, happy at her obvious enjoyment as she luxuriated in his touch. How he wished this could last forever. But something more than passion had brought him here today. He took her hand and waited until she turned to look at him.

"There's something I have to tell you. It concerns everyone in Mapitigama."

"What is it?" she asked, immediately worried.

He stood, pulling her up with him. "Let's go into the village and talk with Mahinda and your mother."

In half an hour they were sitting with Anshu on the bench outside her hut, together with Samitha and the monk. Before they had set off, Phera had tied up her hair and put on her men's clothing.

Henry opened the meeting. "What Mahinda suspected has been confirmed. There is no order for military action against the village."

"That is good news," said the monk.

"Not necessarily," Samitha remarked and looked at Henry. "If your brother wants to attack us, he will, order or no order."

"You're right. I'm afraid my brother decided a long time ago to drive you out by any means necessary."

"So," asked Anshu, "if the paper isn't a military order, what is it?"

"It's a title deed for a plot of land. If Charles manages to have the road to Colombo ready within five years, the governor will gift him the land."

"He's trying to drive us out so he can steal the land," commented Samitha. "Just like the British nation steals our kingdom."

Mahinda was watching Henry, solemnity in his eyes. "At the moment your brother is short of workers, which delays progress and puts his plan at risk. But that won't stop him having his soldiers clear the village."

Henry gave a dejected nod of the head. "That's why I am here. To warn you."

"Your warning won't save us," Samitha said bitterly. "Where is this plot of land that's to be your brother's?"

"Kadugannawa Pass," replied Henry. "It's the stretch of road my brother claimed was impossible to work on."

"And now he wants it for himself?" Phera asked. "What can that possibly mean?"

"Nothing good. That monster has never done anything good." Samitha's voice was full of loathing.

"I'm asking myself the same thing," said Henry. "The land's no good for crops because the topsoil was removed during the excavation. So there must be some other reason for him wanting the land."

"Maybe he doesn't want it at all, but the governor offered and he had to accept?" suggested Anshu.

Henry shook his head. "I don't think so. He wouldn't make a secret out of that. No, I'm convinced this is why he went to Colombo— because he wanted this piece of land."

"Ask him, Henry," Mahinda advised. "And ask him why he lied about the order."

"Because he wants to frighten us," said Anshu.

"Because he enjoys the suffering of others." Samitha sounded wretched.

Anshu turned to her eldest daughter and stroked her cheek, as if Samitha were still her baby girl. When Henry saw this gesture, he was reminded yet again of the brutality his brother had shown this family and swore to keep them safe from any further cruelty.

"You must write to your governor." Anshu's voice broke into his thoughts. "If he really wants to live in peace with us, he'll listen to you." Henry looked doubtful. "Paget doesn't want trouble, it's true. But what's even more important to him is that the road is ready as soon as possible. I doubt whether he'd bother with the concerns of a tiny village. No, we must help ourselves by gathering as much information as we can. This brings me to the second reason for my visit today."

Reaching inside his jacket, he took out a handkerchief and, unfolding it, revealed a small, round stone, which he held up for the others to see. He turned it this way and that, and the others gasped as light refracted on the polished surface and the stone glowed deep blue.

"I found this on Eranga's body."

Phera was confused. The stone bore no resemblance to the insignificant fragment they'd found on the dead mahout.

Henry carried on. "I had it examined and polished in Colombo. It's a sapphire. Yesterday I found a very similar one in my brother's tent. It's even bigger and more beautiful than this one, and definitely worth a lot of money. I suspect a connection between the two stones. They're like two pieces in a jigsaw puzzle."

"What's a 'jigsaw puzzle'?" Phera asked.

"It's an English game where you put together small pieces to make a big picture," Mahinda explained.

"So if we find out more about the two sapphires, that'll help us see the whole thing."

"That's it," said Henry. "So now we have to find the missing pieces." Henry gave her an affectionate look. Phera returned it with a gentle smile.

Anshu watched this exchange and pursed her lips. The Englishman was clearly not fooled by Phera's masculine clothes. What's more, the pair seemed to be harboring some special feeling.

Anshu was not pleased. Of course, she wanted her children to fall in love and lead happy lives, particularly after experiencing so much horror. But could Phera truly find happiness with the brother of a mass murderer?

Meanwhile, the little sapphire was being passed from hand to hand.

"Does anyone know anything about this stone?" asked Henry. "Did Eranga ever say anything about it, or about whether there are mines around here?"

But the others only shook their heads, bewildered.

"This explains Eranga's death!" declared Phera. "He was murdered because of the sapphire."

"By your brother!" added Samitha, looking straight at Henry.

Henry flushed with shame. "If my brother is guilty of a crime, then he should be punished for it."

But this was not well received by Samitha. "Do you really mean that?" she asked angrily. "So your brother's been punished for his crimes against our people, has he? It's been quite the opposite! He is rewarded for his atrocities, while we have to live every day of our lives with the memory of what he did!" She sobbed in frustration.

Her mother placed a soothing hand on her arm. "Don't look back at your suffering. It's behind you now. Only look ahead."

It almost broke Henry's heart to see their distress, and he made a decision there and then. He would do whatever it took to help Anshu, Samitha, Phera, and Thambo, as well as every other resident of Mapitigama, even if it meant risking his own life.

"I'll have a look at my brother's plot of land," he said. "And by God, I hope I find something to help us forward." He wrapped the sapphire in the handkerchief again and placed the little bundle in his inside pocket.

A solemn look on her face, Phera got to her feet. "I'll come with you. To rely on your English god is not enough."

◆ ◆ ◆

"Major?" The orderly was shaking Charles by the shoulder. "Would you please wake up now, sir? I've brought you some tea."

Charles grunted and tried to shrug off the young man's hand. "What time's it?" He opened his eyes, blinked a few times, and then quickly shut them against the harsh sun shining through the tarpaulin doorway. His head was pounding. His mouth was parched.

"It's after midday, Major."

"What?" He sat up in shock. The sudden movement made him dizzy. He supported himself for a moment, his elbows on the desk. "Why are you only waking me now?"

"I just couldn't wake you any earlier, Major, whatever I did. If you've worked all night, it's no wonder you fell asleep at your desk."

Charles stared at him in confusion. He couldn't remember anything about the previous night, but he was pretty sure he hadn't been working. And yet he had not gone to bed. For some reason, he had fallen asleep at his desk, still fully dressed, his head next to his lockbox.

When he tried to remember why, he felt only a stabbing pain in his head and moaned in discomfort. But at least a flicker of the previous evening came back to him—Henry had visited.

The orderly placed a steaming cup of tea on the desk, in front of Charles. "I thought I'd let you sleep, Major. Anyhow, there isn't much going on at the construction site without the coolies. Last night seven more disappeared. Now we've got—"

With an impatient gesture, Charles cut him off. "Where's my brother?"

"Not here, Major. Saw him this morning when I was feeding your horse. He was just leaving camp."

Charles was uneasy. "He hasn't come back?"

"No, Major. I don't think so."

Charles's stomach turned. Somehow, he had lost control over his foolish younger brother. He waved away the orderly. "Leave me alone now."

"Yes, sir! Do you need anything further?"

"No. Thank you."

The moment the lad had left, Charles pulled the key out of his pocket and opened the box. The title deed and the leather pouch were still exactly as he had left them the previous evening. At least he thought so.

He picked up the cup, drank a mouthful of tea, and thought about his visit to the governor. Of course, he had never troubled Paget about a deployment against the handful of natives. His visit had been to pursue another objective, and he had been successful. Paget had awarded him precisely the plot he wanted. Now he just had to build the road. But he needed workers for that, and the bastards had taken off.

Perhaps the only option now was to ask the governor for fresh workers from India, but he did not know how he was supposed to explain to Paget that his had gotten away. In frustration, he slammed his hand on the desk and let the pain sharpen his mind. He decided to start with the simplest job and clear Mapitigama. That way, the village would be done and dusted by the time the construction work got going. What a nuisance that Henry had taken sides with the natives. Henry . . .

Henry had brought whisky with him, Charles recalled. They'd had a drink together, and it had been fun. But what had they discussed? He racked his brains. For him and his brother to have any fun together was unusual. As it was for his brother to visit him of his own accord.

Charles, his head in his hands, struggled to remember more, but he couldn't focus with such a preposterous hangover. Had they really drunk so much last night? And if so, how could Henry possibly have held his liquor so well, getting up early like that, going off into the jungle, while Charles was barely able to get out of his chair?

When he really thought about it, this hangover did not actually feel like the result of several glasses of whisky. He felt strangely befuddled, as if numbed. He had only ever felt like this when his brother had pre-scribed him laudanum for the malaria attacks.

He ran his index finger first over the leather pouch with the sap-phire, then over the document that made him owner of a handsome piece of land by the Kadugannawa Pass. His gnawing doubt grew to serious suspicion.

He locked the box and hid it in his locker, under a pile of shirts. Then Charles finished his tea and forced himself to hold up his throbbing head. It was high time he found out what his brother was up to.

"Is this where the road was meant to go?"

Phera was standing next to Henry on the abandoned section. At its upper end, it was easy to see the work that had gone on. Soil had been shifted and leveled off. Posts marked both sides of the road. These were missing from the middle section, and small rocks still protruded there. There was a mass of holes, too, where larger boulders had been dug out and removed. At the lower end, Phera saw a broad, open strip. Felled trees, some still with roots bared, lay piled up at its edge. But this section was already home to tender green shoots as the primeval forest closed the wounds so crudely opened by man.

"Wherever you British go, you leave the place like a battleground," Phera said. "What's that huge crater there for?"

Henry looked where she was pointing. "There was an especially large boulder there. It was blasted."

They looked together at the almost-circular pit that could have comfortably accommodated Siddhi and another elephant besides. Rubble was littered all around. The huge boulder still loomed above the edge of the crater.

"The hole should have been filled in with soil," Henry explained. "But Charles called a halt to the work and then changed the course of the road."

"I'd love to see this pit close-up," said Phera.

They walked to the crater edge and peered down. The hole was bigger than Henry remembered. Rainfall had eroded its edges, and it had filled up a good two-thirds of the way with water. Flies and dragonflies danced on its smooth, silvery surface.

Phera kicked bits of earth into the water. "What the hell does your brother want with this land? Does he want to live here?"

"Oh no," said Henry. "Charles has no interest in settling here. He hates Ceylon and would get back to England at the first opportunity."

"Yet this land is why he diverted the road and wants to destroy our village," Phera said, grim-faced.

"He's hiding something, but could it really be what we imagine?" asked Henry, prodding the boulder with his boot. He startled a lizard from its sunny position on the warm stone, and it flashed from sight.

Phera watched the little reptile go. "Was this boulder supposed to be taken out of the crater?"

Henry shrugged. "I imagine so."

She took hold of the rope that ran the length of the boulder. Her hand slid along it to the boulder's front edge, where it joined two cords. Phera picked them up and examined them hard.

"These cords were probably used as a harness for an elephant to pull the boulder. But they were cut before the elephant finished the job." She let go of the cords and turned to Henry. "What if that elephant was Siddhi? For her to move the boulder, Eranga had to run a rope under the whole rock. That's why he climbed down into the crater. I bet that's when he found the sapphire, and your brother was spying on him."

"Or it could have been the reverse. Maybe Eranga was watching Charles when he found the sapphire. As a road engineer, he knows how to spot a precious stone even in its unprocessed state. But I was at the field hospital when they were working out here. I don't actually know whether it was Eranga and Siddhi trying to heave the boulder out."

"If your brother stumbled on a sapphire deposit, that would be reason enough for him to steal this land," declared Phera. "And it would certainly explain killing Eranga and covering it up. Do you remember the day when I collected Eranga's body from the construction site? Siddhi went berserk when she saw your brother."

Henry did not reply. He felt for Eranga's sapphire inside his jacket and thought about the larger one he had seen in Charles's lockbox. Henry swallowed hard. Despair stirred somewhere deep inside him, and a soft voice whispered, *Just a little opium, and all your worries will float away.*

He reached out for Phera and was so relieved when he felt her fingers entwine with his. "What are you going to do?" she asked him, her voice soft and gentle.

He sighed. "I'll find Charles and confront him with our suspicions."

"But isn't that dangerous?"

"I'll be careful," promised Henry.

He knew better, but some part of him still hoped his once-loved big brother had an innocent explanation for the sapphire and the land he had been so secretive about.

Phera squeezed his hand. "And I'll ask around amongst the men who were working on the road here. Maybe someone saw Eranga and Siddhi at the crater."

"Good idea," said Henry. "Let's meet again at sunset, by the waterfall, and see what we've both found out."

Hand in hand, they crossed the abandoned stretch of road, went into the forest, and turned again onto the narrow path they had come by.

Phera stopped for a moment and gently stroked Henry's chest. "You look so sad."

He forced a smile. "I'm all right; don't worry." He took her hands and kissed first her fingertips, then her lips.

Something stirred in the undergrowth. They both gave a start, then laughed as a pair of small green parrots fluttered up, almost brushing against their heads, wings flapping noisily. Then Phera and Henry were back in one another's arms, Phera nestling her body close to his. His hands slid down her back and over her bottom.

"When we've gotten all this behind us, I want us to bathe together under the waterfall as often as we can," Phera whispered.

"So do I," murmured Henry, as he kissed her again.

But just a few yards away, Charles was squatting in the foliage. After rushing to the abandoned section of road, he'd spotted them by the crater and hidden himself in the trees.

While he stood there, wondering whether the two of them had discovered his secret, they came closer—hand in hand. Charles rubbed his eyes and blinked in amazement to see his brother and the elephant boy holding hands. Incredulous, he shook his head. He already knew his brother was an obstinate philanthropist with an ill-fated love for opium. But sexual perversion, well, he had never expected that.

Henry took the young Sinhalese mahout in his arms and kissed him passionately. The mahout put his arms round Henry's neck and cuddled up close.

For heaven's sake, surely he doesn't actually intend to lie with this boy, thought Charles, full of revulsion.

As Henry stroked the mahout's backside, Charles squeezed his eyes shut. But after a few seconds, curiosity got the better of him, and he took a surreptitious look. Henry and the boy were still locked in an embrace. Henry's hands worked their way upward to loosen the mahout's hair. Long, beautifully shiny, it tumbled down the boy's back.

They're actually going to mate!

Just then the boy laughed, a girlish giggle. Now Charles heard Henry saying, "You are the most enchanting woman I've ever met."

Charles nearly let slip a gasp of astonishment, clapping his hand to his mouth in the nick of time. He took a good look at the soft facial features of this young mahout, the graceful neck and narrow shoulders. He scrutinized the curves beneath the loose shirt.

He could have burst out laughing. So the elephant boy was really a woman. An attractive one at that. While his brother had obviously seen through the disguise, he had let himself be taken in and, not to mention, scared off by her ghastly elephant.

He stared at Henry and Phera, who had now finished their long embrace. When he saw the happiness on their faces, he seethed with resentment. His brother and the little slut would regret getting in his way. He would teach them both a lesson they would never forget.

Chapter Fourteen
November 1822

Phera stepped out of the forest and crossed the Mapitigama village square. In its center, as ever, stood the Bodhi tree. Like a bent old man with his walking stick, it leaned heavily on the posts supporting its branches. As the wind stirred its green canopy, it seemed to Phera that the ancient tree was greeting her. She realized how contented she felt to be back here, leaving behind, for a while, the loneliness of her forest hideout.

She saw her mother come out of her hut on the other side of the square. Anshu was resting a basket on her hip and began scattering its contents. Phera guessed this to be the chopped shells of cashews, their subtle aroma helping to keep mosquitoes away. Thambo came out of the hut next. He was clutching a tiny broom made of a palm frond and eagerly helped spread the shells. It was heartwarming for Phera to watch the pair of them. Just then Thambo spotted his aunt. He squealed with glee, threw down his broom, and rushed over to her. Anshu waved.

"Any news?" she asked once Phera had twirled Thambo around in fun.

Phera gave a solemn nod. "We're pretty sure Eranga's death is related to a sapphire vein in the land Odell is trying to claim, but we have no hard evidence. I'm here to ask our men if they noticed anything when they were working on that part of the road."

Anshu set down her basket. "I'll come with you to the men's hideout. As widan, I would like to hear what they say." She bent toward little Thambo. "I'll be back very soon. Meanwhile, you can spread the shells nicely around our hut."

The two women crossed the spice-tree plantation and passed rice fields where the tiny emerald-green plants were growing. Children sat high on the raised points around the edges of the fields, doing their usual job of drumming and shouting to stop elephants from nibbling the young plants. Behind these lookout points was a visible path, only the breadth of a human foot, that led mother and daughter into the jungle.

Anshu walked behind, looking at her daughter's back. The tender looks she had seen between Henry and her daughter were troubling. If Phera gave her heart to someone, they should be Sinhalese from a good family and their own caste—not a Briton whose brother was a vile murderer.

"You and the British doctor," she began. "What's between you two?"

Phera brushed aside a branch hanging across their path. "I don't know how to answer that, Mother," she replied indignantly. But then added, "Between us is something special. A deep feeling."

"Your father would not approve."

Phera marched on, exasperation in her voice. "How can you know? We can't exactly ask him. And anyway, Henry was the only Briton who tried to prevent the massacre in Uva."

"A massacre carried out by his brother!"

Phera stopped so abruptly that Anshu bumped into her. "Do you think I don't know that?"

"I know he's a good man," Anshu tried again, "but you shouldn't be so close."

Phera gave no reply, but pride and despair were written all over her face. It broke Anshu's heart to know that what she was going to say next would hurt Phera. And yet as mother, head of the family, and widan of Mapitigama, she could not remain silent.

"His brother will always stand between you. Between you and your family, between you and your people. I cannot accept Henry Odell and his brother into our family."

When she saw the pain in Phera's eyes, she almost regretted what she had said. She went to embrace her daughter, but Phera pulled away.

"That monster has long been part of our family," she reminded her mother. "Or have you forgotten what he did to Samitha?"

Anshu went pale. She shook her head but didn't say a word.

"Henry Odell is doing everything possible to help us and the people of Mapitigama," said Phera. "He is taking a stand against his brother, against his own flesh and blood. That terrible man will not come between us."

Without waiting for her mother's reply, she hurried on. The remaining ground was covered in oppressive silence.

The men's hideout was on the bank of a stream. From a distance, it was almost impossible to make it out, so well did its little huts of palm leaves and branches blend into the forest. Some men were dozing in the open, others washing their clothes in the stream. A few of them had gathered palm fronds to patch their roofs. When they saw Anshu and Phera, they swiftly gathered round their widan and her daughter.

Phera described her visit to the abandoned stretch of road. Then she said, "We believe that Eranga found a sapphire in the blast hole.

And that he died because of it." She looked around the whole group. "After the explosion, did any of you see Eranga and Siddhi at the hole?"

Two of the men looked at one another and nodded.

"We saw them," said one. "Siddhi was supposed to drag the boulder out of the crater. We used poles to raise it a bit so Eranga could run a cord underneath. When we were ready and he'd harnessed Siddhi, along came Major Odell. He jumped inside the crater and stayed down there a while. When he came up again, he ordered all construction work to stop."

At the same moment, Henry was stepping inside Charles's tent. He did not greet his brother but came straight to the point. "There is no order for military action against Mapitigama. Why did you lie?"

Charles rolled up the site plan spread before him on the desk and turned. "Oh, but surely you found out everything you wanted during your visit last night, didn't you? Perhaps you should offer me another whisky with laudanum."

Henry was surprised he'd been found out, but he did not let it show. "I still have plenty of questions," he replied coldly. "Let's start with the supposed order."

Charles adopted his most scornful expression. "Merely a trick. I wanted to scare the brown monkeys a bit to make them leave of their own accord."

Henry did not believe this, but he did not pursue it, posing instead the most important question. "What do you want the land for, and why did you keep it a secret?"

Charles did not flinch. "As you well know, I suffer from malaria and so will soon have to take my leave of the military life. I have sought this land for my own future. The climate in the uplands is supposed to be magnificent for the cultivation of coffee plants. And as you certainly already know, I'm getting the land at a good price, possibly even for nothing. I haven't spoken of it for fear of stirring up envy."

"Don't be ridiculous!" Henry snapped. "You're not going to grow coffee. On this land, you think you've found a sapphire vein. I know you've got one gem already. I don't suppose Paget knows what's under the soil of your future coffee plantation?"

Charles leaned back in his chair, looking icily at Henry. "These are very interesting things that you think you've found out. Pray continue, little brother."

Henry was ready to take Eranga's sapphire from his pocket and wave it under Charles's nose as evidence. But he thought better of it. Instead, he said, "I believe that Eranga, the dead mahout, had found you out." What he actually wanted to ask was, *Did you kill him?* But he could not say it. He was too fearful of the answer.

A vein pulsed hard at Charles's left temple, but his face remained unmoved. "I think there have been a few misunderstandings here," he said with a studied nonchalance. "Let me make a suggestion. We'll go over to the plot together. Then I can show you what I'm planning."

He stood up and left the tent. After some hesitation, Henry followed.

The brothers walked in silence through the forest. Only when they had reached the abandoned section of road did Henry speak up. "What do you intend to show me here?"

Charles only gave a secretive smile and headed for the crater.

"What's this about?" asked Henry again, unnerved. "What's here that you couldn't have told me about back at the camp?"

Charles stood at his side, very close. "At the bottom of this hole is a layer of gravel and sediment in which I did indeed find a sapphire. You saw it in my box." He threw Henry a sidelong glance. "Where there's one stone, there're probably others. I stand a good chance of sitting on a rich deposit."

Henry summoned his courage. "And you'd walk over dead bodies for that, wouldn't you? Or, to be more precise, over the former widan of Mapitigama."

"Please," replied Charles, his voice full of disdain. "Aren't you making too much fuss about a native's life?"

"So you admit you killed Eranga?"

Charles gave a dismissive shrug. "The fellow spied on me and stuck his nose into things that weren't any of his business. And he's not the only one."

Charles raised his arm and, before Henry realized what was happening, punched him hard in the temple. Henry stumbled and collapsed. Charles kicked his boot in his unconscious brother's side, then drew his knife and used it to cut the two cords, once part of Siddhi's harness, from the rope that still ran the length of the boulder. He knelt down and used one of the cords to tie Henry's hands behind his back. Then he rolled his brother over the crater's edge. When Henry's body hit the water with a loud splash, Charles looked around, but the jungle was quiet. He and his brother were alone here. He looked at Henry, facedown in the water and slowly sinking.

"I ought to let you drown, little brother," he said. "But where's the fun if I make it too quick?"

He leapt down into the hole, grabbed Henry by the collar, and fished him out of the water. "Wakey, wakey!" He shook his brother roughly, and it was only after a few punches that Henry came around, groaning as he did.

"Let me go! What's happening?" He tried to get free and stand up fully, but Charles hit him again, so hard that Henry lost his balance and toppled backward.

"I do enjoy seeing you struggle!" Charles laughed at his brother, now thrashing around as he attempted to stay on his feet.

"Are you planning to kill me, like Eranga?" Henry cried, once he had managed to stand again. "Do you really think some stupid stones are going to make you happy?"

"I don't just think it. I know it!" Charles took out his handkerchief and gagged Henry with it. Henry fought, but the ties bound him too tight.

When Charles was ready, he pulled his defenseless brother over to the boulder and forced him up against it. Then he took the second cord, wound one end around Henry's wrist, and secured the other to the rope that ran around the boulder.

"That'll stop you sniffing around after me," he said with a sickly sweet smile.

Desperate groans and grunts came through Henry's gag. Charles had secured him to the boulder so tightly that he had to keep his knees bent instead of standing. He was up to his neck in water. Swarms of flies arrived and greedily settled on his face. He shook his head furiously, but this did nothing to deter the bloodthirsty creatures.

Charles was having a fine time of it. "Vikrama Rajasinha made his opponents sit on young bamboo plants, then took pleasure in watching the shoots grow through their bodies. But it's much better to be eaten by mosquitoes, don't you think? Or maybe you'll drown first, just like a rat. I think we're in for rain." He gave an exaggerated bow. "Farewell, little brother, it's been an honor!" With this, he spun and clambered out of the crater. Once on solid ground, he turned for a final look at Henry, who stared fixedly up at him as he kept trying to pull himself free.

"By pure chance I have come across a colossal treasure. I'm not letting anyone ruin that for me," said Charles. "I've given the best years of my life and my health for this wretched country. This here"—he gestured grandly to the land—"is my reward." He grinned broadly. "Early tomorrow morning, little brother, I'm going to teach the brown monkeys in that damned rebel village a real lesson. But before that I'll be teaching your Sinhalese whore what a real man is."

"Where on earth is Henry? He should have been here ages ago," whispered Phera to Siddhi.

She stood on the edge of the clearing and peered anxiously into the jungle. The sun had already dipped behind the treetops, and darkness was falling rapidly. A monsoon rain shower threatened. Leaden clouds massed, in the distance thunder rumbled, and the wind rushed through the canopies of the trees. Siddhi whipped her tail nervously and stamped her front feet. Sensing how uneasy her friend was, she did not leave Phera's side.

There were several flashes of lightning, thunder crashing right behind. Phera's heart raced, but she was not afraid of the storm. She was afraid for Henry. She squinted harder, but the light was too dim. Siddhi trumpeted a warning and tried to use her trunk to push her friend toward the small shelter. With reluctance, Phera turned to go. She had only just reached her hiding place when the gale let rip.

Sleep did not come to Phera that night. Her hut offered little protection from the rain, anyway, so she crept out to find Siddhi, waiting close by. She crouched between the elephant's front legs and stared into the darkness. The storm was deafening. It was so dark, she could not see her hand in front of her face. When lightning flickered across the heavens, the earth momentarily blazed an eerie, sulfurous yellow. She caught glimpses of the trees dancing wildly like black ghosts at play.

"I know he won't come while the weather's like this," said Phera, leaning against Siddhi's leg. "I hope so much that he's safe somewhere." She let out an anxious sigh.

The elephant reached down with her trunk, gently seeking out the girl's hand and squeezing her fingers reassuringly.

More lightning, and in the flash, someone seemed to dart across the clearing.

"Henry!" shouted Phera, against a clap of thunder. But she was mistaken. It was not her beloved, only the slender trunk of a young tree bent by the wind.

Disheartened, she dropped her head against Siddhi's leg again. "If only he hadn't gone to find his brother this afternoon," she lamented. "What if that monster has done something to him? I've only just found Henry. I can't lose him now."

Henry knew he was going to die that night. The water level now reached his lower lip. And still the rain poured down.

He had already been stuck in this crater for what felt like an eternity. Initially, he had hoped Charles would return to set him free, having satisfied his cruelty. But this hope was fading by the minute. His own brother, out of pure greed and malice, was determined to let him perish.

Cautiously, he shifted his weight. An agonizing pain shot through his muscles. His cry of pain was muffled by the gag. With his legs forcibly bent, he had endured agonizing cramps for hours now and knew he had to move them a little to keep the blood circulating.

For a long time, he had doggedly tried to break free, pushing grimly against his bonds. But the palm-fiber cord that Charles had used to tie his hands had swollen in the water, making the binding even tighter. He had eventually given up, exhausted by the obvious pointlessness of his efforts.

Now that he had resigned himself to being dead before the sun rose, he felt a tremendous sense of calm. As an army doctor, he had witnessed the deaths of so many colleagues that he had no fear of the end. He was ready to meet his maker.

His one worry was Phera. He knew she'd been waiting for him since sunset. Through the dark night, his heart went out to her. He pictured his love flowing from his heart to hers so that she could always remember their brief but glorious happiness together.

He had lost all sense of time but guessed it was not long until morning. The water now covered his mouth, and he could breathe only through his nose. Soon he felt the first tickles at his nostrils.

He bent his head back as far as he could manage. The water surrounded his face like a perfect circle.

Is drowning torture? he wondered. Death would not be quick. But even this would pass, and eternity was waiting.

Rain fell on his face. The water level in the crater rose higher and higher. Then it covered his face and eyes, flowed into his nose, and seeped through the gag in his mouth. His lungs ached and felt as though they would burst. In one last desperate attempt, he pushed against his bonds. In vain.

He had journeyed here from England over many months and thousands of miles, had lived through his ship being becalmed one day and storm tossed the next, only to die now, in the jungle of Ceylon, in a water-filled hole as deep as a man is tall. He found it almost comical.

Toward sunrise the storm moved on. When the first light appeared in the east, Phera climbed onto Siddhi's back and rode to the construction site. Before reaching the huts assigned to the few remaining workers, she told her elephant to halt.

"Wait here," she whispered and vanished into the undergrowth.

Soon she was at the first of the huts. She crept in, reached out her hand to the man still sleeping inside, and shook him awake. With a shriek of alarm, he sat bolt upright on his mat.

"Quiet!" Phera grabbed his arm. "Tell me where the doctor is."

In the darkness, she heard the terrified man's breathing and whispered, "Don't be scared; I'm from Mapitigama. Just tell me where Dr. Odell is. Quickly!"

"Yesterday afternoon the doctor and the major went off toward the stretch of road we abandoned," the man whispered back. "But in the evening the major came back on his own."

"Thank you," he heard a soft voice say in the darkness. Then he was alone again.

The horizon was streaked with silvery blue when Charles stepped out from his tent. He yawned hugely as he looked at the patches of mist lifting from the mountain peaks. The weather seemed to be improving. Although thunder and lightning had robbed him of sleep that night, he was not tired. Quite the opposite: he was in thrall to a feverish unease.

He was thinking about his brother, who had doubtless drowned overnight in that stupid hole. He felt a moment of regret but swiftly dismissed it. No point fussing over an inveterate philanthropist like Henry. He would still have to get rid of the body, though. Best throw it in the jungle for the leopards. But first he needed to deal with that nest of vipers in Mapitigama. More than that, he would teach his brother's whore a lesson. He looked forward to that most of all.

"Major Odell!" The corporal hurried toward him. "Do you know where the doctor is?"

"Am I my brother's keeper?" Charles asked with a scowl.

The corporal looked at him with irritation. "One of the engineers has slipped and broken his leg. Looks bad."

"I don't know where Henry's put himself. Get his assistants to take care of the clumsy fool."

This suggestion seemed to bother the corporal even more, but he was as obedient as ever. "Yes, sir!"

Just as he was turning to go, Charles roared, "Attention!"

The corporal stood tall and saluted.

"Call your platoon together. Saddle up and bring a nice little keg of black gunpowder and a fuse. We ride in fifteen minutes."

"Yes, sir!" The corporal saluted again. "What's our commission, sir?"

Charles laughed. "That's a surprise. But I'll tell you this much—we're going to have plenty of fun today."

A gunshot echoed across Mapitigama. Charles pulled up his horse on the village square, his pistol still smoking.

"Out of your huts, you good-for-nothings! I've made up a lovely play, a stupendous play, and I've made sure each and every one of you has a part." He signaled to his corporal. "Fix the gunpowder keg to that tree there." He gestured toward the ancient Bodhi tree. "Then set the fuse! The rest of you, ensure none of the brown monkeys get away."

The corporal eyed the rotting tree and thought to himself that it was likely to come down of its own accord if someone simply removed the props from beneath its boughs. Why waste precious gunpowder? But he obediently dismounted, unfastened the powder keg from behind his saddle, and tied it to the tree. Then he went back to his horse for a leather tube packed with reeds doused in brandy and gunpowder: the fuse. He took out the reeds and placed them on the ground all the way up to the Bodhi tree.

While he was doing this, his soldiers were driving terrified women, children, and old people out into the square. Only the young men were missing, still off in their hideout.

When the redcoats stormed the village, Mahinda was on his way back from his morning ritual at the river. He quickly grasped what was going on and dived into a thicket of oleander before the commander looked his way. Mahinda had never encountered Charles Odell, but he had heard enough to recognize him immediately. He peered anxiously from his hiding place and saw Anshu and Samitha. He did not see little Thambo. The women had probably told the child to stay hidden in the hut.

Mahinda wondered whether he should sneak away and get help from the men of the village. But what could they possibly achieve against the redcoats with their horses and guns? If Odell and his soldiers clapped eyes on the fugitives from the construction site, it would probably mean a bloodbath. The monk desperately racked his brains.

In his anguish, he turned to his wooden prayer beads, whispering a line from the ancient Sutta Pitaka. "*Buddham saranam gacchami.* I take refuge with you, Buddha."

Anshu broke away from the crowd and stood before Odell. "What gives you the right to force your way in here and disturb our peace?" she asked, her voice unwavering.

"It takes more to frighten me than a woman playing at village leader," Charles said mockingly, looking down at her from his horse. "Tell me, woman, why isn't everyone accepting the invitation to my lovely play?"

"We are all present," replied Anshu. Behind her, the villagers moved involuntarily closer together.

"Why are you lying to me?"

Before she could duck, Charles had slammed the barrel of his pistol against the side of her head. She stumbled backward and would have fallen had two women not caught her in time. Cries of horror and rage rang out from the crowd.

"Why are you lying to me?"

Anshu gathered herself, wiping the blood with the back of her hand. "I'm not lying to you."

"You obviously want me to take a different approach. So be it. Corporal! Have every hut searched!"

"You can't do that!" shouted Anshu.

But the soldiers had already dismounted, and ran, their pistols drawn, toward the villagers' tiny homes.

Anshu grabbed the reins of Charles's horse. "Call your men off!"

"What the hell are you doing, woman?" Charles made to strike her again with his gun, and she let go to avoid a second blow.

Mahinda watched the scene in horror. He knew Anshu was trying to protect Thambo. The soldiers hadn't yet reached her hut, so perhaps he could still prevent the worst. When Odell had his back turned, Mahinda gathered up his robes and ran. Within seconds he reached Anshu's hut and slipped inside.

"Thambo," he whispered. "Quick! Come with me!"

In the gloom, he saw something moving under a pile of blankets near the altar. Then Thambo's head emerged. Mahinda rushed to pick the child up. "I'm taking you with me, Thambo. We must hide from the strangers somewhere else. But keep quiet, do you hear me?"

The boy nodded without a word. Mahinda pressed the child's head against his shoulder, ran to the door, and peeped out onto the village square. He spotted Samitha not far from Anshu. She was staring straight at him. Mahinda nodded slightly in her direction, held the child even closer, and ran. He dove back into the oleander bushes and carefully set the child down next to him.

"Mama," the child whispered.

Mahinda quickly placed his hand over Thambo's mouth, urgently shaking his head. Then he took the distressed child in his arms again, and together they looked out at the village square from their hideout.

Odell had reloaded his pistol and was herding the villagers together like a wild dog would its prey. Inside the huts, the redcoats were creating havoc. There was clattering and crashing as sleeping mats flew out of front doors and crockery smashed to smithereens.

Mahinda felt enraged and yet powerless. Ever since his novitiate, he had upheld the teaching that hate breeds hate and murder leads to murder. And yet it took all his strength to control his emotions. On no account could he let rage make him do anything foolish that would further endanger the lives of the villagers and the little boy.

"The huts are empty, sir!" the corporal announced.

"Oh, they are, are they?" Charles's pistol hand trembled with rage. He whipped around and aimed at Anshu. "Where is your daughter?"

Samitha shrank in fear. Since Odell had turned up in Mapitigama three months ago, she had been terrified he would recognize her. Now the moment had come. She stared at the pistol in Odell's hand, certain the nightmare in Uva was about to be repeated.

"I'm here." She stepped forward and stood next to Anshu, ready to endure any torture if only this demon would let her mother live. She felt Anshu squeeze her hand and heard her mother whisper, "Be brave."

Charles jumped off his horse and approached them. "You two! Don't you dare think of plotting against me." He raised his pistol and aimed—first at Anshu, and then he turned the barrel on Samitha.

Anshu let go her daughter's hand and stood in front of the man. "Leave her!"

"I'm sorry?" Charles said with a laugh. "You're giving orders? To me?"

She raised her chin proudly. "Do you still not recognize me, Mr. Englishman? I am Anshu Maha Nuvara, widow of Jeeva Maha Nuvara, who you murdered in Uva."

His eyes narrowed. He looked at her, long and hard. "Yes," he said quietly. "What a happy coincidence." A twisted smile played on his thin lips.

She took a deep breath, pushed aside all her fear, and said, "I'm offering you my life for that of my daughter's."

"No!" cried Samitha.

Anshu turned to her. "Every day I have reproached myself for not being able to protect you that day in Uva. Today I shall protect you."

A muscle twitched in Charles's face. He took a slow walk around the two women, then halted in front of Anshu. "It's not only you

I want. I want your daughters as well. Not just her." He glanced at Samitha. "I want the other one, the one you passed off as a son. Yes, I've found out your sick little secret. Out with it. Where is she?"

"Not here," whispered Anshu.

She should have known that a devil like this would never be satisfied with one life when he could have three. He had killed her husband and one of her children, and violated the second. Now he was demanding her youngest. In her mind, she sent a message to Phera, begging her to stay away.

Anshu's reply enraged Charles. "So you want to play games with me? Go ahead. I'm eager to know how high your stakes will go."

Slowly, he turned to Samitha.

Her beauty never failed to excite him, and her expression of pure loathing mingled with absolute terror sparked his desire. Today he would make up for what he had not been able to do at their last encounter because of his damned malaria.

"We already had such fun in Uva," he remarked, delighting in the way his words stoked the young woman's fear. "Today we'll have even more fun, you and me—and your sister." Smiling broadly, he turned back to Anshu. "I'll ask again, where is your other daughter?"

"She is not here," repeated Anshu.

Charles pretended he was thinking hard. Suddenly, his pistol arm shot forward, and he fired.

Anshu's left hand flew to her right shoulder. Then she collapsed without a sound. Samitha cried out, falling to her knees beside her mother. She grabbed a corner of Anshu's sari and pressed it to the wound. A dark stain formed rapidly on the pale material.

"It's all right," gasped Anshu. "I am only injured."

"I could've killed you, woman," bellowed Charles. "But I'm not going to make it that easy for you." He waved over one of his soldiers and handed him both pistols for reloading. "I'll give you five minutes. If you still refuse my request, I'll shoot you in the other shoulder. Then another five minutes and it's your right arm, then your right leg. Next we'll do the left side. I'm intrigued to see how long you'll hold out." He took back from the soldier his freshly loaded weapons, pushed one in his holster, and kept hold of the other. "And in order to be done with your rebelliousness once and for all, I have sharpened up my conditions. I want not only your daughters but also the men who absconded from my construction site. All of them. For every man who hides from me, one of you will die." With this, he waved his pistol at the villagers. He took his watch from his uniform pocket. "The clock is ticking."

Nobody moved. Neither the stunned villagers standing beneath the Bodhi tree, nor Anshu, nor Samitha. Mahinda crouched in his hideout, frozen. Only now did he fully grasp how powerless they were against this British tyrant. With his superior weapons and the protection of his soldiers, he was unassailable.

Charles strolled back and forth, his hand playing with the pistol. Suddenly, he stopped behind Samitha, still kneeling by her mother, then bent forward and pulled her up by the hair. He made her turn and face him so she was forced to look into his eyes. "Do you know, my beauty, you're the best slut I've ever had?" He laid the pistol barrel against her throat, then slid it slowly over her neck, her breasts, and her belly. Now he was at her abdomen. "Did it please you as much as it pleased me?"

"You're poisonous, more than all the cobras and vipers put together," Samitha snarled. She pursed her mouth, then spat full in his face.

"You filthy bitch!" exclaimed Charles. "You'll pay for that." He reached back and slammed the pistol barrel hard into her groin so she bent double with pain.

Anshu managed to pull herself up. "Have mercy!"

Charles only laughed. "If you want mercy, look for a priest." He wound his arm around Samitha's neck and tightened his grip until she could hardly breathe. "I promised you a play, didn't I?" he shouted to the villagers. "Here comes act one."

All of a sudden, a clod of earth came flying out of the crowd and hit Charles in the arm. "Who did that?" he roared. "I want an answer, or this slut will die before you can count to three."

A number of soldiers had already stepped toward the villagers, weapons ready.

"Mama!" came a little voice, and Thambo clambered out of the bushes. Mahinda tried to pull him back, but he wasn't quick enough. The little boy ran across the village square, hurled himself at the man tormenting his mother, wrapped his little arms around the man's legs, and bit hard. Charles yelped angrily and tried to shake him off, but one arm was still around Samitha's throat. Charles attempted to aim his pistol at the boy, but with Samitha struggling and kicking, he couldn't get a clear shot without risking his own feet.

"Corporal!" shouted Charles. "Shoot the little rat!"

"A child, sir? Must I?"

Charles raised the pistol in his free hand. A shot rang out. The corporal tottered backward and collapsed. His red uniform was pierced at the heart, and blood ran from the wound. He drew only a few, faltering breaths; then his eyes froze over. The fifteen soldiers under his command watched in horror.

Charles threw the empty pistol to one of the soldiers to reload, pulled his second pistol from its holster, and held the barrel firmly against Thambo's head. "Now it's your turn, you little rat."

"No," gasped Samitha. "I beg you. Don't shoot your son."

Chapter Fifteen
November 1822

Seconds after Henry stopped struggling against the water, something plunged into the crater next to him. His eyes shot open, but he could make out nothing. A body pressed against him, a hand pulled down the gag, a mouth pressed on his, and air streamed into his lungs.

His emotions threatened to overwhelm him as he recognized the mouth giving him this gift—Phera's.

He felt her hand at his back, trying to push him up higher. In vain. The rope Charles had used held him down. In silent agony, Henry writhed for more breath, dumbly twisting and turning. Phera understood immediately, and gave him the gift of her own breath once more. Moments before, he had surrendered himself to death, and yet now he was fighting with all his might to remain alive.

She let go and moved away. He felt her pushing at his back while she tried to cut through the rope that bound him to the boulder. He summoned all his strength and bent his upper body forward to help her by putting some tension in the rope. He felt the rope give. He rocked forward, braced himself against the base of the crater, and stood tall. His cramped leg muscles wavered, but he managed to stay upright. Coughing and gasping, he took in as much air and life as he could.

"Henry!" Phera clung to him and covered his face with her kisses. He almost lost his balance again, his hands still tied behind his back.

"You have saved my life," he gasped.

Grinning, she replied, "You're still one up on me." Then she was serious once more. "Thank goodness I have my father's dagger on me. Otherwise I'd never have been able to cut through the rope." She swam behind him and set about freeing his wrists.

When at last the rope dropped into the water behind him, he rubbed at his wrists in relief. The skin was chafed and raw. The powerful tingling caused by his blood starting to flow again was nothing compared to the pain in his legs.

Deep puffing sounds came from above. Henry looked up and saw Siddhi, watching him and Phera as if wondering what strange game they were playing in the water.

"Let's get out of here," said Phera.

But when he tried to climb out of the crater, his legs failed him. Phera took hold of the crater edge with both hands and pulled herself up. Then she instructed Siddhi to let her trunk hang down so that Henry could get a firm grip on it. The elephant hoisted him up. Once he had at last left his watery cell, he was so happy that he hugged first Siddhi, then Phera.

She took hold of his wrists and gently caressed his damaged skin. "He did this to you, didn't he?"

Henry nodded. "I'm such an idiot. I should never have let my brother bring me here."

Her voice shook with loathing. "If you'd died, I'd have hunted him to the ends of the earth, no matter how many lives I'd have had to spend atoning for it."

Henry placed his hands on her shoulders and looked earnestly into her eyes. "Leave Charles to me."

"I don't know if I can."

"Please. Promise me."

She hesitated, then snuggled up against him. "I promise."

He kissed her wet hair. "How did you find me?"

"When you didn't come last night, I knew something was wrong. I went to the building site, and a laborer there told me where you'd gone."

"It's a miracle that you found me in the nick of time," said Henry quietly.

She nodded. "It is. And that's why I'm going to offer my thanks to the Enlightened One as soon as we're back in Mapitigama."

"Heavens!" He had suddenly remembered. "I must get to the village straightaway! Charles has planned something terrible."

Phera looked up in alarm. "We'll go together. It's faster with Siddhi."

"No! I will not allow you to put yourself in danger."

He remembered the words Charles had spat out before he left. His brother's threats were never empty, and more than anything Henry wanted to protect Phera from harm. But there she was, already astride her elephant.

"Do you really believe I'd go into hiding when this devil is threatening my family?" she said, sitting tall and proud on Siddhi's neck. "Climb up. We don't have much time!"

"My what?" Charles lowered his pistol, and Thambo immediately took refuge behind his mother.

"Your son," repeated Samitha. "You know how he was conceived."

Charles looked at the boy. Did he really have a son? Or was she serving up lies to save her child's life?

Though his skin was pretty light for a native, the boy looked more Sinhalese than English. And yet, his features seemed strangely familiar to Charles, almost as if he were looking in a mirror. His heart quickened, and he could almost have reached out to stroke the child's hair.

I'm turning into Henry, he thought in dismay, shaking off the impulse. Maybe he had created a bastard with the Sinhalese whore. Maybe he hadn't. But under no circumstances would he allow stupid sentimentality to thwart his plan of dealing with this rebel village once and for all.

"Your brat is of no interest to me," he informed Samitha, his voice icy. He beckoned over two soldiers.

"Tie him up!" He pointed at the Bodhi tree.

"I'm telling you the truth!" Samitha grabbed him by the arm. "Do with me whatever you please, but spare your son."

Charles brushed her off with impatience. "The woman as well," he ordered. "Tie her to the tree with her bastard son. And prepare a torch."

The soldiers exchanged nervous looks.

"Get on with it!" bellowed Charles. "Or do you want to end up like your corporal?"

One of the soldiers hurried off to fetch a rope from his saddle. The other seized Samitha and Thambo.

"It's a waste, I admit," Charles said. "Glad I've still got your sister to look forward to." He turned to Anshu. "And I know she'll be here any minute."

"Just kill me!" Anshu stumbled toward him. Weakened by pain and blood loss, she sank down on her knees before him.

Charles took out his watch. "The five minutes are up, woman. Where shall I shoot you? Still in your other shoulder? Or would you prefer a leg or an arm?"

"Wherever you want," replied Anshu, her voice breaking. "Just let my daughter and grandson go."

This broadened Charles's smile. "An attractive offer. Now listen to my counteroffer. If you give me your men and your other daughter, these two will live." Here he gestured toward Samitha and Thambo, and then the soldier standing nearby with a readied torch. "If you refuse—*boom*!"

"You cannot let your son die! A tiny child! Is there nothing that can make you see reason?"

Samitha's cries and Thambo's screams filled the square.

Now a commotion broke out amongst the villagers. They feared the Englishman, but their anger was taking over. They stood shoulder to shoulder and marched on the soldiers. The soldiers had their guns ready and leveled, but it was clear from their faces that none wanted to be the first to fire.

Charles flew into a rage. "What are you waiting for, you cowards? Shoot them!"

But before the first shot could be fired, a voice thundered behind Charles. "Drop your weapons or you'll bring about your own end!"

Charles spun around, and his soldiers wavered when they saw a monk, complete with flaming-orange habit, walking out of the forest at the head of a group of men. They were armed with nothing more than their determination, the authority of the monk who led them, and their voices as they recited the words of the Enlightened One, asking him for strength and fortitude.

When Mahinda saw that Odell would not even spare the life of his own son, he had raced to the men's hideout. He had explained his plan to them on the way back to the square. "Our one chance of success is getting our hands on the British commander ourselves. Then we can negotiate for the redcoats to withdraw. And there's only one way to get him. Some of us will concentrate on the soldiers and distract them, while the rest of us must overpower Odell. And remember, we must be quick and show no fear!"

When the men reached the village, Mahinda knew he had to seize the moment or the bloodbath would begin. He raised his right hand to signal to his men.

Charles realized he was trapped between the two groups of villagers. He had Anshu as hostage, but only one pistol—and that meant only one shot remained. And he dared not order his soldiers to shoot, as he himself stood in their line of fire. Then he spotted the fuse, just a few steps away, and he smiled. It took more than this to outwit Charles Odell.

"You're clever, monk," he shouted. "But not clever enough." He grabbed the torch from the soldier's hand and hurled it at the fuse. The flame hissed and shot up, licking its way to the Bodhi tree like a raging cobra.

Chaos erupted in the square. Soldiers and villagers alike ran frantically to escape the explosion. Riderless horses galloped, terrified, into the jungle. Samitha fought against her bonds and screamed. Only Mahinda stood still in the middle of the confusion, staring at the burning fuse, and cursing himself for not having foreseen what his opponent might do.

"Mama!" He heard Thambo's desperate screams. "Mama!"

Mahinda grabbed a sharp-edged stone from the ground, gathered up his robes, and ran.

Anshu saw the monk running and realized he could not make it in time. Too weak to stand, she wriggled on her belly, determined to halt the flame's progress. At the moment her fingers brushed the reeds, Charles appeared in front of her. With a malicious grin, he looked down, lifted his leg, and brought down his boot heel on her forearm, pinning her to the ground. She yelled with pain and rage and tried to use her other arm to push Charles away. But he just laughed.

We're all going to die, she thought as she lost consciousness.

With a harsh trumpeting sound, Siddhi charged into the clearing and headed straight for Charles, ears forward, trunk at full stretch.

Aghast, he spotted Phera, Henry behind her. Charles fired a shot, just missing Siddhi as she bore down upon him.

That damned rebel whore. He was sick to the stomach that he had no bullets left to blast them both off that elephant.

Siddhi had almost reached Charles, and he could see her eyes glinting as she raised her trunk to strike him down. He dodged in the nick of time and fled. Phera let out a shout of pure rage, spurring Siddhi on. But Henry held her back.

"Look!" he yelled, pointing to the tree and the powder keg. Only seconds remained before the explosion would rip Samitha and Thambo to shreds.

"Ho!" shouted Phera. "Ho, Siddhi!"

Henry slid off Siddhi's back while she was still in motion. He hit the ground, rolled swiftly away from the elephant's feet, jumped up, and ran. One step more, another, and he kicked aside the last reed just as the flame reached it. With a groan of relief, he fell to the ground.

Panting and gasping, he clenched his fists, then bellowed, "Charles! Where are you hiding, you damned swine?"

Phera slid from Siddhi's back and ran to Henry. "Where is he? He mustn't get away!"

"I don't see him," said Henry as he stood up. He cupped his hands around his mouth and roared, "I'll find you, Charles! And God help you then!"

She touched him on the shoulder. "We'll find him. Samitha and Thambo are safe; that's the most important thing for right now." She looked at the Bodhi tree. The monk was sawing at their ropes with the stone. "I'll help Mahinda. Look after my mother."

He nodded and hurried to Anshu, who was motionless on the ground.

Phera drew her dagger and ran toward the Bodhi tree.

"Watch out! Behind you!" yelled Samitha.

Phera felt a painful blow on the back of her head. She cried out and fell. Stars danced before her eyes. Then a hand grabbed her and pulled her brutally to her feet. In one swift movement, the attacker took her dagger and brought it to her throat.

"Who have we got here, then?" Charles hissed in her ear. "Isn't it my brother's pretty little slut?"

She felt his hot, wet breath on her neck and writhed desperately against his grip. But he forced her backward, then placed the tip of the dagger on her neck, under her left ear. "Henry! Look what a delicious fruit has fallen into my arms!"

She used all her strength to fight against him. But Charles laughed. "You're even wilder than your sister, you little bitch. But I'll tame you as well." He dug the tip of the dagger deeper into her skin until it drew blood, then slowly began to trace it across her neck.

"Let her go!" Henry yelled, nearly crazed with anger. "If you harm a single hair on her head, you'll pay for it!"

"When did you ever beat me, little br—aagh!"

Something that felt like a rifle butt hit Charles's head. The dagger slipped from his fingers, and he staggered sideways, raising both arms to shield himself. Phera stumbled as the vicelike grip around her neck was released. She turned and saw Siddhi.

Charles tried to crawl out of the elephant's reach. But she got hold of him, lifted him impossibly high in the air, and hurled his body to the ground with all her strength. Bones cracked loudly. He lay motionless for several moments, but then his whole body twitched, and, slowly, he raised his bleeding head.

"Shoot—that—beast—dead," he croaked, before falling back to the ground.

The British soldiers watched in horror. They could do nothing for their commander because the villagers, every last man, woman, and child, had formed a tight ring around them.

Siddhi's victorious trumpeting resounded through the clearing. She lifted her right foreleg. She held it in the air for a few moments, quite still, then brought it down on Charles's broken body. He howled in agony.

Siddhi turned her head, looking all around her. Once she spotted Henry, she used her trunk and forelegs to roll Charles's unmoving body over to his brother's feet. Then she turned and went to Phera.

Phera placed her hands on Siddhi's trunk and pressed her forehead against Siddhi's strong, gray head. "Thank you, my friend," she whispered through her tears.

Henry crouched down near his brother. Charles's eyes were shut, his face white, his uniform spattered with muck and blood. His arm and leg lay at terrible angles, and Henry suspected some internal organs had also been crushed. Carefully, he placed two fingers on Charles's neck and noted his pulse was weak and faltering. He bent close and whispered, "It's Henry. Can you hear me?"

A muscle twitched in Charles's face. He opened his eyes. "Am I going to die?" he wheezed.

"Yes," said Henry. "This is your last chance to repent."

"I repent nothing."

Henry leaned forward again, this time to close his brother's eyes. Then he looked at Charles's face, frozen in the agony of death. *Never again will you rape, torture, and murder,* he thought. *I only regret that it was not my own hand that stopped you, and sooner.*

He felt a touch on his shoulder and turned. Phera was there behind him. He lifted his hand and traced his fingertips along the thin strip of blood that ran across her neck from one ear to the other.

"Dr. Odell!"

Henry turned and saw a soldier. "What do you want?"

"What should we do now, Doctor?"

With Charles dead, the villagers had formed two rows to allow the soldiers, their heads lowered, to pass between them. Now they were standing behind Henry, looking at him uncertainly.

He thought for a moment. "Take the corporal and my brother back to camp; place them both in a tent with a guard outside. And do not speak to anybody of what happened. I'll talk to my brother's proxy myself when I get back."

"Certainly, Doctor!" The soldier saluted.

The soldiers went over to the few remaining horses. They loaded the two corpses and disappeared into the jungle.

Henry's face betrayed his exhaustion, but his voice was resolute. "I must attend to your mother."

Phera took him by the hand, and together they went to Anshu. She had regained consciousness and was sitting up, supported by Mahinda. He had cleaned the bullet wound and dressed it with a strip of cloth torn from his habit. Sitting with him were Samitha and Thambo. The child clung to his mother, his face buried in the folds of her sari. She had one gentle hand on his head, and held her mother's with the other.

"How are you feeling?" asked Henry.

"My daughters and my grandson are alive," Anshu said. "That takes away nearly all the pain."

Henry knelt down beside her and examined her wounds. The bullet wound was expertly dressed and had stopped bleeding, as had the cut on her face from Charles's pistol. Fortunately, Charles's boot had not caused any grave injury to her arm. "No bones broken," Henry confirmed. "But the arm will hurt for some time."

"I'll prepare a cooling ointment that will help soothe the pain," said Mahinda.

Anshu looked at Phera and Henry. "Without you two, I don't think they'd have left anyone alive."

"Siddhi stopped the worst from happening," said Phera and looked proudly at her elephant as she stood under the Bodhi tree, her trunk examining what was left of the fuse.

Led by an elder, the villagers now walked toward the little group.

Anshu gestured to Mahinda and Henry. "Help me up, please."

With great care, they lifted her up. She was a little unsteady but could stand without assistance.

The elder stepped forward. "With your help, widan, and with the help of your family, the Englishman, and the elephant, we are saved. Nothing has happened to our sacred tree or to us. We thank you, widan, for you have endured injury and pain to save our village." He bowed deeply, first to Anshu, then to her family and to Henry. Last of all, he turned to Siddhi. "We owe you our thanks, too, daughter of the god Ganesha, the bringer of goodness and happiness."

Siddhi lifted her trunk and puffed contentedly.

As the clearing emptied, Anshu stayed behind with her daughters, her grandson, Henry, Mahinda, and Siddhi.

"My dearest children." She reached out to Samitha and Phera. Both went to her, and they all embraced, while little Thambo cuddled up to their legs. They stayed like this, arms wrapped around one another, for some time.

Phera was the first to speak. "After today it won't be as hard for me to think about Father, Mihiri, and Eranga."

"My son will grow up without fear of that man," added Samitha.

Anshu smiled. "And we'll live in peace from now on."

The following day, Henry buried his brother at the edge of the construction site, beneath the overhanging boughs of a mahogany tree. Beside him lay the corporal. Two oblong mounds of earth, each with a crudely made wooden cross, were the only markers of their final resting place.

That evening, when Henry sat alone to meditate in the half-light of his tent, his thoughts strayed to Charles. He knew the death was a justified deliverance. But it was still hard for him to grasp that the beloved and admired big brother of his childhood was the same person who had tortured, exploited, raped, and murdered. Henry wanted now to live in peace, so he chose to embrace the future. He hoped this future would be at Phera's side, even if he had little idea whether two people from such different cultures could successfully build a life together.

Soon after sunrise the next day, Phera came to see him at the construction site just as he was on his way to a meeting with Charles's proxy, Captain Daniel Brooks. She looked lovely, graceful in her yellow sari and with matching ruk attana blooms in her long, dark hair, worn loose. He went to kiss her but then held back. He could not take his eyes off the wound his brother had made with the dagger, the dark-red line, now scabbed over. He touched it gently with his fingertips and murmured sadly, "For that alone, I'll never forgive Charles."

"Mahinda prepared me a special ointment. It'll heal," she said, smiling. She took his hand. "When are you coming back to Mapitigama?"

"I'd love to go there now with you," he replied. "But there's a lot to sort out here, and reorganize. For the time being, Charles's proxy, Brooks, will take over the construction project. I'm going to try and dissuade him from running the new road through Mapitigama, but I haven't got the measure of him yet and don't know what he'll say."

Phera's jaw dropped. "You mean Mapitigama is still under threat?"

He held her closer. "Every delay costs the British government a lot of money. That's why I'm going to tell him the men of Mapitigama will start work again immediately if he will pledge the protection of their village."

"How dare you just decide like that? The men haven't agreed to this."

"I'm going to tell Brooks to pay them."

Phera was puzzled. "They don't know anything about money. Maybe they don't want it. Only the king and nobles used to own coins."

"Those days are over," said Henry. "The British government plans to introduce money through the whole country. It'll be best if they can get used to it as soon as possible."

"Will you come back to Mapitigama soon?" asked Phera.

"As soon as I've spoken to the new site manager."

"Make it fast," she said, kissing him.

Soon afterward Henry and Brooks sat in a quiet corner of the mess tent over a cup of tea. "Your brother, God bless him, has left quite a mess," said the engineer with a sigh. "First of all, we had the epidemic; then nearly all the workers ran off. Now a whole platoon has come back from Mapitigama with the bodies of the site manager and his corporal. I tried to question the soldiers, but they said you had forbidden them from talking about it. What does all this mean, Odell? Are there serious problems to be had with the people from this village?"

Henry stirred his tea while collecting his thoughts. For the people of Mapitigama, a lot rested on the outcome of this conversation, and he did not want to make any missteps. He related with calm and objectivity what had played out in Mapitigama. He remained silent only about Siddhi's role, for fear Brooks would call for the supposedly dangerous cow elephant to be put down.

"It's not easy for me to say this," Henry concluded, "but the violence stemmed entirely from my brother, and from him alone. The people of Mapitigama never attacked us. The soldiers will confirm that for you."

"Was your brother really trampled by a wild elephant? I've never heard of any coming near the construction site."

"Yes, a lone bull elephant, Captain. A huge beast that suddenly stormed out of the jungle," Henry assured him without batting an eye. "There was nothing anyone could do."

Brooks leaned back in his chair and gave him a long, hard look. "I've always considered you to be an honorable man, Odell, and I have no reason to doubt your word. I'd be pleased to have your continued loyalty as medical officer for the construction site."

"I'll stay for the time being. But this road will take many years, and I can't promise I'll be here until the end," said Henry.

"I can't blame you for having other plans," said Brooks. "Building a road through the jungle in this climate pushes us all to our limits. None of us can say how long we'll hold out."

"As long as I'm the site doctor, I'd like to take care of everyone working here," said Henry. "Whether they're British, Indian, or Sinhalese. More than that, the workers need plenty of nourishing food and some decent accommodations if we expect them to perform such hard labor."

"I share your opinion one hundred percent," said Brooks.

Encouraged by this, Henry went on. "What would you say to paying the workers?"

The engineer scratched his head. "You're asking a lot, Odell."

"I don't think so," countered Henry. "There are rumblings in London about slavery in the colonies having to stop. An upstanding man like you must agree everyone should be paid for their labor. Further, it contributes to people's willingness to do the job and to the quality of their work."

Brooks laughed and held up a hand. "Very well. I can't disagree with you, Odell, but at the moment I don't even have any workers to pay."

"If word gets around that we're going to give them better working conditions, a lot of the men will come back of their own accord. Of course, you will have to guarantee no punishment for their disappearance."

"I'll do that provided we can resume construction immediately."

"I'll make all efforts to get the men back, if you guarantee payment, food, and accommodations." Henry extended his right hand to Brooks.

After a moment of hesitation, the engineer accepted the handshake. "I shall write to the governor today, asking him to officially name me as site manager. And I'll commission new coolies from India. But I don't yet know how I'll explain to Paget why we need more. It wouldn't be very clever to tell him all the workers absconded."

"Tell him people died of typhus, fever, and malaria," Henry advised. "In this climate that's not unusual at all."

"Good idea." Brooks was toying with his teaspoon. "Incidentally, I'm giving some thought to resuming the original route. It would save us a detour of many miles—and time and money, to boot. My colleagues in the Royal Engineers never understood why your brother altered the course. Yes, the subsoil is stony, but that's why we've got explosives."

To make sure his pleasure wasn't too obvious, Henry asked, "Are there any other alternatives to the old route?"

Brooks shook his head. "We have to build it in sweeping curves. Otherwise, our beauty of a road will slip down the mountain with the first monsoon rain. The old route or the stretch toward Mapitigama offer the best conditions for this. To be honest, I expected to see you rather delighted by my proposal. It'll allow your Sinhalese friends to stay in their village."

Henry held out his cup toward the boy with the teapot, waited until he had poured, then said, "The final stretch of the old route belonged to my brother. He bought it from Paget."

"Good Lord!" exclaimed Brooks in amazement. "What did he want with that land?"

Henry took a mouthful of tea. "He said he'd grow coffee."

"Forgive me, Odell, but I'd never have thought your brother harbored the desire to be a farmer!"

"Nor would I," remarked Henry.

Brooks rubbed his chin, taking all this in. "That makes you the heir. Why are you not in agreement? Or do you want to grow coffee, too?"

Henry made a dismissive gesture. "I wouldn't want the land. And I'm not the heir. My brother leaves a young son." Phera had told him about Thambo. She had made it clear the family was united in the belief that the child must never know the tragic circumstances of his conception.

Brooks whistled through his teeth. "That makes it complicated."

Henry drained his cup and got to his feet. "I have in mind a solution whereby nobody loses out—neither the British government, nor the people of Mapitigama, nor my brother's child. But please give me a day to work things out."

When Henry rode into the village early that afternoon, he saw Phera and Siddhi first. The elephant was standing under the Bodhi tree. Phera was on her back, closing up with beeswax the wounds Charles had inflicted on the tree.

Although Henry had seen her just that morning, the sight made his heart beat faster. He stopped his horse so as to watch her as she tended to the injured tree, enjoying the uplifting feeling of being completely and utterly in love.

But Siddhi had already spotted him, greeting him like an old friend by lifting her trunk. Phera turned, too. When she realized it was Henry, she slid off Siddhi's back and ran toward him. She looked so fresh, so enchanting, all he wanted was to lift her onto his horse, ride together to the hidden waterfall, and make love with passion and tenderness. But right now there was important business to attend to.

He slid down from his horse in time to hold out his arms just as she flung hers around his neck. She was beaming with happiness.

"I'm so pleased you're here! Do you have good news for us?"

"I hope so." He played gently with the yellow ruk attana bloom in her hair. "I have a plan, at least. But its success depends on all of you."

A little later the whole village stood beneath the Bodhi tree and looked expectantly at Henry, who was standing before the shrine of the Enlightened One. Phera stood close to him on one side, and on the other were Samitha, Thambo, and Anshu. One of Anshu's arms was heavily bandaged, the other was in a sling, and on one temple was a large bruise. Anshu was in pain, and yet she felt good. Henry had assured her the wounds would heal fully. More than that, she would never again live in fear of Charles Odell, a blessing that made all discomfort pale in significance.

"The new site manager respects your wishes," Henry announced. "He wants to take the road not through your village, but along the original route."

Cheering broke out. The villagers were laughing and hugging one another.

Then Henry raised his right hand. "I bring yet more news." When the noise had died down, he told them how the new chief engineer had promised not only better accommodations and food but also payment for the workers.

"I know money hasn't been familiar to you before," he said. "But things are going to change. Very soon you won't be able to exchange rice and spices for other goods in Colombo. You'll have to sell your wares, and the Moorish merchants will only part with their goods for money. The chief engineer has agreed to pay road workers a wage now, which you can treat as an investment for the future. You could build a hospital for the village, or a school." His eyes ranged over the assembled villagers, who had been listening intently. "Will you accept?"

They all looked at him uncertainly. Eventually, some of the men gave hesitant nods of assent. But others loudly declared they would never work for the British again.

Henry nodded. "I can understand your reservations. Think it over, and tell me when you have decided." His eyes sought out Samitha. "As it is, the site manager needs your agreement in order to build on the original route."

When she looked back at him blankly, he explained. "Charles had purchased the abandoned section of road, which now belongs to him, and Thambo is Charles's heir. As his mother, you have to decide for him whether he accepts the inheritance. But know that, on that land, there's a sapphire deposit that would make Thambo a rich man."

Samitha shook her head in confusion. More than anything, she wished for a happy and carefree life for her son. She feared his father's legacy could bring Thambo more trouble than joy.

Henry cleared his throat. "Apart from us, nobody knows about this sapphire deposit. However, if the governor were to find out, he would claim that land for the Crown. Then Thambo would lose his inheritance."

"Can they so easily take what doesn't belong to them?" asked Phera.

"In theory, no," Henry conceded. "But I fear they would find a way, given the scale of riches. If that happened, the only route for the road would be straight through Mapitigama."

Samitha put her arm around her son. "Those precious stones have already brought enough misery. That's why I'm refusing it on behalf of Thambo. I know he'll understand my decision when he's old enough. What do you think, venerable hamudru?" She looked at Mahinda, who gave a deliberate, considered nod.

"A wise decision, and one which will be of great benefit to your son."

"Thank you." Samitha smiled with relief and bent to kiss her child's head.

"So is it decided, then?" asked Anshu, taking in the circle of village residents. "The sapphire deposit will remain our secret so that we might preserve our village?"

They all nodded solemnly and murmured agreement.

The elder directed his comments to Samitha. "We thank you for the gift of peace to this village. You and your son will have a home here forever."

"But how can we stop the British finding out about the sapphire vein?" she asked.

Henry had already thought of this. "We could meet tonight at the abandoned stretch and fill in the hole," he suggested. "But all the men must help, so that it's quick."

The men all agreed. Henry turned to Phera. "And we'll need Siddhi to pull the boulder out of the crater."

"Of course."

"Won't the site manager notice the hole's been filled in?" asked Anshu.

"We'll make it look like erosion after the monsoon," said one of the men.

Henry took a deep breath. "Let's get to work."

He reached into his jacket pocket and brought out Charles's sapphire. "Samitha, even without the sapphire mine, your son will never be poor." He took her hand and placed the stone in her palm. She stared at it, lost for words. The sapphire had a breathtaking beauty and a pleasing smoothness. It glowed dark blue, like the night sky, and the fine, milky lines radiating out from its center resembled a star.

"This is the sapphire my brother found in the crater. Now it belongs to his son. Its value will ensure Thambo's prosperity, and that of his descendants, for many years to come."

Slowly, Samitha closed her fingers around the stone to make a fist. The gem was cool as a hillside stream and smooth as glass. She did not want to own anything that had once belonged to her torturer, but she knew she could not reject this legacy on her son's behalf.

While she was still thinking, Henry took a second gemstone from his pocket and held it up between thumb and forefinger for all to see. "This is Eranga's sapphire. Because he has no descendants, this now belongs to the whole village, and I'm handing it to your widan for safekeeping." He went to Anshu and gave her the stone. "Nobody outside this village must know about this sapphire," he warned her.

The village elder looked at everyone in the circle. "Do we really want the stone? Yes, it's valuable, but it means danger, too. Why don't we commit it to our river waters, give it to Nanu Oya?"

"We shouldn't be too quick to reject such unexpected wealth," reasoned Anshu. "Let's bury the stone beneath our sacred tree, near our shrine to the Enlightened One. It'll be safe there until we need it."

"But if someone dug it up in secret and made off with it, that would be the end of peace in the village," said the elder. "However, if the river takes the sapphire, nobody will ever be able to steal it."

"I've got a better idea." Phera placed her hand on the crusty bark of their ancient tree. "We'll sell the stone and use the money to build our own temple here, next to the tree, in thanks for the salvation of our village."

Everyone looked at her, filled with relief at finding such a good solution. Henry nodded in loving approval.

Tears stood in Anshu's eyes. "My dear daughter," she said softly. "Have you at last subdued all your thoughts of revenge?"

Phera looked to Mahinda. "It hasn't been easy to trust in fate. But I've done it. And now everything's as it should be."

"Just as water can't hold on to an upward slope, nor can revenge hold on to a generous heart," responded Mahinda, brimming with pride.

"I could sell Eranga's sapphire for you in Colombo," Henry said. "I'll be sure to negotiate a good price."

After the villagers had accepted his offer, the gathering broke up, and they all dispersed. For the first time since Charles Odell had invaded their village and taken the men for forced labor, the people went off to work in their rice fields feeling calm and safe.

Anshu stayed back with her family, Mahinda, and Henry. "Do you have to return to the building site now, or would you like to stay a while with us?"

Since his courageous actions at the Bodhi tree, Anshu's reservations about Henry's relationship with Phera had eased. Most importantly, his brother no longer stood between him and her family.

While Thambo marveled at Henry's horse, the grown-ups went to Anshu's garden. They were greeted by Siddhi, who stood at the fence, helping herself to the tempting fruits of Anshu's banana palm.

Samitha went into the hut to prepare some refreshments. Mahinda, Anshu, Phera, and Henry sat together in the shade of the overhanging roof.

"Venerable hamudru," said Phera, "do you remember my birth horoscope and how you prophesied an extraordinary destiny for me?"

"I certainly do," replied the monk. "I had never seen a horoscope like yours, with opposites so clearly defined. Cancer and Scorpio, the Moon and Mars, sensitivity and toughness mark your life. Your path has been determined by destiny to this very day, but when you renounced all thoughts of revenge, you became mistress of that destiny."

"But in this world, isn't it better to be able to defend myself like a Scorpio than to be a sensitive Cancer?" she asked.

"Cancers have a tough shell to protect them. And, true, if that isn't enough, you can use the scorpion's poison—but use it wisely. Remember, child, you must always strive to follow the path of the eight virtues. Seek out knowledge and righteous thinking. Do no harm to your fellow creatures, and take care of the body given you. Make honest efforts to avoid all evil, and meditate daily."

"That sounds hard." Phera sighed.

Henry put his arm around her. "Don't be discouraged. You'll have plenty of lives where you can learn all that," he said solemnly.

"Are you making fun of me?"

"Heavens, no! I'm quoting the Buddha," protested Henry, a mischievous twinkle in his eye.

Even Mahinda gave a big smile. "My friend, I think you're right. While I urge Phera to pursue the noble path to enlightenment, it should not make her forget the joys of life."

Just then Samitha came back with a tray of coconut water, and everyone reached for a bowl, most drinking appreciatively.

But Anshu sat, looking at hers. "I'm going to step down as widan," she said.

Everyone looked at her in amazement. Phera spoke first. "But why, Mother? You're a wonderful widan. The people love and respect you."

Anshu shook her head. "There are others here equally able to take on the office. Since we had to flee Senkadagala, I've been so homesick for the place where I spent the happiest years of my life. I miss it and want to see it again. And now that Charles Odell is dead, we don't have to hide anymore."

"But where will you live? We have nothing there now!" asked Samitha.

"I know," conceded Anshu. "But my roots are in Senkadagala. That's where I belong. I'd love to know whether our house is still standing."

"If it's still there, other people will have been living in it for years," said Phera. "Have you forgotten we were completely dispossessed?"

Henry stroked her arm. "I could ride to Kandy and gather information. If we're in luck, the house could even be for sale."

"We'd have to buy back our own house?" Phera was outraged.

"We can't, in any case. We have no money," said Anshu sadly.

Henry cleared his throat and turned to Phera. "I've been giving thought to the future, too. I've saved some money, maybe enough to buy your father's house so that we could all make it our new home—your mother, your sister, Thambo, you, and I. And Siddhi will have a stall in the garden. Phera"—he was looking straight at her—"can you see yourself living in Kandy? As a doctor's wife?"

Mahinda, Anshu, and Samitha gave encouraging smiles, but Phera did not notice. She lowered her head, clasped her hands, and did not say a word. Cautiously, Henry lifted her chin.

"What do you think?" he asked softly.

She shook her head, and he felt all his courage drain away. He must have been out of his mind to think she would ever marry an Englishman.

But then she spoke. "My heart's pounding so hard, it feels like thunder in the monsoon! That's probably because I'm the happiest person in the world."

He beamed at her. "No, I'm the happiest person in the world! But only if"—he turned to Anshu and Samitha—"only if everyone accepts my proposal."

Anshu nodded enthusiastically. "Thank you. Through you, I have been able to see that amongst all the British, there are some good people."

"I want to thank you, too," said Samitha. "And I have one request. Take your brother's sapphire and use it to buy us our house, or any other, in Kandy." She tried to press the stone into Henry's hand, but he shook his head.

"Keep it for your son. When he's old enough, he can decide for himself whether he wants it. I shall buy us a home with my own savings."

"Wise counsel," said Mahinda.

"And you, dear friend, will you come to Kandy with us?" asked Henry.

The monk shook his head. "Our paths crossed, and for a short time we walked together. Now I shall return to my monastery in Colombo."

He looked at Henry, and the two men exchanged a smile. Mahinda added, "Meditate every day so the vice in your soul can never stir again. You now have a family to think of."

"What are you talking about?" asked Phera.

"About the demons living not just around us but within us," said Henry, kissing her.

Then he raised his bowl of coconut water to Mahinda. "My friend, just promise you won't leave until you've married us!"

Authors' Note

The kingdom of Kanda Uda Pas Rata, named Kandy by the British, was in the heart of Sri Lanka. In the sixteenth and early seventeenth centuries, the Portuguese and Dutch took possession of first the coastline and then the rest of the kingdom. They did not, however, manage to conquer Kandy's high mountains and impenetrable jungle, nor did the kings of Kandy manage to drive out the colonial powers. However, because cinnamon, precious stones, and elephants were among the most sought-after export items in the country, a variety of trade agreements resulted.

The British were the colonial rulers of Sri Lanka from 1796, but they failed more than once in their attempts to march into Kandy.

In 1817 the native population, particularly the people of Uva, rebelled against their new rulers. It was a year before the rebellion was subdued and only through extreme brutality, with crops ruined, rice fields destroyed, cattle slaughtered, and villages burned to the ground. All men over the age of eighteen were hunted down and murdered. Many British officers displayed merciless cruelty. Lieutenant John Maclaine, of the Seventy-Third Infantry Regiment, was known to delight in watching the executions of Sinhalese prisoners while he breakfasted.

As early as 1802, Sri Lanka was made a Crown colony and named Ceylon by the British. After they had subdued the Uva Rebellion, the new rulers wanted tighter control over the island and began its development. Virgin forest was cleared to make way first for coffee plantations, then later for tea. Bridges and modern roads were constructed. In 1864 the first railroad in the land came into service, running from Kandy to Colombo.

The road described in our book is today the A1. Its construction started in 1820 under the leadership of Captain William Frances Dawson. When Dawson died of exhaustion in 1829, the road was still not ready.

Anyone reading our description of Kandy's Temple of the Tooth, and who has also been there in person, may be surprised how much today's temple differs from our depiction. This is because the temple was altered and extended in the early nineteenth century. After fire damage, only the lower section of the royal palace remains, while of the elephant stables there is nothing. We took as a model the architecture and scale of other stable blocks, such as those of Vijayanagar in South India.

In several places, we have changed historical facts for the benefit of our story. Uva Ravine and the associated ambush is our invention. Sylvester Wilson was one of the British present, and the Sacred Tooth of Buddha was taken to the highland fortress of Hanguranketha, not to Badulla.

For the kingdom of Kandy, we use its original name of Kanda Uda Pas Rata while it remains under Sinhalese rule. The same applies to the city of Kandy, known to the Sinhalese as Senkadagala.

Acknowledgments

We thank all those who have offered their specialist advice, constructive criticism, and helpful comments during the writing of this book and after.

In particular, we would like to thank the whole AmazonCrossing team, especially Lauren Edwards for being our excellent editor; Deborah Langton, who produced a wonderful translation; and P. G. Norman Edwin, our friendly and humorous guide to Sri Lanka, who also happens to be the first local guide to this wonderful country taken on by a German travel company.

If you have enjoyed our novel, do tell your friends. We would love to have your feedback through social media like Twitter, Facebook, or Goodreads.

About the Authors

Photo © 2016 Mirella Drosten

Julia and Horst Drosten write historical novels together under the pseudonym Julia Drosten. In their spare time, Julia loves to do yoga, and Horst runs regularly. Horst is also a very skilled cook, and Julia loves to eat the meals he creates. The authors have written many other works of historical fiction in German, and they greatly enjoy conducting research for their novels—diving into history and making the past come alive. They count flying in a historic biplane, watching the workers in a butcher's shop, exploring Egypt, and being pampered by a beautician among their research pursuits. The authors of *The Lioness of Morocco*, an Amazon bestseller in Germany and the United States, Julia and Horst live in the idyllic Münsterland in Germany. *The Elephant Keeper's Daughter*, originally published in German under the title *Die Elefantenhüterin*, is their second novel translated into English.

About the Translator

Photo © 2017 Stella Scordellis

Deborah Langton was born in Reading, England, studied German and French literature at Cambridge, and has worked in Munich, Berlin, Milan, Abu Dhabi, London, and Manchester. After a rewarding first career teaching and lecturing, she moved into translation while still working at Munich's Ludwig-Maximilians University and loves translating fiction best of all. Deborah now lives in a rural location not far from London and translates in her study with views toward England's South Downs. She shares her life with her husband, Chris, her best critic, and their two fine sons, Joseph and Samuel.